He leaned blocking o the small s whispered against her ear. **"Now I really do need to call Vice."**

"Why's that?" She heard the breathy response and delighted in the raw emotion that coursed between them.

"You've clearly been a sugar pusher a lot longer than I realized."

"I do have a lot of satisfied clients."

His breath whispered over the shell of her ear before he ran his lips down the line of her jaw. "Besotted fools, just like me."

As he finished the journey from ear to jaw, Lilah turned and met his lips with hers. The warmth of his mouth enveloped hers, the sweet moment punctuating a roller coaster of an evening.

And as she allowed the moments to swirl out like the finest threads of spun sugar, Lilah let loose on the tight reins of emotion she normally kept in check.

Here, in this moment, she was safe.

* * *

check out the next books Dallas miniseries:
Texas nights...

TEMPTING TARGET

Addison Fox

HARLEQUIN® ROMANTIC SUSPENSE

Recycling programs
for this product may
not exist in your area.

ISBN-13: 978-0-373-27928-9

Tempting Target

Copyright © 2015 by Frances Karkosak

Printed in U.S.A.

Addison Fox is a Philadelphia girl transplanted to Dallas, Texas. Although her similarities to Grace Kelly stop at sharing the same place of birth, she's often dreamed of marrying a prince and living along the Mediterranean.

In the meantime, she's more than happy penning romance novels about two strong-willed and exciting people who deserve their happy-ever-after—after she makes them work so hard for it, of course. When she's not writing, she can be found spending time with family and friends, reading or enjoying a glass of wine.

Find out more about Addison or contact her at her website—addisonfox.com—or catch up with her on Facebook (addisonfoxauthor) and Twitter (@addisonfox).

Books by Addison Fox

Harlequin Romantic Suspense

Dangerous in Dallas

Silken Threats
Tempting Target

House of Steele

The Paris Assignment
The London Deception
The Rome Affair
The Manhattan Encounter

The Adair Affairs

Secret Agent Boyfriend

Visit Addison's Author Profile page at
Harlequin.com for more titles.

For Carley

Purveyor of Dumbledore defenses, days of fun
and the best damn cakes in Dallas.

Some family we're fortunate to receive at birth
and others we gather along the way.
I'm so blessed to be on the journey with you.

Chapter 1

"You hid a ruby in your shoe?"

If he weren't increasingly irritated about that fact, Detective Reed Graystone would have found it amusing. Alluring. And strangely appealing. Especially since the woman currently storing a priceless gem in her pink Crocs was one of the most fascinating people he'd ever met.

Lilah Castle shrugged before slipping her foot back into her now-empty shoe. "I was going for diamonds but sometimes a gal's gotta settle."

"I don't believe this." Reed fought the urge to tug at the ends of his hair and watched—oddly helpless—as she picked up the bloodred stone and set it on her gleaming stainless-steel kitchen counter.

The ruby was roughly the size of a large summer strawberry. Red facets caught the light, the gem's rich depths reflecting color back in a vivid display of nature's power. A vibrant crimson reflected from the shiny surface of the counter, only adding to the ethereal glow of the piece.

Although large for a gemstone, the ruby and its two mates were, relatively speaking, small. They could be easily hidden in any number of places. Lilah had obviously suffered minimal discomfort with this one shoved in the toe of her shoe.

With a sharp glance around her industrial kitchen, he acknowledged she could have hidden it anywhere with no one the wiser. Sewn into the seam of her purse by her business partner, the seamstress. Effectively dropped into a file cabinet by her other partner, the wedding planner. She could have even left it in the bottom of the series of spatula containers that lined the wall of her kitchen and no one would know.

Who knew a wedding business had so many places to hide the precious and the priceless? Then again, who knew that these particular stones had lain in the floor of an old Dallas warehouse for nearly fifty years?

Half a freaking century.

Reed mentally shook his head at the improbability of that. Gemstones of immeasurable value and purported to hold a curse, hidden away in an old industrial concrete floor. Of course, improbable didn't mean impossible.

Which brought them to today.

This case had surprisingly few answers so far for the three frightened yet determined proprietors—Lilah Castle and her two partners, Cassidy Tate and Violet Richardson.

Reed hated complications. He'd developed the distaste early—his childhood so full of them he'd lost count—and had determined he would avoid them like the proverbial plague of locusts when he grew up.

So how the hell was he caught up in the middle of a major mystery revolving around jewels gifted to the British Crown during World War Two and subsequently buried in the concrete floor of a Dallas warehouse?

It had been just over a week since Elegance and Lace had been first broken into. Five days since they'd discovered the rubies that the thieves had been after. Three since the architect, Tucker Buchanan, had saved his now-fiancée, Cassidy, from her deranged ex.

And two since Reed had glued himself to Lilah Castle.

Things had grown far more complicated than he ever could have imagined.

"You do realize you can't keep them. This one or the ones your girlfriends have stored in safe-deposit boxes. Which, I might add, is where this one should be, too."

"I know." She shoved her hair behind her ear, a long pink streak twining through the blond like an invitation to touch what he instinctively knew would be silky-soft strands.

Pushing away the fanciful thoughts, his voice was a bit harder than he intended. "You sure?"

"Quite."

"Because every time I look at you looking at that rock, I see stars in your eyes."

"It *is* a priceless ruby."

"Not nearly as priceless as your life." As a loud shout drifted toward the kitchen, he gestured in the direction of the sounds coming from the other half of Lilah's business, walled off from the kitchen to meet board of health codes. "All of your lives."

"Which is why, until we figure out who's behind this, we need to keep them safe."

A small snort escaped his lips before he reached for a plate of chocolate-covered madeleines she had set out on the counter. He'd made no secret what he thought of their plan to keep the rubies hidden, but Reed also knew he needed to maintain the proper balance between cajoling and flat-out directing.

Their landlady owned the rubies free and clear and had put them in the care of the women for safe-keeping. Since they were hers to do with as she wished, he had no power to take the gems.

So instead, he'd stuck close, watching and waiting while the women tried to put their business back to rights and get on with their lives.

They might wish the problem had corrected itself but he knew whomever had struck, desperate to have the gems, was sure to have another go at it.

Lilah gave him the eye as he reached for another of her delicious cookies, the calculation clear in those brown depths. "You don't like what we're doing?"

"Hell no." Reed eyed the madeleines, considered a third before he shoved a hand into his pocket. "The people who want those jewels mean business. And they're not going to let anyone stand in their way."

"The rubies give us leverage."

"There is no leverage when you're dead, Cupcake."

Lilah waited for something to register—some fear at the deep, masculine voice that spoke at her, full of righteous frustration—but all she could manage was a delicious little shiver.

Despite the danger inherent in their situation and the threat that hung over them all, she still felt safe. Protected. And, if she were honest, she also felt that sly, subtle shiver of attraction that fired the blood every time she looked into those haunting gray eyes fringed by thick, dark lashes.

All because of the man standing opposite her.

Reed.

No, she mentally chided herself, it was *Detective Graystone.* Which really was the more professional way to think of him.

Lilah knew it bothered him she'd hung on to the ruby. His frustration had been on display multiple times since she and her business partners had found the gems buried in the concrete floor of their wedding business, yet he always maintained a professional demeanor and a polite attitude.

Which only made her want to muss him up.

She didn't trust men who projected absolute control, yet she couldn't deny the appeal of the stoic cop. Nor could she fully deny he was spot on with the rubies, one of which was still warm from her body heat.

A situation she knew she needed to fix, even as she couldn't quite deny the need to keep the ruby in her possession. Yes, the stone fascinated her, the good detective wasn't wrong about that. But it was something more.

She'd lived without any control—or a single bargaining chip—for too long. The idea of placing that control in a safe-deposit box nagged at her.

So while she battled the rational versus the instinctual, she kept the ruby buried in her shoe.

And despite their danger, she couldn't deny how the stones had brought a sense of closure to her best friend, Cassidy.

Even more important, they'd brought with them the love of Cassidy's life, Tucker Buchanan.

Another delicious shiver pulled her from the thoughts of Cassidy and Tucker as her gaze caught Reed's. The man was an interesting one, she mused. Physically impressive, with a broad chest and narrow waist, he wore authority in every muscle and sinew of his body. But it was more than the physical.

Quiet, calm and decidedly by the book, he'd been assigned their case after the first break-in the week before. He'd been professional, and she, Cassidy and Violet had also seen how much he cared about his job.

Reed Graystone was a good cop.

It wove around his shoulders like a mantle, telegraphing his desire to protect and defend.

But none of it changed the ornery need to poke at him. Lilah knew it was no use to pick a fight but the tension of the past week had begun to fray everyone's edges. So she stood her ground and allowed her eyebrows to take a decided lift north. "Cupcake? Is this the sort of sexist nickname you use with all the women in your life? Or is it some derogatory reference to my profession?"

Another cookie disappeared between his lips, followed by a wicked grin a few short moments later. "I'd never insult a woman who spins sugar into gold."

Their conversation was interrupted by the arrival of Tucker's partner, Max Baldwin, with an empty plate in hand. He was as large as Reed—larger, actually, his figure thicker and boxy—and their impressive forms seemed to fill up her kitchen, making the vast space appear small. Max's bright blue eyes narrowed as they roved over Reed. "Are there any more of these bacon cheese puffs, Lilah?"

She didn't miss Reed's raised eyebrows but the detective said nothing as she reached for a fresh tray of Max's favorite appetizers she'd kept warming on top of the stove. "Of course I have more." *Barely.* Lilah made a mental note to bake in greater quantities when Tucker and Max came over for lunch. When a second note quickly followed the first—*make more madeleines for surprise visits from the detective*—she swiftly pushed away cozy images of Reed Graystone regularly sitting in her industrial kitchen.

She scooped several more bacon-and-cheese-wrapped puff pastries onto the plate and passed them over to Max.

Although the casual talk of appetizers seemed silly relative to the problem they were still dealing with, Lilah knew the food helped provide a subtle sense of normalcy. Tucker and Max had spent several days with them after the destructive break-in to help fix the ruined display areas while also providing the simple reassurance of their presence. They'd also managed to subtly redesign those areas and Cassidy had been like a kid with candy as she rearranged several of her creations on a series of raised platforms.

A few treats were the least she could do.

Since the showdown a few days prior with Cassidy's ex-fiancé, Robert Barrington, life had begun to return to normal. The need to look over shoulders or keep an eye on the large display windows that fronted their shop had begun to recede. So had the hard bundle of nerves that had settled deep in her stomach.

What they'd not yet decided was what to do about the rubies. Hence today's visit from the good detective.

Reed's eyebrows rose. "Jeez, Baldwin. Hungry?"

Max's gaze drifted toward the depleted cookie plate and the smatter of crumbs on Reed's black T-shirt. "Pot. Meet kettle."

Cassidy's new fiancé, Tucker, walked in. She might have half the building to herself, but Lilah didn't think this room had seen this many men in one place since it was under construction.

"Did you seriously eat them all, Baldwin?" Tucker asked, looking at the empty plate on the counter.

Tucker's tall form and sweet smile brought about her own grin. Cassidy had chosen well. Tucker Buchanan was a gentleman, in every sense of the word. He'd also protected Cassidy when the threat around the jewels had hit its worst, and Lilah knew they were crazy about each other.

She turned back to the stove and let her new reality settle over her once more.

There were men inside her business. In her kitchen, in

fact. Large men who had seen violence and were equally capable of committing it.

That fact should have bothered her, yet they'd all made her feel safe.

Secure.

Max and Tucker were former military, part of the Army Corps of Engineers. She didn't know all the details, but Cassidy had shared a bit of Tucker's background and she knew his skills in architectural design were only rivaled by his ability to destroy architectural marvels.

As for Reed...

She hadn't pegged his personality yet and she was usually very good when it came to reading others.

Usually.

Lilah shook off the old memories and focused on the matter at hand. She'd made a valiant attempt to read the detective over the past week and while she didn't have all the answers, she couldn't deny that he also made her feel safe.

His devotion to justice certainly went a long way toward cementing that feeling, but it was something more. Something hovering just out of reach. A sense, really, that Reed Graystone was more than the sum of his parts.

And there she had it. Where her business used to be full of estrogen and wedding talk, it had devolved into discussions centered on danger, decades-long deception and men who gave her moon eyes over her gooey, pork-infused pastries.

She wasn't a fanciful woman—she'd lost that skill long ago—but even she wasn't immune to that juxtaposition.

"Come on. Back in the main office so we can discuss finally getting back to normal." She didn't miss the matched looks of longing across all three men's faces at the small scattering of appetizers on the warmed plate. "After, of course, I throw another batch in the oven."

* * *

Reed snatched the last puff pastry—more to piss Max Baldwin off than any real hunger—and watched the by-play between the three women who had descended into his life like Dorothy in the middle of Oz.

While he didn't quite feel as if he had a house on his head, he was increasingly concerned how his world had exploded in vivid Technicolor.

Speaking of color…

Lilah returned, now with a plate of desserts that drew a worshipful expression from Max, and set them down on an oversize coffee table in the main area of what Reed supposed was a bridal salon. A long wall of mirrors and elaborate-looking dressing rooms stood on the far wall and he had positioned himself in a very large velour chair in a shade of red that screamed brothel or a Louis of France. Fourteenth? Fifteenth? Who the hell knew.

Buchanan's boxer, Bailey, watched with equally worshipful eyes until Lilah pulled a boiled soup bone from behind her back. Those solemn brown eyes nearly rolled into the back of his square head as she offered it to him.

If dogs could talk, Reed suspected he'd have heard a prayer of thanksgiving. As it were, the ugly—yet lovable—beast gently took the bone between his teeth and trotted toward a welcome mat near the front door.

The dog had lain near that door since all of them had assembled earlier, his devotion to his task only pulled away by the arrival of the food. While he didn't consider himself a fanciful man, Reed could only think of the boxer's behavior as sentinel duty.

He keyed in to the reassuring feel of his gun strapped to his ankle, but couldn't deny the presence of the large dog offered a damn good bit of reassurance, as well.

He turned back to Lilah, color exploding before his

eyes once more as he looked at her. It wasn't simply the vivid pink streak that stood out in her blond hair, currently brushed behind her ear, but it was *her*.

The woman just transmitted *pink* in everything she was.

Her warm, rosy cheeks. A wide, generous mouth, with plump cherry-colored lips that had drawn his gaze more times than he could count. And her usual pair of thick pink plastic shoes that seemed her perpetual choice of footwear.

Even with her nondescript white baker's coat and black slacks, when Reed looked at her he saw pink. The fact that he found that wash of color so enticing was only the latest surprise in a long line of them over the past few days.

"We need a plan to draw them out."

Reed keyed back in to the discussion, his ears ringing with the mention of a plan. "I went along with you on this once but not again. You need to get those damn stones out of your possession."

"We've been over this." Lilah's voice was quiet, her usual animation gone. "No one, not even the Dallas PD, will be able to protect all of us. And without the stones we don't have any leverage."

"And with them you're all sitting ducks." Reed was done pussyfooting around the argument. He understood the choice to hide the jewels. And while he didn't have to like it, he also knew his jurisdiction to do anything about it was suspect.

But he'd be damned if he was going to sit there and let them talk about drawing out some criminal who was determined to get ahold of the find. *Especially* after their faceless enemy had proven how ruthless he was in his pursuit to acquire them.

The break-in that had started it all had devolved into a body dumped at the back door and an attempted kidnapping on Cassidy. Although they'd determined the responsible party for the body was Robert Barrington, Cassidy's ex-fiancé, the man's lack of history as one of Dallas's criminal masterminds didn't sit well with Reed.

Someone else was pulling the strings.

Reed took a cream puff and considered the rest of the players. Although he'd initially given Buchanan a second look, the man's devotion to helping the women and his subsequent relationship with Cassidy had changed Reed's mind.

Buchanan's partner, Max Baldwin, was an interesting one. Stoic and stiff, he'd obviously come to understand the implications of taking possession of the stones after their discovery. And, in his remorse, had grown gruff and impatient as they worked through various scenarios.

Reed also hadn't missed the byplay between Max and Violet. His career was all about observing people, and the two of them had something going on, even if it was just a massive case of verbal foreplay.

But none of it changed the fact Violet was mad Max accidently focused the mastermind's attention onto the women. She was smart and sharp, but her every exchange with the man held decidedly tart edges and a layer of frustration that his impulsive act had put them in this position in the first place.

Reed rubbed the back of his neck, willing away the tension curled there. This was a case, nothing more. He had no right to be mad or frustrated with the three women who'd had their livelihood—and their lives—interrupted.

But nothing about this case had been easy or smooth and he was increasingly coming to care about what happened to this crew.

So here they were. Four days into an endlessly circulating argument that he hadn't figured a way around.

The women had jewels that they were rightfully allowed

to possess. Said jewels had a bad history and an even worse present. And none of them were willing to give them up.

Damn it.

He always knew how to figure his way around a problem. It was the Reed Graystone way of life. He was *good* at figuring his way around problems.

Cassidy's phone ringing punctuated the tense silence and he saw the quick flash in her eyes that suggested she'd like to ignore it, before a reluctant sigh had her off the couch and headed for the hallway. Bailey glanced up at her with an adoring expression as she moved toward the back of the shop—another sign of just how *in* this together the women of Elegance and Lace and the men of Dragon Designs were.

Even the dog had adopted the women as his own.

Reed's gaze drifted to Lilah and he fought the swell of attraction that always punctuated his interactions with her.

How had it come to this?

His thoughts had been consumed by a woman who lived and breathed pink and who perpetually smelled like vanilla frosting. And even if the vanilla was a side effect of her job as baker extraordinaire, the pink was just a flat-out choice.

He liked long, lithe women who dressed in all black and avoided commitment like the plague.

Instead, he'd found himself increasingly intrigued with a woman who looked like a cross between a guardian angel and a pixie with a Pepto-Bismol addiction.

Cassidy waved from the hallway, the dark expression on her face a match for the somber words she murmured over and over. "When? How? Who would do that?"

Tucker crossed to her, his arms around her as she continued to murmur in shocked surprise.

"What is it?" Violet spoke first as soon as Cassidy had hung up the phone.

"Robert was found dead. Out in an empty field near Fair Park."

Robert, the ex-fiancé who'd tried to kidnap her.

"Murdered, more like." The words were out before Reed could pull them back or soften the implication, and he was already reaching for his phone to contact the investigating officer.

Lilah spoke first, her vivid features going ashen with the question. "But wasn't he in jail?"

"Which means whoever's been behind all this got to him or managed to post bail for him." Reed dropped his phone back into his pocket. The call could wait.

"Where the hell did he find a judge who would let him post bail?" Tucker's anger exploded like a gunshot. "The bastard attempted premeditated murder."

"That's what I need to find out."

Lilah busied herself in her kitchen, the long, sleek countertops shining like a homing beacon as she set out trays of ingredients. Cupcakes today, for a wedding shower in Highland Park, followed by a delivery of a luscious Italian crème cake for a ninetieth-birthday party. The grandmother of a happy bride they'd taken care of the previous spring.

It was a light day, relatively speaking, and Lilah thought she might work on a few designs for an upcoming holiday wedding. She'd tried several poinsettia designs in fondant and hadn't yet settled on what she wanted.

Anything to keep her mind off the matter at hand.

Attempted kidnapping. Stolen jewels. Murder.

A hard shiver gripped her shoulders as she thought of Cassidy's former fiancé. She'd never liked Robert Barrington, even if she'd never been exactly sure why, but she certainly had never wished the man dead.

Of course, that was before he'd attempted to kidnap and attack her best friend.

Lilah wrapped her arms around her midsection at the all-too-recent memory. She was deeply grateful Cassidy was okay, but knew her friend still had a long road ahead. Robert had almost gleefully shared the horrific news that Cassidy's sister had been murdered by her husband years earlier.

Cassidy had worked so hard to move on from the loss of her sister. To have the truth revealed in such a callous manner only reinforced what an evil man Robert had truly been.

She fought off another shiver at the memories of her ex that always hovered just beneath the surface. The angry words. The dismissive statements. But when the statements had turned to fists…

"Fitzgerald shower?"

Cassidy's statement pulled Lilah from her dark place, the memories skittering back into the shadows. "Yep."

"Champagne frosting?"

"Of course."

"Yum." Cassidy ran a hand down Lilah's back, the comforting gesture at odds with their casual words.

Lilah should have known her friend had seen the memories reflected in her eyes.

True to form, Cassidy hovered an extra moment—waiting—but when Lilah said nothing, she moved on, pouring a cup of coffee at the counter before refilling Lilah's own mug. "I'd offer to help, but since a Betty Crocker box mix and Rice Krispies treats are the limits of my baking abilities, I'll keep you company instead."

"Never underestimate a woman who can microwave marshmallows."

"It's a gift." Cassidy laid the coffee down.

"And the company's always welcome."

They drifted through odds and ends of conversation. An upcoming wedding they each had a role in. Violet's latest report from the Design District's last town hall, including a collective promise from the nearby businesses to help keep a closer watch. And a new boutique that had opened in Uptown that they wanted to do some advance recon on.

Normal. Comfortable. And deftly avoiding the elephant that sat on their chests like a lead weight.

"You didn't stay on long with your mom last night." Lilah disengaged the paddles from her hand mixer, scraping each with a spatula before giving them to Cassidy. She knew her friend and her pleading puppy-dog eyes were a match for Bailey's. Cassidy let out a small sigh of contentment.

"No one's batter tastes like yours."

"Naturally."

Lilah waited her own beat before pressing her point. "You haven't told your mother what happened yet."

"No." Cassidy shook her head, her blue eyes going wide.

Lilah knew she wasn't one to tell others how to make their family decisions, but, well, this was *them*. They were a unit and she'd be damned if she was going to keep her mouth shut.

The news of Robert Barrington's death was one more confirmation that things were spiraling out of control. "You need to tell her. For her own protection, she and your father need to know."

"She won't keep it to herself."

Lilah began to transfer the rich, cream-colored batter into cupcake trays. "Then we need to convince her why she has to. We'll give her enough information to make her understand and keep the rest to ourselves."

"She won't. Not coming on the heels of the news about

Leah." Cassidy hesitated, her throat constricting as her eyes grew red at the rims. "I can't tell her."

"Then we'll help you."

Lilah kept her gaze focused on the neat, even rows of batter as the mixture filled each well of the muffin pan. She knew her friend struggled—from the close call with her ex to the even more startling revelation that her sister, Leah, was killed by her former brother-in-law.

The news had come as a shock—Robert's confession coming as he attempted to kidnap Cassidy—and Reed had begun working that murder angle, as well. Not that he'd been willing to share much the night before, which had been the ostensible reason for his visit.

"You okay?"

Lilah glanced up from the pan. "Yeah, why?"

"You just looked really annoyed there for a minute."

Willing that strange mix of frustration and intrigue over the stoic detective to stop messing with her focus, Lilah smiled. "I'm just glad you're okay. And I'm really glad Tucker is here."

"Me, too." Satisfied the telling moment had passed, Lilah shifted to the next pan and continued the precise deposits of batter.

"What did Robert get himself involved in?" Cassidy crossed to the sink and busied herself with rinsing off the beaters. "And how could I have been so oblivious?"

"You were in love."

"No." Her friend shook her head before turning at the sink. "I understand what it truly means to be in love now, and what I felt before wasn't even close."

"It doesn't mean you didn't have feelings. Or a basic belief that your fiancé was above theft, kidnapping and possible murder."

Cassidy scrubbed at her cheeks, the tears fading in the

bright morning sunlight that flooded the kitchen. "You sound so rational when you put it that way."

"Because it *is* rational. You didn't do anything wrong." The words were honest—she meant each and every one— even as a tiny voice rose up and whispered what a hypocrite she was.

Not to mention terribly inept at taking her own advice.

"You're right. I know you're right. Maybe if I say it enough times I'll believe it."

"Don't worry." Lilah ran a spatula around the rim of the bowl, capturing the last bit of batter for the cupcakes. "Tucker's hell-bent on convincing you. And what he misses, Vi and I can manage."

"He's surprisingly stubborn." A tremulous smile tilted Cassidy's lips. "Sort of like two friends I know."

Lilah dropped the now-empty bowl into the sink, then gave Cassidy a quick squeeze. "Skills, we've got 'em."

"*And* you bake like an angel." Cassidy's arm wrapped tight around Lilah's waist. "Is there no end to your talents?"

"Nope."

Lilah reveled in the gentle affection, the love and comfort of her best friend going a long way toward banishing the dark memories that had accompanied her earlier.

Basking in the light of a pretty summer morning and the love of her best friend, she doggedly fought off the memories of a congenial man with the personality of a monster. The deception that lived behind a jovial wink and a knowing nod for the rest of the world.

She'd left that nightmare behind over four years ago, and there was no way in hell she was ever going back.

Chapter 2

Reed scanned the paperwork on the clipboard and tried to make sense of what he saw. A hastily scribbled signature at the bottom of official papers ensured one Robert Barrington was released from jail three days ago.

The printed name underneath the scrawl was no doubt fake, but Reed tapped it quickly into his phone before shoving it back into his pocket.

"Thanks, Gannon."

The officer nodded, his face bright and eager, such a huge departure from the man he'd been a few years before. "Glad I could help."

"How's the baby?"

"Jade's crawling already." Gannon's deep brown eyes sparkled brightly, a happy haze filling them up as he spoke about his daughter. A picture soon followed the words and Reed found himself oohing and aahing over a chubby little girl with mocha skin, eyes that matched her daddy's and the sweetest smile he'd ever seen.

Reed let Gannon talk—partly because he was happy for the man and partly because it was good to see his old friend engaged in life again—and smiled through a story of how the baby had managed to wedge herself behind the couch while learning to crawl. "She's amazing."

Reed could only nod his agreement. "Of course she is."

He let the conversation run out naturally, ending it with a quick handshake before he headed out into the noon sun. August was blazing in full force and he briefly toyed with marching back into the office building and finding something else to work on.

He'd lived in Dallas his entire life. But even with thirty-two years of Texas summers under his belt, every time he thought he'd gotten used to the heat, about a million degrees rose up to slap him in the face.

Or give him a full body hug was more like it.

Reed slipped into his car, the quick blast of air from the vents keeping him company with his thoughts.

Thoughts that had taken a decidedly dark turn as images of three bloodred rubies rose up to edge out the heat.

He paid his way out of the downtown parking lot and then used his voice controls to call his partner.

"Jessie, it's Reed. I need you to look up a name for me."

He rattled off the spelling of the name Gannon had given him and the sound of tapping computer keys on the other end was audible.

"Okay, the computer's searching. How's Gannon doing?"

"Raving about his baby daughter with a smile that could rival a beauty queen's."

"I could eat that baby up with a spoon she's so sweet."

Reed didn't know if he quite agreed with the analogy, but any attempt at protest faded as Jessie started in on a funny story about the three of them from high school. They'd both worried over their old friend and were happy to know Gannon's return to civilian life from the service had begun to take a more positive turn.

He shook his head to himself at Jessie's easy transition from cop to high school gossip. She wore one as simply as the other, and—oddly—both suited.

"Sasha and Jade are good for him. Real good."

"That they are."

The veteran's organization they'd finally convinced Gannon to join had done its part, as well. An image of his friend and his wife filled Reed's thoughts before morphing into an image of him and Lilah, his arm wrapped around her shoulders.

And where the hell had *that* come from?

"You got anything yet, Jess?"

Her voice grew flat at his gruff bark. "Yes, bossy. It's just coming up now."

"Well?"

"That's odd." He heard her frowning through the phone before another round of key tapping, this time louder than the last.

"What's going on?"

"I don't see any paperwork under that name. Nor do I even see any paperwork on a Robert Barrington."

A hard clench fisted his stomach in knots and he reached for the roll of antacids he kept in a small well under the radio. "Jess, I just looked at the papers in Gannon's hand."

"Then we need to figure out who the hell processed Barrington, because nothing is here."

Reed continued turning the paperwork issue over in his mind as he navigated the Design District. Jessie was already looking into who might have taken care of Barrington's arrest and he'd decided to head back to Elegance and Lace.

The shop wasn't that far from the jail and he mulled over the mystery of Robert Barrington's life and death as the storefronts slowly morphed from fast food, dingy bars and bail bondsmen establishments into the more refined— yet still edgy—storefronts of antiques shops, design firms and newly built apartments.

The district sure as hell had come back. He remembered coming down here as a kid with his mother, her hunt through the endless design shops—open only to professionals—some of the longest days of his life.

She'd been a lone single mother back then, taking whatever job she could to keep them afloat, desperate to keep a roof over both their heads as she tried to get her design business off the ground.

Then she'd met Tripp Lange on the job while decorating his new home after divorce number two. Tripp had quickly tumbled into marriage number three, and Reed and his mother had moved from a small apartment in the suburbs to a mansion in the swankiest part of Dallas.

All things considered, Reed knew, things could have been far worse. Tripp wasn't a bad guy. A bit of a caricature, with his oversize cigars and small sports car, but the man was fairly decent all the same.

Tripp had embraced Reed and his mother, and while he'd shown no interest in becoming a father again at fifty-two, he had provided a home and anything Reed could have asked for. And he'd made his mother happy, which had gone even further toward putting him in the good-guy camp.

The large windows of Elegance and Lace filled his view as he pulled into the street parking in front of Lilah's store. The damage from a week earlier was nowhere in evidence, with mannequins covered in frothy wedding gowns back in their place of honor in the windows. Beyond that he could see the thick-cushioned couches that made up the seating area, and even farther back, Cassidy Tate was visible, carrying one of those frothy confections with the same delicate steps of the Dallas bomb squad.

Weddings.

He shook his head as he stepped out into the heat and headed into the store, a discreet security bell ringing to announce his arrival. He got marriage. And while he wasn't anxious to dive headfirst into one, he got the idea of it all. That one person you were crazy enough about to link up with.

But a wedding?

Waste of money, as far as he could tell.

A dress you wore once. A cake someone slaved over for days. And an open bar and rich food you used to anesthetize your guests into some sort of zombie pack who danced to dopey songs, half of which the radio refused to still play.

"Detective." Cassidy's voice reached him over the dress in her arms as she caught sight of him from the hall. "Come on in."

"Miss Tate?"

"Just give me a minute to put this down." She ducked into what he knew to be a studio off the main hallway of the shop, full of all the things she used to cut, measure and sew dress after dress.

In moments she was back, dress-free, her gaze tense. "I saw that dark look on your face when you walked in. Everything okay?"

Reed glanced around her business and knew he needed to tread lightly. But his strange walk down memory lane over his mother and the odd thoughts that had gripped him as he looked up in the windows won out.

"I'm trying to figure out the appeal of a wedding."

The tension vanished, fading away in the face of what

she loved to do for a living. "You mean you're not a fan of happily-ever-after?"

"The happy part, sure. Yeah. But the wedding part. I don't get it."

"It's a celebration. A way to tell the world you're in love and share that with the people you care about most."

"Then why do couples fight over the guest list?" He distinctly remembered how Jessie had bitched for weeks about Dave's family and how they'd upset several relatives who didn't rate an invite.

"The fight's just about the tension of the moment. People get over it. Plus—" she added a wink "—making up's so much fun."

Recognizing a lost cause, Reed shrugged and pointed toward the couches. "Do you mind if we talk for a few minutes? I do have some details on Barrington I'd like to ask you about."

The warmth of her excitement faded. "I'd like Lilah to be here with me."

"Sit down. I'll go get her."

Lilah smoothed another sheet of fondant, already envisioning the elaborate ivy that would rise up along the side of her latest project. The shade of green had come out perfect and the slender white lines she'd experimentally painted on a few of the leaves cut from the first sheet gave just the look she was going for.

Adrenaline kicked in her veins as the vision began its slow progression into reality and she danced toward her already-blaring docking station to switch from the always-kicky Donna Summer to some Aerosmith.

Steven Tyler's voice had just screeched when she let out a screech of her own as a large hand settled on her shoulder.

Immediately, she swung out, her arm a hard arc against the muscled, solid chest behind her.

"Whoa!"

Fear and panic warred with confusion as Lilah twisted once more to see her attacker, reality pushing through the moment as the image of Reed Graystone registered in her mind.

He had backed up several feet and was already reaching for the music dock on the counter when she stopped, her heart racing like a Thoroughbred.

"What the hell are you doing?" His loud voice echoed even louder with the loss of music.

"What are you doing sneaking up on me?"

"I'm not sneaking! You were dancing like a manic fairy in here and I was trying to get your attention. I hollered your name about four times."

"Oh." Lilah stilled, the initial panic fading into a wash of embarrassment.

Which only managed to piss her off.

Her shoulders hunched and she mentally shook off the weight, standing straighter, even though her voice remained petulant and gruff when she spoke. "Why not just turn the music off, then? I regularly carry a knife in my hand. You should watch yourself, Detective."

"So noted." The light of battle still sparkled in his gray eyes, but she saw something else.

Concern.

"I need to talk to Cassidy about something and she'll do better with someone with her."

The lingering panic in her belly faded in full at the mention of her friend, along with that gentle awareness in his eyes. "What's wrong?"

"I've got some questions about Barrington. I also have an update."

Lilah glanced at her workstation, then to Reed. "Give me a minute to cover everything and I'll be right out."

He followed her to the counter, his gaze on the work already laid out. "Those are gorgeous. They look like real leaves."

"That's sort of the point."

"But I mean, really real. Like I could smell them if I were close enough. Are they edible?"

"Yep."

"Can I try one?"

She lifted one of the already completed leaves with a small cake knife. "Take this and go. I'll be right out."

The leaf had already disappeared through his lips and Lilah struggled to hold back a smile at the grimace on his face. "It's chewy."

"It's fondant."

"Do people really like that?" That deep voice was still distinctive, even around a mouth full of gummy sugar.

"Some people do. And it makes for stunning decoration, which is why it's one of the weapons in a baker's arsenal."

"I'll keep that in mind." He swallowed hard, then backed toward the door. "Speaking of weapons… Why don't you do me a favor and leave the knives in here?"

Lilah watched him disappear through the kitchen entry into the main store. The urge to go to her friend was strong, but she gave herself a moment to give in to the equally strong urge to linger.

Every time she thought she had a handle on her reaction to Reed Graystone, the damn man showed up again and had her rethinking her position.

Nearly beating him up in the middle of her kitchen likely wasn't lost on the good detective, either, Lilah suspected.

Ignoring the embarrassment, along with that small swirl

of desire that flamed to life every time he showed up, she covered the leaves with plastic wrap and headed for the main salon.

No reason to keep the man waiting.

Lilah had known Cassidy Tate and Violet Richardson since the first day of college. The three of them had immediately bonded over their living space, their common interests and an innate ability to talk about anything and everything that struck their collective fancy.

So the wide-eyed friend who sat on the couch, her slender frame set in fragile lines, was a surprise.

Cassidy was many things, but delicate to the point of frail wasn't it.

Lilah sat and took her hand before turning her attention fully on the detective. "What did you find out?"

"We've been looking into Robert Barrington's background, especially who might have sprung for his bail."

"His parents, I'm sure," Cassidy said.

"I'm afraid not."

Lilah listened to the details, shocked by the pervasive sense of something foul and malicious that filled Reed's words. Paperwork they couldn't quite find, signed off on by a nameless, faceless individual who had paid for Robert's release.

All resulting in a second dead body in less than a week.

The fact they knew both of the deceased had only pushed the creep factor off the charts.

"So I need to ask you again, what knowledge do you have or could you possibly have on Robert Barrington?"

Fierce, protective urges rose up first at the leading question, stilled only when she caught the sincerity in Reed's gaze. Measuring her words, Lilah kept her tone even.

"We've been over this and over this. None of us had contact with Robert Barrington until he reappeared last week."

"I understand that, but is it possible Cassidy's former association with the man could lead to a few more strings to tug?"

"Tucker and I have discussed this, as well." Cassidy offered up a tremulous smile before she leaned forward, her innate strength forcing itself to the surface. "And after I got over being mad at him for asking me basically the same question, I got to thinking."

"And what conclusion did you come to?" Reed probed.

"There *are* connections and have been for a long time. How deep they run is the bigger question."

Lilah sensed the shift in Cassidy's demeanor before her friend took her hand, the grip of her fingers tight with support.

The whirling flash of panic that had come upon her in the kitchen returned in full force.

She *knew* that look.

It was pity veiled behind a layer of sympathy. She'd thought their relationship well past looks like that, but apparently she'd been wrong.

As wrong as thinking she could stay several steps ahead of her past.

"I think Lilah's ex-husband, Steven DeWinter, might be the connection."

Chapter 3

From the start, Reed had figured Lilah Castle for secrets. He made a living out of sizing up individuals with quick, precise impressions and using those impressions to figure out their true motives. He'd honed the skill young and he was good at it.

Damn good at it.

But over the past few days, he'd increasingly suspected the secrets Lilah carried held pain and abuse. The visceral shock that painted her pale face in deep, grooved lines only confirmed his instincts.

What he hadn't counted on was the raw, pulsing fury that gripped him at the confirmation.

Shifting from his position on a plush, purple velvet chair, he took Lilah's free side and pressed a hand to her back. "Breathe. Slowly in and out."

He caught Cassidy's gaze over the top of Lilah's pink-and-blond hair, a world of acknowledgment in that one look before the same rough voice that greeted him in the kitchen barked back at him, "I'm fine."

"Of course you are. So humor me by sitting still and taking a few deep breaths."

The tense set of her shoulders never waned, but she did take the breaths as he'd asked. "Good. Nice and slow."

She might have grudgingly taken the breaths, but there was no way he could miss her white-knuckled grip on Cassidy's fingers.

But it was when her friend shifted her free hand to brush several strands of hair behind Lilah's ear that Reed truly understood the bond between the two women. "I think it's time we gave Detective Graystone a bit of background."

"Like he can't look it up if he wanted to."

Cassidy ignored the continued gruff responses. "Oh, I don't know. I think it might come better from you."

He saw Lilah war with the truth of that statement as something strange worked itself into his chest. He wanted her to open up to him. Even more than that, he wanted her to believe she could trust him.

And as someone who'd spent his adult life around victims of violence, he knew trust was the very last thing Lilah Castle would ever give him.

With that fresh in his thoughts, he gave her space, returning to the gaudy chair. He kept his gaze level, focused on hers. "Cassidy's right. I can look it up. But I'd rather hear it from you."

The convivial baker who kept things light and breezy with a smart mouth and airy confections was nowhere in evidence as Lilah seemed to sink into herself. Even the pink streak in her hair seemed duller somehow. As if the color were a mood ring to its owner.

Ignoring the inane observation, Reed kept his focus on Lilah.

"I was married to Steven for almost two years. We met when I went to work in one of his restaurants."

Reed nodded, encouraging her to continue. He knew the name DeWinter, but until she said *restaurants*, he hadn't made the connection with the popular local restaurateur who had risen to near-stratospheric heights in the past few years.

"He was temperamental and moody and an amazing creator. His star was on the rise then and I was hooked. All that temperamental moodiness focused on me. Directed toward me. It was amazing and passionate and fiery and I fell for all of it."

Reed would confirm the timing later, but based on what he knew of the women's ages, he assumed Lilah was no more than twenty-two or twenty-three when the relationship took place. And while he knew no one was immune to a heady dose of passion, it was especially alluring at that age.

"There's nothing wrong with caring for someone."

"No." She shook her head, her eyes dark with memories and pain. "But there is something wrong when you make excuses for the bastard every time that passionate moodiness turns dark and twisted."

"Lilah—" Cassidy reached for her friend as if to pull her close, but Lilah was already up and off the couch.

"It's a story as old as time and I fell for it. Bright-eyed innocent in love with an older man."

Before either of them could stop her, Lilah was already down the back hall toward the kitchen, hollering over her shoulder, "The rest is in a nice fat juicy file at the Dallas PD. I suggest you look it up."

Reed watched her go before he turned to Cassidy. "I'm sorry to have to dig underneath all this. I know it's a sensitive subject."

The slim redhead hesitated and Reed gave her the space. He knew her reluctance for what it was—loyalty to a friend—and he only admired her more for it.

"Sensitive. And incredibly raw, despite the passage of time."

"I take it you haven't shared your connection theory with her before."

"No." Cassidy shook her head. "I didn't even put it together until Tucker and I were talking last night. And if you weren't here, I'd likely have waited to bring it up until Violet was back and we could tell Lilah together."

"What connection do you think there is?"

She cocked her head, interest sparking in her gaze. "You're a Dallas native, aren't you?"

"A dubious honor, but yes."

"Then you know, for all its size, Dallas is a small town. Social circles overlap other social circles and all that."

Not if you hopped circles.

Reed thought about his own childhood. The friends and life of his youth had absolutely nothing to do with the social circle cultivated for him after his mother remarried.

Brushing off the stubborn old memories, he forced his attention onto the present. "From Lilah's comments it sounds like she met DeWinter after she went to work. I'm not making the connection with your broader social life."

"Steven knew my late brother-in-law, Charlie."

Seeing as how the man was still lying in the morgue, an image of Charlie McCallum rose easily in his mind. "By all accounts, DeWinter was a rising star and your brother-in-law wasn't. What was the connection?"

Cassidy's smile was gentle, but her voice remained flat. "It's amazing how often wastrel behavior is excused on youth. It was only after Charlie married Leah and he maintained his inability to keep a job that we began to figure it out."

"I still don't follow the connection to Lilah and De-Winter."

Cassidy shrugged. "It's just one of those odd social-circle connections. Leah had already met Charlie and they were dating. Lilah was just out of school, working for DeWinter and crazy in love. I hadn't met Robert yet but had heard his name mentioned a few times. And then one Friday afternoon on a rare day off for all of us, we made the connection over margaritas in Uptown."

Reed ignored the irrational spurt of irritation at the idea of Lilah crazy in love and focused on Cassidy instead. "DeWinter and Charlie were friends?"

"Very distant cousins, actually. They had been distant as kids and then started hanging out together as they got older."

Reed sat back, the plush velvet of his chair sucking him in just like the damn twists and turns of this case.

Who were these women?

And how was he ever going to get to the bottom of what was happening to them if the sands kept shifting?

Lilah had no interest in her fondant leaves, and after ruining half a tray with her distracted thoughts, she finally wrapped what was left and vowed to work on them later.

Lazy.

Incompetent.

Unwilling to give the work your all.

She shoved the tray into the fridge as the words looped through her mind, whip quick, and delivered in the deep male voice of her nightmares.

Steven.

Her hands fumbled over the edge of a carton of eggs as

she grabbed the box, then a large container of heavy whipping cream. Still trembling, she set both on the counter and slammed the fridge door closed with her hip.

This was *her* kitchen. Hers.

She fought to remember that as the battle with her memories increasingly took over.

His criticisms had started in a kitchen. *His* kitchen.

She'd been surprised at first, hurt even, but she knew he ran his restaurant with an iron fist and had already observed how he spoke to the rest of the staff and crew. She certainly shouldn't be immune because they were sleeping together.

So she'd worked harder. Come in earlier. Tried more elaborate creations.

And when she'd won an award as one of Dallas's premier up-and-coming pastry chefs, Steven had exploded instead of being excited for her. He lamented her suddenly large head instead of focusing on the increased prestige that drove even more patrons into his restaurant, all determined to add several expensive desserts to their already-sizable dinner checks.

Still, she'd soldiered on. Their wedding was only a month away and their nerves were all frayed. The daily grind of the restaurant, his distracted focus with the new location he was opening across town and, of course, the four-hundred-person guest list would take a toll on anyone.

But it was the hard slam into their Sub-Zero refrigerator in their gleaming dream of a kitchen three weeks after they got married that finally began to open her eyes to the man she'd bound her life to in marriage.

He'd apologized, of course. Had told her it was an accident and he'd slipped on the floor and fell into her and, besides, he was so tired. So worn-out. So full of the work and the stress of their new life together that she *had* to know he hadn't meant it.

And she'd believed.

Lilah methodically cracked and measured egg yolk after egg yolk into her mixing bowl, their rich yellow breaking on contact with the hard, ceaseless paddles. Sugar followed, blending with the eggs and thickening the mixture into a thin paste.

Not only had she believed he'd changed, but she began to believe him when he told her a new crust she'd perfected wasn't very good. And she'd trusted when he told her he was going to get some good press when he brought in a guest pastry chef for a few weeks to create a bit of buzz around the restaurant. And she'd blindly followed when he told her he wanted his wife by his side each night greeting his guests in his restaurants and not in the kitchen.

And oh, how she'd paid.

"You want to talk?"

Lilah heard Cassidy's voice a moment after she registered the slamming beat from her music dock had stopped. She never looked up; instead she kept her gaze on her bowl. She measured the cream by sight, adding it smoothly into the mixture. "It's nothing we haven't talked about before."

"Doesn't mean we shouldn't talk about it again."

"It's the past, Cassidy. And it's well behind me."

"Well, that's the biggest load of crap I've ever heard and that includes the pile of bs Melinda Crosby's cheating fiancé tried to level on me when I caught him in the dressing room with Melinda's maid of honor."

Lilah looked up despite herself, shocked at the news. "He was getting it on with Shanna Thomas? Why didn't you tell Vi and I that part?"

"Because I am a discreet proprietor who can manage my clients in their less-than-stellar moments."

Lilah shook her head, sad at the news. "And she still married the dog."

"Despite my best efforts to gently persuade her to re-think this major life decision, yes, she did."

"It's not for us to fix. Even when we see the glaring signs of a future of misery."

"Which is the reason I'm standing here, actually."

Lilah flipped off her mixer. "What's that supposed to mean?"

"You did escape a future of misery yet here you are, wallowing in it."

A renewed shot of anger bloomed in Lilah's stomach, a preferred counterpoint to the sickly coating of nausea that had lingered along with the bad memories. "Don't go there with me. You have no right to go there with me."

"I have every right. I'm your friend. And I'm here for you. And it's my job to keep you honest when you're fall-ing back into the idea that you somehow brought the whole damn thing on yourself."

"Of course I brought it on myself."

"And there we go with the piles of crap again." Cassidy gentled her voice before reaching out.

Lilah wanted to reject the kindness and understanding and keep on with her misery, but the promise her friends had made to her several years before echoed in her ear.

We're here for you.

Cassidy and Violet had made the promise and they'd lived it each and every day since.

Lilah took the proffered hand and squeezed tight before pointing to her mixer. "I'm at a delicate phase."

"Is that your Bavarian cream?"

"Yep."

Cassidy took an exaggerated step back. "Don't let me

be the one to keep the angels from weeping. I'll wait until you're done."

Lilah finished the mix quickly, the cream one of her trademarks, as she caught Cassidy's movement from the corner of her eye. Her friend kept out of her way, crossing to one of the kitchen's work spaces to snag a stool.

The paddles kept up their work, as well, mixing the cream into thick, stiff peaks as she dropped in the last few ingredients.

"Please tell me I can dip in a clean spoon for a taste."

"I'll do you one better."

Lilah snagged a small bowl from underneath the counter and scooped out a small serving of the cream. Handing it over, she still saw the concern in Cassidy's gaze, but was pleased to see it warred with avarice over the fresh treat.

She hated pity.

Give her a crazy bride, a demented mother-in-law and a side order of wedding drama and she'd handle it like a pro. Pull three all-nighters in a row to finish up the cake and desserts for the wedding of the season and she'd push through like nobody's business.

But put her oldest friend with a pair of sad eyes and a concerned tone in her light Texas twang and Lilah froze all the way through.

Pity suggested weakness.

And she'd vowed after finally leaving Steven that she'd never be weak again.

"Where's the detective?"

Cassidy smiled before licking the edge of her spoon clean. "You mean Detective Yummy?"

"I believe his last name is Graystone." Lilah scooped her own small bowl, breaking one of her usual requirements to avoid indulging in her own creations.

"Only if you're blind." Cassidy's gaze sharpened, no sign of pity in sight. "And you're not."

"Let's put his attributes aside for the moment. What did you tell him?"

"The long-standing connections between Charlie and Steven. And if you add in Robert, there's a merry little threesome going on there."

"Two of whom are now dead."

"Yep." Cassidy set her empty bowl on the counter, her gaze flitting briefly to the mixer before looking away. "It's suspicious."

"But not that surprising. Yes, they were three men who knew each other, but they also knew a heck of a lot of other people around town. I'm not making the connection."

"Someone didn't just happen to know there was a cache of faked British crown jewels underneath our shop floor. Someone found out. It would make sense it was people who know us."

Lilah shook her head, puzzling through what they already knew. "But Mrs. Beauregard said several times she and Max's grandfather never told anyone after they buried the cache."

"They did pull in an appraiser before they buried the fake crown jewels and the real rubies. Maybe the guy talked."

"But he was a friend." Lilah stopped, knowing full well it was futile to speculate. Mrs. B. and Max Senior might have said nothing, but it didn't change the fact they brought a third person into the mix. Even someone with an innate understanding of when to keep his mouth shut couldn't necessarily be expected to keep a secret over fifty years in the making.

"Has Reed run down the old appraiser?"

"I didn't ask."

"Where is he, by the way?" Lilah meant the question as an innocent one, but instantly regretted the words at her friend's sly smile.

"He had to go to the precinct. He said he'd be back later."

"He's nosy."

"He's doing his job."

"His nosy job."

"Lilah. This thing isn't over. I'm glad Reed's taken an interest in us. He's committed to finding out who's responsible and making sure we stay safe in the process."

"I know. Damn it—" Lilah broke off, her ridiculous petulance fading in the light of the truth.

"Look. I know we're in danger. And I know there's someone out there who'd like nothing more than to remove us as a collective obstacle to getting what they want."

"Which is why we're going to stay one step ahead and figure out who this mystery person might be."

"I'm sorry I wigged out over Steven."

"I'm not." Cassidy laid her bowl on the counter. "You're not a robot. And hiding in here day after day or racing around town making deliveries doesn't mean you can run from the past."

"I'm not hiding." At Cassidy's wide-eyed skepticism, Lilah pressed her point. "Come on, I'm serious. I'm not hiding. This is our business and I want to see it be successful."

"I know you do."

"Then why the sudden accusation that I'm working too hard? Last time I checked, you and Vi clocked as many hours as I did."

"We still find time for outside interests."

"One week with Tucker Buchanan does not make you an expert on outside interests."

At the mention of Tucker's name, Cassidy seemed to come alive. Electrified from the inside out. "No, but it does make me see hearts and flowers everywhere I go. Which is why I suggest you hit on Detective Yummy as fast as you can."

Steven DeWinter surveyed the quiet interior of his restaurant with a satisfied nod of his head. They were closed for lunch this week to manage the city's annual Restaurant Week festivities and he had a full house scheduled for the night.

He smiled to himself as the previous evening came to light in his mind's eye. They'd crushed it, with a packed house from five o'clock on. His sommelier had busted his ass, as well, securing several sales of some of their most expensive bottles.

It was a subtle fact Steven had learned his first year in business—people did love to spend when they felt they were being oh, so generous to the city's homeless. Even if his only requirement for participation was a small portion of the meal. He did his part and gave his fair share to the food bank the event benefited, but the drink revenue was all his.

He glanced down at the receipts his manager had prepared, a dark cloud spoiling the good news from the dinner crowd even a few high-priced bottles of wine couldn't assuage. The damn dessert revenue was still down.

He'd have to fire Wilhelm after this week was done. The guy did a decent soufflé, but his pastry crusts were thick as sand and about half as tasty.

A fleeting image of Lilah drifted through his mind, a quick shot of anger following on its heels. She'd been damn good. Better than he'd wanted to believe.

She'd also been his one weakness.

Her light-as-air mousse had flown off the menu and he still, even after all these years, had patrons asking about her Bavarian cream puffs.

His staff had been threatened to within an inch of their lives not to mention those same cream puffs could be had for a quick call across town to that damn warehouse hole she and her girlfriends now called a business.

Suddenly irritated, the triumph of the previous evening vanishing as if it had never been, he stomped toward the kitchen and the jovial voices of his prep team. He zeroed in on Wilhelm, the big man's smile as wide as Texas as he mixed up a batter for his evening's creation.

"Wilhelm."

The man snapped to attention at the sound of his name, the smile fading in full. It was only when he belatedly realized his mixer still beat in heavy, thwapping circles that he shut off the machine. "Yes, sir?"

"Dessert sales were off last night."

"I beg pardon, sir? We've got the small trios as part of each patron's meal. I plated them myself last night. Everyone received a dessert plate."

"We had very few add-on desserts."

A quick slash of fear heightened the color in the man's cheekbones as he pondered the criticism. "But we have offered dessert as part of the special menu for Restaurant Week, sir. I've used the desserts as a springboard for the fall menu and will be writing up the guest commentary. They were selected carefully to gain learning for fall."

"And I'm focused on now. Today. Fall sales don't matter to me if August sales are crap."

Wilhelm grew quiet, his eyes wide with fear. Steven reveled in that look, the large man so stymied by common business sense he appeared on the verge of tears.

None of his comrades in the kitchen staff were all that eager to help, either.

Further proof of their loyalty.

"See that you visit the tables personally this evening. I expect to see a difference in tomorrow's receipts."

He moved off, the quiet kitchen coming back to life with the rustle of pots as he headed for the main dining room.

Wilhelm needed to go. He toyed with firing the man on the spot, but common sense won out. They had a full set of reservations for three seatings a night through the end of the weekend. He detested the sniveling bastard but he needed him.

And he hated needing anyone.

Another shot of irritation speared through his midsection, cut off only by the hard buzz of his phone in his pocket. Steven dragged out the slim piece and nearly barked out a hello before he caught sight of the name on the screen. Pulse galloping, his throat was already dry as bones picked clean by vultures as he lifted the phone to his ear.

"DeWinter."

"My place. Thirty minutes."

"Of co—"

The phone had already clicked off before he could complete his sentence and Steven was oddly grateful for that fact. Conversations with the Duke were blessedly rare, but when they came it was better to take your lumps and move on.

As he dropped into the seat of his low-slung sports car five minutes later, the heat radiating around him like an oven, Steven DeWinter was forced to acknowledge the same thought in a matter of moments.

He truly hated needing anyone.

Chapter 4

Reed skimmed the police report, the sounds of the precinct fading as he dived into the data. Robert Barrington might not have a rap sheet, but Charlie McCallum wasn't so lucky. He'd been fairly clean since hooking up with Leah Tate, Cassidy's sister, but before that he'd had some issues.

Disturbing the peace. A few suspicious vice notations about his presence at parties with drug paraphernalia, even if he managed to slide on actual possession. And a nice big DUI the summer he got out of college. Was it possible the love of a good woman had made him go straight?

Reed fought a snort and knew the facts already gathered told a vastly different tale.

Charlie's present home in the city morgue, along with the confession Robert gave Cassidy that Charlie had been responsible for his wife's death, suggested McCallum had never gone straight.

He'd just gotten better at hiding it.

"So what were you doing all that time, Charlie?"

Reed brought up a state database on his laptop and fiddled with a few search queries before shifting gears to focus on the mysterious disappearance of Robert Barrington's bond paperwork. He'd already ordered up the video feeds from that day and should have them later this afternoon.

In the meantime, he was going to do some old-fashioned detective work and go visit his mother.

While he avoided dragging her into his cases, her knowledge of Dallas's elite from both inside and out made her an invaluable resource. And while he wouldn't quite say Charlie McCallum and Robert Barrington had been part of the city's elite, they'd played in that world.

Desperately wanted in, if his suspicions were correct.

Twenty minutes later he pulled into the driveway of the Park Cities home his mother and Tripp made theirs. Despite the oppressive heat, the flower beds that surrounded the massive structure were full of bright, perky flowers that practically winked in the still air.

His mother answered the door herself and he was caught—as always—by the sheer, genuine beauty in her face. Diana Graystone Lange had always seen the world in vibrant, rich colors, and those same colors seemed to reflect back on her, projecting a vivid warmth. "Reed! Darling, come in."

She ushered him inside before dragging him into a tight hug. Her head came just below his chin and her petite frame was slight in his arms. As always, she gave him one last tight squeeze before she pulled back, her smile warm and her gray eyes sharp.

She'd always had that ability. To keep her smile as a vivid beacon of distraction while her eyes did all the work.

"While I'm delighted by it, what's brought this midday visit?"

"I can't have lunch with my mother?"

"You *can* have lunch with your mother. But since you rarely do so on a random weekday, I suspect you're here for a bit more."

He pulled her close in a side-armed hug as they walked down the long foyer toward the kitchen. "I think they need to give you the detective's shield."

"I'm a mother. It amounts to the same thing."

A large pitcher of iced tea sat on the table, a thin cotton cloth wrapped around it to catch the sweat, and she poured them two glasses. "Tripp's not joining us?"

"He said he might, but he was still at the club when I spoke to him a few minutes ago. I think it'll just be us today."

While he and Tripp had come to care for each other, Reed suspected the older man understood better than he let on that he needed to give the two of them space today.

"As a matter of fact, I do need to ask you a few questions."

She handed him the glass and gestured him toward a seat at the kitchen table. Although they had a formal dining room that could seat the Dallas Cowboys football team, when it was just the two of them, his mother always insisted on the more insular warmth of the kitchen.

"Well, don't keep me in suspense."

"I caught a case last week. One that isn't what it appears."

He quickly filled his mother in on the past week, surprised to realize in the retelling just how much had occurred. The seemingly run-of-the-mill break-in at Elegance and Lace that had opened the strange turn of events that included fake copies of the British crown jewels in the floor, three genuine rubies that had lain nestled in with the fakes and two dead bodies.

"*The* crown jewels? As in the royal family and British crown jewels?"

"According to the landlady, yes."

His mother refilled their glasses before crossing to pick up a quiche cooling beside the stove. "You realize just how unbelievable this is? I knew there were fakes made during the war, but they've always been a closely guarded secret, including the hiding place of the real jewels. But to think they saved the copies and that they were buried here all this time. In Dallas, Texas. How did they even get there?"

"Josephine Beauregard. The landlady. It was her father who made the fakes."

"So why not destroy them? I can't believe they'd want them around after the threat of war had passed."

"That's what I asked. Apparently it's got something to do with the rubies."

"The real ones?"

"Yep. They wanted them out of England, too, so hiding them with the fakes was the method everyone settled on to get them out without suspicion."

The large helping his mother set down before him still steamed from its time in the oven, and a fleeting image of Lilah drifted through his thoughts as he took in the feather-light mix of eggs and piecrust. Pushing the enticing picture away, he focused on the plate. "Jeez, Mom. I'm not a growing boy anymore."

"You'll always be a growing boy to me." She took her seat opposite him and leaned forward, the large strand of pearls around her neck nearly in her slice of quiche. "Come on, come on. Tell me more. Have you seen the rubies?"

"Yes."

Her back went poker straight, the pearls slamming

against her chest with a thud. "Reed Edward Graystone, you've seen royal jewels and it took you all this time to tell me?"

"I'm doing my job."

"And I'm a woman who loves a good piece of decoration. Tell me about them."

"They were gifted to George and Elizabeth by a maharajah or someone of his ilk."

His mother went off in a fit of fancy and he gave her a minute, stuffing himself with the delicious quiche while she ranted about the Queen Mother, Queen Elizabeth and him touching something that belonged to royalty.

"Can I see them?"

He glanced up from his now-empty plate, the last bite already vanished between his lips. "They're evidence."

"I'd still like to see them." She lifted her fork and pointed it at him. "And don't talk with your mouth full."

He washed the last of his lunch down with the iced tea and nodded his acknowledgment. "Well, they're not mine to show. The women have the stones. The ones who own Elegance and Lace."

"But you just said they're evidence."

"Technically, they're property. Of the landlady, who is fine with the women holding on to them."

"But you need them for this case. And if someone's already ransacked their business, I'd think they would want the police to hold on to the jewels."

"It's a bit more complicated than that."

"How complicated?"

"How much time do you have?"

Lilah had forgotten the consult.

She never forgot their schedule, and the very fact she'd nearly missed the meeting Violet had scheduled for them with one of their October brides had left her already-raw nerves flustered and frayed.

"What are we going to serve Amanda and Quinn?"

"I've got it, Vi." Lilah stomped around the kitchen, dragging a glass serving dish from one of the cabinets. She had the Bavarian cream and she had a tray of the thick pastries. All she needed to do was add the rich mixture and she'd have cream puffs.

"Can I help you?"

Lilah eyed Violet over her shoulder. "Touch my food and die."

Violet's gaze never wavered, but she finally gave one hard nod. "You sure you're up to this today? Gabby's coming over to cover off the catering portion, and Cassidy and I can run interference for the items Elegance and Lace is responsible for. I can come back and get the cream puffs in a few minutes."

"Get out, Vi."

"Lilah—"

"Out."

Violet stalked off on the stilts she habitually wore, their heavy clicking only adding to the tension headache throbbing in her temples.

She'd be ready. She'd be fine. And she'd be brilliant, to boot.

Oh *hell*.

Lilah glanced down at her chest and saw the evidence that she was anything but fine. Her chef's coat had a large smear of cream and eggs running down dead center, both of which had crusted over into an unappealing yellow roughly the color of baby vomit.

"Damn it."

Powering through the cream puffs—she had a little over a dozen plated in moments—she then raced for the small collection of clothes she kept in her office alcove for just this reason. Her anger at Violet's prim and annoying tone still simmered as she stomped into her office. Mad with self-righteous anger, Lilah shrugged off her unbuttoned coat and flung it on the ground as she bent over, digging through the bottom drawer of her desk.

Her hand closed around a pale pink sweater set and she grabbed the cashmere like a lifeline. Who cared if it was a billion degrees outside? Violet had the AC cranked up to roughly match the air in the frozen tundra anyway.

Fingers tight on the material, she had the sweater up and out of the drawer and was already spinning around when she came face-to-face with Reed Graystone.

As she stood, unmoving, in her pale pink bra.

She'd already given him the satisfaction of a scream that very morning and she'd be damned if she was going to do it again. But neither could she stop the jackrabbit hammer of her heart in her chest as Reed stood stock-still, those delicious gray eyes wide in his face.

"You—" he managed to get out before he took a few determined steps away from her. "You should probably change."

Despite the awkward moment, she couldn't quite shake the satisfaction that bloomed in her chest at his appreciative gaze. Nor could she fully shake the tight ball of heat that had taken up residence in her stomach. He was an attractive man, and at the moment, she had his full attention.

Her gaze dipped lower, pleased to see she appeared to have all of his attention.

Ignoring the small thrill that shot through her, Lilah shut the door, even if it was an unnecessary formality. He'd already turned his back and had moved into the main part of the kitchen. She slipped into the sweater set, adding a quick fluff to her hair before she opened the door once more.

And felt her breath catch as she took in the long, lean lines of him.

Damn, but the man really was a vision. Trim waist, long legs and a rather impressive set of shoulders. He wasn't skinny, but she suspected he'd leaned that way in school. No longer. Mother Nature, puberty and what she suspected was a fair amount of gym time to keep up with his job had sculpted him into a rather impressively built man.

Shaking off the persistent attraction that stuck to her like molasses, she pushed her way into the kitchen. "Twice in one day, Detective. To what do I owe the honor?"

"I told Cassidy I was coming back this afternoon. Didn't she mention it?"

Cassidy *had* mentioned it, but admitting that—or the fact that she'd watched the door for the past three hours— wasn't on her agenda. "So here you are. And I've got a meeting. We're trying hard to remember we actually do run a business around here."

"Then go to it. I can wait."

"You don't have anything better to do?"

"I have several calls to make. I can do them here as easy as I can at the precinct. Mind if I use your office?"

She gestured toward the small alcove off the kitchen. "Be my guest."

Lilah passed him, the heat of that large body warming her through the already-oppressive cashmere. Why had she selected the sweater set again?

Ignoring the discomfort and chalking it up to her penance for nearly missing the meeting, Lilah grabbed her plate of cream puffs. In her haste, she'd plated everything she had, which amounted to fourteen puffs.

With a quick glance toward the clock, she snagged a

small plate from the cabinets and removed two of the pastries. She rearranged the gaps on the serving plate—Violet would never know—and handed Reed the desserts. "Don't get into too much trouble while I'm gone."

Reed stared at the empty dessert plate and marveled at the pastries he'd just done his level best not to shovel into his mouth. The cream puffs had to be the best thing he'd ever tasted and he could have sworn he heard his blood humming on a satisfied sugar high as he methodically polished off both desserts.

Damn, but the woman could cook. Bake. Create. What exactly was he supposed to call the food he just ate?

He was an eater and he came from a family of foodies. One of his earliest memories after his mother married Tripp was the three of them out on a Saturday night for a steak dinner at one of Dallas's finest restaurants the weekend before school started. He'd been wide-eyed and scared of making a mistake—both at the restaurant *and* at school—but Tripp had kept a bright smile on his face as he'd walked him through the various cuts of meat on the menu.

That night was one of the first times he'd recognized his stepfather wasn't all bad. The man had been trying in his own way, and the gentle coaching that was never overbearing had gone a long way toward cementing their budding relationship.

That evening had also set him on a path as a food lover. And in a town full of some of the world's best restaurants, he had a ready supply of offerings at his disposal.

Which was why, Reed realized, he'd been to both of Steven DeWinter's restaurants in Dallas as well as the man's properties in Las Vegas and Chicago. He pulled out his phone and did a quick search on the restaurateur, curious to see if the press-ready bio matched his memory. As he tapped in the search, his mind filled with the big man in the chef's coat. Attractive and fit, DeWinter didn't look like someone who spent his day around food.

In fact, come to think of it, DeWinter had more the build of a gym rat than a foodie.

Reed clicked into the bio, the man's impressive list of credits, including a stint as the chef for several major events in the previous Hollywood awards season, running the length of the screen. Reed kept scrolling, curious to see any references to a personal life, only to find nothing.

Shifting, he opened a standard search app and did a deeper dive into the man's background and that was where he found it. A small reference to having been married to a Lilah DeWinter for just shy of two years.

Which, from what he'd pieced together, made sense and matched the timeline Cassidy had provided.

A wholly irrational spear of anger lanced once more, a hot spill of frustration and—jealousy?—at the thought of Lilah married.

She was a grown woman. Of course she had a past. Hell, so did he. And while his might not come with a walk down the aisle and the proverbial picket fence, he'd had his fair share of relationships. He had no right to judge.

Or be jealous.

The distinct sound of heels interrupted his thoughts and he glanced up to a loud voice and an overall general impression of dynamic movement. A woman spoke on her cell phone, gesturing with her free hand as a loud wave of half Spanish, half English spilled from her lips.

She didn't even realize he was there until she'd nearly sat on the edge of Lilah's desk. Her dark brown eyes went wide in her face as she leaped up, nearly stumbling over heels that added several inches to her already-considerable height. Reed moved up to help her, steadying her motion before her windmilling arms carried her right over to the floor.

"Mama! I said I understand." The woman gripped his hand, her long fingers curling around his before she squeezed to let him know she was fine, then she promptly marched off toward Lilah's kitchen.

Fascinated, Reed kept his attention on the heated conversation before it finally ended with a firm "I love you and will discuss this with you later."

Assuming she'd disappear now that her conversation had concluded, Reed was surprised to hear the sultry tones that floated down the hallway. "You can come out now, Detective Yummy."

The moniker nearly had him stumbling as he stepped through the door. "What was that all about?"

"Parents. Mothers, more specifically. Do you like yours?"

An image of the warm, fascinating woman who'd shared lunch with him filled his mind's eye before the answer spilled forth. "Absolutely. I love her."

"I didn't ask about love. I asked about like."

"Well, yeah. I like her, too."

"Lucky." The woman sighed, shoving a mass of curls behind her shoulder before extending a hand. "I'm Gabriella Sanchez."

"Are you the bride?"

Her loud snort and dark expression suggested immediately that he'd overstepped, but Reed wasn't quite sure why. "Hardly. I'm the caterer. Although the fact I'm not the bride was half the reason for that call." She gestured with her phone.

"I'm sorry?"

"Never mind. So you're the dreamy detective. Violet and Cassidy can't stop talking about you."

Not Lilah? Forcing the thought aside, Reed decided to let the comment play out. "Oh."

"They've been very impressed with your help and, I believe Violet said it, 'your God-given patience to deal with the lot of us.'"

"They've had a bad scare."

"One that's not over."

The buoyancy that had carried her into the kitchen—even in the midst of a heated family conversation—vanished at her words. Reed saw her conviction as clearly as he saw the exotic beauty that painted her face and shaped her long, lithe body.

And in that moment he suspected people sorely underestimated Gabriella Sanchez.

Before he could say anything, Lilah marched through the door with the now-empty tray of cream puffs. Reed was surprised at the depth of disappointment that gripped him at the evidence the pastries were gone.

"Gab. Is everything okay?"

"Yeah. I'm sorry. I had to take that. It was my mother's fifth call this afternoon and I was starting to worry something was really wrong."

Reed didn't miss Lilah's penetrating gaze as she took in the sight of the two of them alone in the kitchen, but her comment was casual when she spoke. "Amanda was wrapped up in the discussion of her dress with Cassidy, and Quinn had excused himself to take a work call. No one noticed."

When Gabriella didn't offer up anything else, Lilah added, "Is everything okay?"

"Same old same old with my mother."

"Who's getting married?"

"My cousin Marcie."

"Sorry."

Gabby shrugged, those thick curls bouncing lightly against her back. "She's been dating the guy forever. We all knew it was coming."

With a quick hug for Lilah, Gabriella turned toward him and gave him an impulsive hug. "They're lucky to have you, Detective Yummy."

"Thanks."

The woman moved out of the kitchen as fast as she'd come in, and it took Reed an extra moment to realize Lilah had already picked up her empty plate and crossed to the large, stainless-steel sink on the far side of the room. "Did it go well?"

"Fine. They're excited."

"And hungry, obviously." Reed moved up next to her. "The desserts are gone."

"They're the groom's favorites. I'm doing about forty dozen for the wedding."

"You're doing four hundred and eighty cream puffs for a wedding?" The words were spoken to her back as she moved toward her long counter to pick up her abandoned mixing bowls from earlier.

"There are nearly four hundred people invited to the wedding. You can count on people to take seconds and, besides—" she shrugged "—that's how many they want."

The number boggled his mind. "How do you package that many?"

The dark cloud that had seemed to settle over her never wavered, even as a puzzled look stole over her face. "This is what I do. I've got large cardboard boxes we'll put together for the event. I'll layer them with parchment paper and then transport the pastries in my truck along with the cake for the wedding."

Reed realized he had no idea what went into a wedding and his always-curious mind was already thinking through the implications of how someone made that much food. "It's impressive."

"You want impressive, you should go see Gab's setup. She's the one who has to feed four hundred people an entire meal."

"That's what she does? Food? I didn't realize you had a fourth partner."

"I don't. I mean, we don't. But we've been working with Gabby for a few years now. A few odd jobs here and there and now it's become more consistent. She can't get into the big hotels because they want to cater on their own, but there are a ton of venues in North Texas that want wedding revenue but don't necessarily want to manage all the catering themselves."

"Where's this wedding?"

"The Arboretum in October."

Reed thought of the endlessly beautiful acres at Dallas's botanical gardens, particularly gorgeous in fall. He let out a long, low whistle. "That must be costing them a pretty penny."

When she said nothing, he added, "The height of wedding season at one of the city's best venues. And with four hundred people? I'd say a small fortune, more like."

"Weddings are expensive. And. Well." She shrugged again. "They appear to have the money for it."

She busied herself with the dishes and Reed found himself amused at her complete freeze-out. "You're busy."

"We're always busy." She scrubbed the mixing bowl of crusted cream. "And we lost nearly a week dealing with the break-in and—"

"And the attack on Cassidy." He kept his words gentle, but he pushed all the same.

He didn't want her scared—far from it—but he knew in his gut whatever had landed in their laps was far from over. Becoming complacent was the worst that could happen.

"Robert's gone now."

"But the person who shot him isn't."

She continued scrubbing and only offered up a light shrug of her shoulders. "That's why you're here."

"And you're running around in your damn underwear, letting anyone and everyone inside your shop."

Her hands stilled on the dishes, her eyes going wide. He still only saw her profile, but even from that angle he could see her dark brown eyes were wide orbs in her face.

That shock was nothing compared to his own surprise at the harsh words that had spilled from his lips, catching him unaware.

"You have no right."

"I have every right. I'm trying to keep you and your partners safe and you're not taking this seriously."

"Seriously?" She snapped the water off with a hard twist and grabbed a towel to dry her hands. "I'm not the one back here making eyes at our caterer."

"What?"

Lilah whirled, the irritation in her voice punctuating the gesture. "You heard me. I realize she's an attractive woman, but you couldn't wait to flirt all over Gabby."

Whatever self-righteous anger had carried him this far faded in the face of her resentment.

And a sudden awareness of just why she was upset.

"I wasn't flirting with your caterer. I can't say the same for her."

"Just because she looks like a supermodel doesn't mean she deserves to be objectified."

"I couldn't agree more."

Her mouth was already open to keep on arguing when she snapped it closed at his agreement.

Without checking the impulse, Reed leaned in, delighted when those dark eyes went wide and round once more. "But I don't think that's why you're upset."

"It's anger for my friend."

"Oh, really." He took a moment to just breathe her in, the light scent of sugar that hovered around her simply intoxicating.

"Of course."

He pressed a light kiss to her cheek before dropping another along the line of her jaw. "It wouldn't be jealousy?"

Whatever initial acceptance she might have had in the moment vanished. "It's most certainly not that. And why don't you ratchet down that swelled head while you're at it?"

Reed couldn't stop the smile, especially now that he was virtually high on the scents of vanilla and warm sugar, coupled with the cream puffs that were still humming in his veins.

Could sugar really make someone reckless?

"I wasn't the one who called myself Detective Yummy."

"That was—" She broke off. "Gabby was just being funny."

"Consider me amused."

Awareness filled her dark gaze and in that moment Reed felt something shift deep inside of him. He knew what it was to want—to need—but the look in Lilah Castle's eyes was something more.

In her gaze he saw the desperate craving of someone who knew what they wanted yet were afraid to let go.

On sheer instinct, he closed the distance once more and dragged her small, slight frame against his own. At the actual feel of her—muscle, sinew and bone under his hands—he realized his initial estimation was spot-on.

She was a pixie.

As his lips came over hers, her head already tilted up to meet him, he amended that thought. She might be small— a mere slip in his hands—but she had a woman's curves and a woman's needs.

The instinct that pushed him on was greeted with full acceptance and he groaned as she opened her mouth, an invitation to deepen the kiss.

The moment was hot—desperate—and he took full advantage.

Heat radiated off her, through the thin material of her sweater. One of his hands was large enough to cover nearly the entire span of her back while the other drifted down toward her derriere, pulling her close.

Her hands gripped his waist, her fingers restless at the waistband of his slacks, and he saw a wash of stars when her stomach bumped hard against his groin.

What had begun as impulse—and a deep need to finally taste her—had turned on him, and Reed felt himself fast losing control. With one last rush of teeth and lips and tongue, he took advantage of the moment and deepened the kiss, lingering over her luscious mouth with satisfying urgency.

Then he pulled away and added a few steps of distance for good measure. As he took in the passion-glazed gaze and soft color high on her cheeks, Reed came to a startling realization.

He was wrong.

Her cream puffs weren't the best thing he'd ever tasted. Lilah Castle was.

Chapter 5

Lilah was still trying to make sense of the whirling storm in her mind when Reed ended the kiss and stepped away from her. Her normal twin shields of humor and sarcasm had deserted her and she was left staring at the man like a gaping fish.

She knew the gaping-fish look. She'd seen it one night when she helped Gabby filet a last-minute request of four dozen Dover sole and she knew it wasn't pretty.

So she clamped her mouth shut.

As soon as she managed to get a few breaths back.

Damn, but the man could kiss. And no matter how desperately that irritated her, stuffing her brains back into her ears had to be her first priority.

As she righted the waistband of her sweater set—and holy cow, the cashmere was now hotter than her ovens—Lilah took a moment to scan Reed's face.

And took a small measure of solace that he looked as

shell-shocked as she felt. The cocky grin he'd sported as he'd teased her about being jealous of Gabby had faded, replaced with a serious look that she didn't quite know how to take.

Shielding up, Lilah smoothed the sweater once more and fought the unseemly urge to wipe the light sweat on her lower back. "Why are you here, Detective?"

"I had lunch with my mother."

The comment about his mother stymied her and whatever hardball she was winding up faded at the sweet, gooey bubble that opened up in her chest. "How nice?"

"It was nice, but that's not why I bring it up."

Lilah waited, not trusting herself to say anything further.

"My mother has a unique perspective on Dallas society." He reached for the dishrag and began drying the items she'd already set on the drying board earlier.

"How so?"

"She was a decorator to the city's elite when I was a kid and then married one of those elite customers when he had his home redone after he divorced."

Reed handed her one of the heavy mixing bowls she'd used earlier and she took it, not sure what else to do with it. Or him.

"So she's seen both sides of the fence, as it were."

"Exactly. I figured she might have some insight into this case. Who runs with who. What others say about them. She doesn't do a lot of decorating any longer, but she keeps her ear to the ground with her charity groups."

"Wait—" Lilah turned from the open cabinet where she was busy stowing the bowl. "Is your mother Diana G.?"

Reed winked. "Her street name."

Before she could stop it, a hard giggle spilled from her lips at the image of his small, petite, elegant mother with a "street name."

"I met her several months ago at a function. She's lovely. And, as I remember, she put the event caterer squarely in her place for serving day-old bread for the sandwiches."

He waved a couple of now-dry mixing paddles in his hand. "The horror."

"She was lovely to me, though. I only just put the name together because everyone called her Diana G., but her name on the event program was Diana Graystone Lange."

"Of course she was lovely to you. I'm quite sure you don't use day-old anything."

Echoing his words, she laid one hand on her breast, extending her other for the paddles. "The horror."

The tense moments—both pre- *and* post-kiss—had vanished as they worked in companionable silence.

"What did she tell you?"

"I filled her in on the case and told her about the rubies."

A small shot of panic filled her at the knowledge yet another person knew about the jewels, but Lilah pushed it aside. Quite a few people—bad people—knew about the gems that had lain buried beneath the floor of her business. Putting a few good guys on their side who might be able to help could only work in their favor.

As if sensing her indecision, Reed added, "She's a vault, so you don't have to worry about that."

"I believe it. I'm quite sure she's forgotten more gossip about Dallas's elite than any of us even know."

"You'd be surprised how quickly she can conjure it up, though." Reed picked up the last item on the drying rack. "She wants to see them. The rubies."

"Who wouldn't?"

"I also asked her about Steven DeWinter."

Lilah stilled at that, the comfortable camaraderie fading at Steven's name. "Steven's a discreet person who prefers to keep his humiliation private. I'm sure she hasn't heard much."

"On the contrary."

She looked up at him, not surprised to see his gaze squarely on hers. His eyes were all cop. Dark gray storm clouds, swirling with energy and life and a driving need to bring justice.

From what she knew about Reed Graystone, she suspected he wore that look often. She'd done a bit of information gathering of her own after he'd taken on their case. Although the Dallas PD kept information about their staff on pretty tight lockdown, there were a few articles mentioning him.

Several acts of bravery while he was still in uniform and a particularly difficult human-trafficking case two years prior that he'd broken wide-open. The case had gained national attention and the department had awarded him several accolades for the work.

She'd been filled with a strange shot of pride reading the articles and had spent far more time than she'd realized before she'd shut down the search program in a rush. Confirmation she, Cassidy and Violet had a strong detective on their case was one thing. Dreaming about his accomplishments was another.

"You don't seem curious about what my mother knows."

The mention of Steven threw a bucket of ice on her thoughts and brought her firmly into the present. "My curiosity about Steven DeWinter ended a long time ago."

Lilah knew the words to be true, but curiosity and preparation were two different things. While she'd had no interest in the restaurants he opened or the events around town where he was photographed, she'd made it her business to keep a close eye on the man's comings and goings.

She paid attention to the events he was scheduled for so

she could steer clear of any catering requests, and she kept a close watch on any public appearances he was planning around town. And she knew full well that Violet paid attention to the guest lists of the weddings they covered to avoid any inadvertent interactions.

Vi denied it, but Lilah knew her best friend's MO and she was more than grateful for the interference.

"Humor me, then. Forget curiosity and call it basic detective work. I went to my mother because dealing with those who run in the elite circles of our fair city isn't always found in files or case records."

Lilah held back the harsh laugh, even as she knew that simple point to be more than evident. Steven hadn't been on anyone's radar. Clearly, Robert Barrington hadn't been, either. Yet here they were, with the overwhelming reality that Robert had played fast and loose with the law.

And the increasing suspicion that Steven either knew what Robert was involved in or had been the conduit to Robert's introduction into the criminal underworld.

"While I appreciate you keeping us informed, what do you want me to do about it? I've had no contact with the man for over five years."

"No, but you did live in his world. Look. I understand this is painful. But if you'd talk to my mother, walk her through what you know and see if the two of you can jingle any bells, that'd be helpful."

Before she could even muster up an argument, Reed pressed on. "Besides. She's only going to nag at me until I show her one of the jewels anyway. Since you're so determined to carry one around in your shoe, we can kill two birds with one stone."

Lilah wanted to say no. Really, she did. The thought of revisiting any of her time with Steven left a dull coating of nausea lining her stomach.

But she wanted some answers even more.

"Let me go change."

"You look fine."

"It's about a thousand degrees outside. Since it's roughly the same temperature in this sweater, I'm going to go change."

She took off in the direction of her office, stopping at the sound of his voice.

"You sure you don't need my help this time?"

With a small smile she couldn't quite suppress, she turned around. "Nah. I've got this one."

Although he'd meant the joke about her clothing to lighten the mood, Reed couldn't shake the image of Lilah in her bra. The woman was a vision. She had high, perfect breasts—small, but not too small—and creamy pale skin.

And she was toned.

He'd never thought about it until seeing her physique, but the woman was ripped, with thin layers of muscle clearly visible underneath her shoulders, biceps and back. Obviously working thick dough and managing frosting and large trays of cakes all day did something to one's muscles.

Some very attractive things.

Reed shook off the vision, only to have it replaced by an image of that small, firm body tight in his arms, her lips feverish on his.

With an act of will he didn't realize he possessed, he pushed *that* thought aside, as well. The kiss had been a bad idea. He didn't get involved in his cases and coming on to the victim was a really shabby idea all the way around.

Now that he'd tasted her—satisfied his curiosity, really— he needed to let this crazy fascination go. She needed his help, not his come-ons.

He'd nearly convinced himself when she sauntered out of her office. The thick plastic shoes had been traded for a pair of nude pumps with heels roughly the size of ice picks. Her hair was twisted into a quick knot at the nape, and a thin silk blouse the color of rich emeralds shimmered around her when she moved.

With the exception of the bright pink streak in her hair, all sign of the baking fairy had vanished. The woman in its place was an attractive goddess, one who'd be readily accepted at any high-society function in town.

"Ready?"

It took him a moment to answer, his tongue having firmly implanted itself on the roof of his mouth, especially when he caught sight of her slender, muscular legs beneath a slim black pencil skirt. "Yeah. Sure. Let's go."

She wended her way through the kitchen and into the main area of Elegance and Lace. He'd observed the design already—the long, rectangular shape of the shop, firmly cut off from the kitchen.

"This partition?" Reed asked as they moved through the entranceway to the main showroom. "This keeps the business officially separate?"

"Yes. It's a fully functional kitchen without interference from the public areas. That's why this space had worked out so well."

She turned to look at him over her shoulder and he managed to shift his gaze from the delectable curve of her backside just in time.

"Had?"

"I'm not sure any of us would say it's working out all that well right now." She offered up a small wave at Cassidy, whose head was down, fully focused on a pattern on her worktable. "Headed out, Cass. See you in a bit."

Cassidy waved, the motion abstract until she caught

sight of Reed. She scrambled away from a long roll of material that lay on her worktable. "Where are you going?"

"A quick errand. Detective Graystone has a few questions and he thinks his mother might know the answers."

"His mother?" Violet stepped up to the door of her office, her gaze on high alert.

Reed watched the byplay between the trio, amused to see the questions arcing between them, nearly deafening even though no one spoke a word.

"It's a new detecting method." Lilah's tone was breezy and he could have sworn he saw her wink. "Apparently it's all the rage."

He wanted to say something—really, the woman was infuriating—but the twin smiles on Violet and Cassidy held him back. He'd be damned if he was going to be the butt of their collective joke.

"My mother knows people."

"She must." Violet actually did wink, the cheeky move only adding to the discomfort of the moment. "And you must be getting itchy for some answers."

"What makes you say that?" He offered up the question, quite sure he wasn't going to like the answer.

Violet took the few steps out of her office, coming over to smooth the lines of his sport jacket. "Men usually bristle at taking strange women home to their mothers."

"Hey! I'm not stra—" Lilah broke off at Violet's quelling glance.

"What makes you think I'm bristling?" he asked.

She gave his shoulder one last brush with her fingertips. "Are you?"

Reed was still digesting Violet's words as he turned onto his mother's street twenty minutes later. The afternoon traffic hadn't hit its peak and they'd navigated the relatively short drive with ease.

He wasn't bristling. Or bristled. Or... *Damn.*

He was wound up because he knew damn well his mother saw everything and she'd no doubt grill him later this evening about one Lilah Castle.

Pushing away the thought, he latched on to another one.

"I'm curious about something." He slowed for a four-way stop and used the moment to turn toward Lilah. "Violet would make a good cop."

"Oh?"

"She doesn't miss much."

Lilah laughed out loud at that. "No, she doesn't."

"So why does she do weddings for a living? It seems—" He broke off, not wanting to insult her friend. "It seems a bit frilly for someone so sharp and all-knowing."

Lilah grew thoughtful before she answered. "Vi's a realist. Eminently practical and always full of plans. Lots and lots of plans. It makes her exceptional with details. And don't let her fool you. She likes the frilly, too. And she keeps us on track and in business with her terrifyingly organized brain."

Reed took it all in, the clear affection and respect more than evident in Lilah's words. But it was her next question that caught him totally unawares.

"The real question, to my mind, is was she right?"

"About what?" Reed pulled through the intersection, his focus once again on the road.

"Have you ever brought a woman home to your mom?"

"I'm thirty-two years old." He turned into the driveway, surprised at the snappish tone. Dialing it back, he softened his voice. "Of course I've brought women home."

"How many?"

The question stopped him. How many women had he

dated that he'd brought home to meet his mother? As he began doing the math, he realized the number was awfully small. "Two."

"And how many of them were in high school."

On a resigned sigh, he nodded. "Two."

"I guess Vi was right."

Lilah already had her door open and was out of the car before he could reply.

His mother *had* met several women he'd dated. At dinners. Summer barbecues. Even at various weddings they'd all attended.

So why hadn't he brought any of them home?

He puzzled over that as he followed Lilah to the front door. Which, he suspected, was her point.

The man known as the Duke sipped an ice-cold glass of vodka as he waited for his team to escort DeWinter in. The shades were drawn in his home office, the oppressive summer heat to be battled at all costs.

The combination of dark paneling and drawn curtains kept the room in perpetual darkness and he had a small lamp angled toward his guest chairs as the only source of light.

He hadn't seen DeWinter in a few years—not since he joined him for the man's Chicago restaurant opening two years before. It had been a promising evening and he'd left pleased that he'd continued to invest in Steven DeWinter.

The Duke was always ready to back a winner and the restaurateur had big dreams and a maniacal willingness to see them through. The man ran a top-of-the-line kitchen and tolerated nothing but discipline and genius from those who worked for him.

But it was DeWinter's solid streak of ruthlessness that really sold him as an investment.

An image of dealing with Robert Barrington flashed through the Duke's mind and he nodded to himself. Oh yes, he prized ruthless discipline above most anything else.

The soft knock at the door—just as he preferred—punctuated his thoughts.

It was that discipline and attention to detail that mattered. Too many had lost that, so focused on their phones, their electronic toys and their endless rush to get somewhere only to find they'd gone nowhere.

He'd learned long ago it was only when you sat still that people actually paid attention.

"Come in."

He ran his life with an order that appeared deceptively calm on the surface but was the outcome of rigorous expectations. On himself and on his staff.

Alex, his man of business, opened the door. The man still sported a fading bruise around his eye, delivered the week prior after one of his failed attempts to go after the women of Elegance and Lace. It still irked the Duke each time he looked at the mark, the evidence of what they'd still not accomplished. "Mr. DeWinter is here, sir."

"Send him in."

Steven came through the door, his standard-issue black slacks, black shirt and black Italian loafers pristine. For a man who worked with food, he was impeccable in his dress. Nary a stain in sight and covering a large, fit body that spoke volumes about the man's discipline.

More traits the Duke admired.

"It's good to see you." Steven extended his hand and the Duke shook it, breaking his standard protocol in his private office. He played at the social game in polite society, but in his private world he preferred to avoid contact.

"You, as well. Word has it your Restaurant Week menu is a hit."

"I'm pleased with the response. My new pastry chef's not working out, but he'll see us through the week."

"Weak link?"

"Yes. The man's got no creativity or innovativeness."

The Duke knew DeWinter's ex-wife had developed quite a reputation while they worked together and for all his success, he'd gone through his dessert chefs like water ever since.

How interesting that their recent project would now bring them full circle.

"Barrington and McCallum failed at their tasks."

"Robert?" Steven leaned forward, surprise etching itself in his features. "He's a good guy and deeply committed. I know I haven't seen him in a while, but I recommended him with my full endorsement. What happened?"

"He failed."

Whatever surprise had carried Steven into the conversation vanished. The Duke saw his mouth shift before he calmed himself, stilling any movement. "I see."

"I'm not sure that you do."

"Excuse me?"

"Charlie McCallum failed. Failed at his attempts to penetrate your ex-wife's store and then further failed when he gave me false intel."

"Charlie's always been a bit of a doofus, but he's committed. You must know I'd never recommend anyone I thought was subpar."

"Yet you did, Steven."

"Let me call them. I can get them both back in line."

"I doubt that."

"But I can. I'll make it right." Steven leaned forward and rested his elbows on the edge of the desk. The Duke fought the urge to swat at him and instead reached for the slim folder beside him.

His motions deliberate, the Duke slipped two photos from the folder. The first showed Charlie McCallum, his eyes wide-open, the kill shot marked at the base of his throat. The second was Robert Barrington, where he lay in an empty field at Fair Park, a bullet hole square in the center of his forehead.

Steven leaped away from the desk, fumbling the chair in his haste to stand. "They're dead?"

"Yes. Quite."

"But I don't—"

"They were your recommendations."

"Yes. As guys I trusted to do the work you asked. Clearly, they weren't given enough time."

The Duke pushed the photos farther across the desk, pleased when Steven's gaze skittered over them once more.

"They were given ample time and resources. And they failed."

"But—"

The Duke held up a hand. "I'd suggest you keep any further recommendation and endorsement of their skills to yourself. As you can see, further defense is moot."

Steven nodded, the motion counter to the sudden shaking of his shoulders.

"Sit. Please. We have some details to work out, you and I."

Chapter 6

Lilah took in the posh surroundings of Diana Lange's home and marveled at how warm and comfortable it all felt. The house had to be over eight thousand square feet, but instead of feeling cold and distant, it was warm and inviting.

Just like Diana.

The woman's gray eyes were a match for her son's, but that was where the resemblance stopped. For all Reed's impressive size, his mother was a tiny little thing. But any thought that tiny meant weak vanished as his mother invited her into the sitting room, then summoned Reed to the hall.

"Reed Edward…" Lilah had heard a hiss as his mother dragged him out of the room. Although she hadn't heard the rest, the tone and the addition of a middle name had Lilah convinced Reed was getting taken to task for bringing a woman home without calling first.

Served him right.

Especially since he hadn't brought a woman into his mother's house since high school.

When she stopped and thought about that fact, that persistent warmth filled her chest, spreading outward in a wave.

Who was this man?

And why did he keep catching her off guard?

He was a cop, for Pete's sake. And the only reason he'd come into her life was because she and her business partners were in grave danger.

They'd worked hard to put that sense of imminent threat out of their minds, but it was there all the same. Violet had set the alarm behind her as she and Reed left Elegance and Lace. And she also knew Tucker was scheduled to come down to the shop and stay there as soon as he finished an afternoon meeting at a job site, his partner Max likely in tow.

Despite their best efforts to keep busy, they were on high alert. Her fight over the afternoon's wedding consultation with Violet had been just one example in a string of many over the past few days.

While she hated the not knowing, she was having a hard time believing Reed's mother held any answers. The woman seemed lovely, and even with an ear to the ground, Lilah had no idea how Diana could ever manage to help them figure out who was behind the attacks.

With one hand on her purse strap, she walked around the room, looking at one photo after another. Several photos of Reed through the years filled frames. A small baby with chubby hands was framed next to what had to be his first day of kindergarten. His smile was broad as he waved from the entrance to the school bus.

She continued through the room, stopping at his graduation photo as well as one of him in his dress blues.

Breath catching, she stilled as she took in the photo. No matter how she sliced it, the man cut an impressive figure. Tall, steady and sure. He couldn't have been more than twenty-two or twenty-three in the picture, but it was evident, even then.

He was a protector.

Muted voices carried down the hall, drawing Lilah's gaze away from the photo of Reed and onto one of Diana in a wedding gown. His mother stood next to what had to be her current husband.

They were a striking couple and Lilah took an extra moment to look at them both. Reed's stepfather appeared to be well into his fifties at the time the photo was taken, and she could see the trim, fit strength of him. He was several inches taller than Diana, with a piercing gaze and that slight smile the elite were fond of giving the camera.

Too toothy makes one look too eager.

The words leaped up and slapped her, effectively ending her review of the photo.

Steven had given her that advice the first time they made the society pages. Even now, she could remember how excited she'd been to be photographed with him *and* mentioned by name.

And then he'd ruined it by admonishing her about having too wide a smile.

"Lilah?"

Reed's voice was quiet at her ear, the warm, rich tone pulling her fully from the memory. "Yes?"

"Would you care to sit down?"

She turned to face him and didn't miss the questions stamped in his gaze. She could see he warred with asking again how she was, but a quick glance at his mother had her smiling broadly.

"I'm sorry. I was caught up in the photos. So many good ones, Mrs. Lange."

"Diana. Please."

Reed's mother waved them over to the seating area, where she busied herself with a pitcher of iced tea and a tray of cookies.

"Here. Let me," Reed said as he reached for the pitcher, gesturing his mother to sit.

Again, Lilah was struck by the simplicity of his gesture. She knew—*knew*—that Steven DeWinter wasn't the typical man. While spousal abuse wasn't exactly uncommon, it wasn't in the mainstream, either.

There were good men out there. Men like Cassidy's Tucker and his partner, Max. Men who worked hard and who wanted to share their lives with the right woman.

But even despite knowing that, the simple sweetness in Reed's gesture still caught her off guard.

"It's good to see you again, Lilah." Diana leaned forward. "I must admit I've thought about your petits fours more than once."

"If they're even half as good as her cream puffs, I know why." Reed settled the heavy glass pitcher of iced tea on the table in a small dish to gather any moisture.

"Oh?" Diana's gaze drifted to her son, along with a small smile. "Perhaps I need to put in an order for my next function."

"We'd be happy to help you." Lilah hated putting on the sales show—she normally left that to Violet—but it never hurt to present a pleasant front when an opportunity arose.

"Thank you. Now. First things first. Did you bring the ruby?"

"Mother!" Reed had just settled into one of the large wingback chairs that flanked the sofa.

Diana adopted an innocent expression, but Lilah didn't

miss the sly smile that accompanied the protest. "You can hardly blame me for asking."

"We came here for help."

"And to show off." Lilah patted her purse. "I'm happy for you to see it."

Although *happy* was a bit of a stretch, Lilah was anxious to gain another opinion on the rubies they'd discovered in the floor of the shop.

"Reed filled me in on much of the story. How your landlady's father was the designer of the fake crown jewels during World War Two?"

"Exactly." Lilah filled in the story's gaps—namely, that the fake jewels were smuggled out of England with a trio of real rubies at the Queen's request after the war.

"She thought the rubies were cursed?" Excitement rode high in Diana's eyes as Lilah pulled out the small wrapped cloth from her purse. "We're talking about the actual Queen here?"

"Based on the story we've been told, yes."

The stone was heavy in her hands as she unwrapped the polishing cloth it nestled in. The stone—roughly the size of a small strawberry—winked bloodred as she lifted the last corner of material and Diana let out an audible gasp.

"Oh, my gosh! It's really real." Excitement telegraphed off her like a sparking live wire as her gaze stayed on the stone. "May I hold it?"

"Of course."

Lilah handed it over and, not for the first time, felt slightly bereft to let it go.

Which was silly.

She wasn't keeping the stone. No way, no how.

Diana lifted the ruby, the color winking in the late-afternoon sunlight that flooded the sitting room. Lilah knew hanging on to the stone bordered on stupidity, but unlike Cassidy and Violet, who were more than happy to stick theirs in safe-deposit boxes, she couldn't quite hide the need to hang on to hers.

Not that they owned any of them, but they'd made the agreement to each keep one safe. And she took that responsibility seriously.

"It's breathtaking. Look here." Diana ran the pad of her little finger over the broad, flat surface of the ruby before she handed it over. "The lack of inclusions is incredible. See how perfect this facet is?"

Lilah leaned forward to look at the same time as Reed. His knee bumping hers as he extended himself toward the couch. "I don't see anything."

"That's my point." Diana tapped the edge of the ruby once more. "No stone is perfect, but this one is close. Especially for a piece this large, there are no obvious inclusions. No stress on the piece at all."

Lilah wanted to disregard the shot of warmth where her leg connected with Reed's as nothing more than lingering heat from their kiss but it was the electric hum beneath her skin that had her questioning if her thoughts were that casual. She hardly believed in love at first sight, but she couldn't deny there was something about Reed Graystone that made a woman sit up and take some serious notice.

Forcing her attention and focus back onto the ruby, she concentrated on Diana's comment. "We haven't had them appraised, but we spent a fair amount of time looking at them. I'd say the other stones are comparable."

"Oh my. Oh—" Diana broke off before she handed the stone back. "Give me a minute."

Diana raced out of the room as if she had a demon on her heels, and Lilah didn't miss Reed's soft smile. "She does that."

"Often?"

"Often enough."

The ruby cut into the edge of her palm as she gripped it and Lilah made a concerted effort to loosen her fingers. His knee still brushed hers and she fought the twin urges to push him away and move closer.

Opting for the high road as memories of their kiss threatened to swamp her senses once again, she shifted into a new position on the couch, breaking contact.

"Why have you dismissed the idea of a curse?"

His gaze drifted to where their bodies had touched before she moved away, and she didn't miss the distinct tightening of his shoulders. With stiff movements, he settled into his own seat and gave her a hard stare. "Why are you entertaining it?"

"You can't deny these stones have brought us a heap of trouble."

"And you can't deny you've had no trouble until a week ago. Before that, they'd sat beneath your office floor, no one the wiser, as you three worked to build your business. A rather successful business by all accounts."

"I guess."

"Come on, Lilah. If there's any curse, it's shameless greed that has someone insistent on going after these jewels. And more than willing to hurt whoever gets in the way in the process."

"Can't it be both?"

Reed was prevented from saying anything when his mother scooted back into the room, three large books in her hands. She had her finger lodged in one and resumed her seat, flipping open to the page she'd marked. "Right here. I knew I'd seen this before."

Lilah followed the bold chapter heading. "The Renaissance Stones?"

"Discovered by the British East India Company in the late seventeenth century."

"But that's one stone." Reed's natural curiosity had him leaning over her shoulder once more and Lilah finally gave up and moved over to give him room on the couch.

"Keep reading," Diana urged them both, pushing the book so it lay between them.

Lilah scanned the passage about the actual discovery of the stone, her gaze skipping toward the bottom of the page. "It says here it generated several smaller stones after cutting."

"And that there was considerable thievery between the Dutch and the British over who believed themselves rightful owner," Reed added.

Lilah unwrapped the stone once more and held it up. "All three pieces came from a larger stone?"

"There's more. These stones were steeped in drama even then." Diana passed over one of the other books she'd carried down. "The stone and its subsequent cutting has a nasty history. The original jeweler in Antwerp who worked the stone was found murdered a week after the rubies left his possession."

Lilah glanced at Reed, not entirely surprised to see the skepticism that painted his face in grim lines. "Really, Mom. Are you going down the curse route, too?"

"I'm just sharing what I know. I've not done a ton with jewels in my work, but I've often done Eastern-inspired homes or wings of homes. These jewels come up from time to time in any reading of the era."

Lilah scanned the page once more, several words like *bloodred* and *murder* leaping out at her from the page like a scream. "If they ended up in Britain anyway after this discovery, then how were they gifted to the Queen? That's been Mrs. B.'s story all along."

"Maybe they were returned to their homeland at some point?" Reed offered up the guess, but it was Diana who pointed toward the closed books.

"You're welcome to take these with you, but I suspect you'd be better off seeing what you can come up with on the internet. These books are old and I'm sure more's been written since these were published."

Diana ran a finger over the stone, her gaze distant. "It is incredible. But even if you trace its provenance and find out how it made its way back to its home, I still don't see why the Queen gave them away. It seems like it would be easy enough to hide them in a wing of the castle or stick them in a museum and just be done with them."

"That's what we've not been able to figure out. Violet's done a bit of research over the last week and has discovered that royalty is gifted things all the time. Most find their way into public displays or photo ops and then become a small footnote in the annals of history, never to be seen again."

"Which only reinforces the idea of a curse. If the Queen wanted these out of Britain—"

"Mom—" Reed was kind but firm as he eyed his mother. "You're a practical woman and you've spent more than enough time in people's homes to know they put sentimental value on the dumbest things."

"True, but a curse is a different matter altogether."

"Fine. Call it sentiment or superstition. Either way, we're not going there."

"Wait." Diana held up a hand. "Think about it, Reed. Something must have spooked the Queen if she wished to have these removed from her country. Smuggled out, as a matter of fact. And you can't deny recent events sort of support the concept of the jewels having a poor effect on others."

"Greed is greed, Mom."

Lilah reached for her iced tea and gave his mother a knowing look. "He gets touchy when I push this angle, too."

"My boy likes what he can see and touch. What's real."

"Exactly." Reed nodded.

"Which only reinforces all my efforts to explain to him that sometimes it's the things we refuse to believe that teach us the most."

Reed was still turning his mother's words over an hour later as he opened his passenger door for Lilah. His mother had been all too eager to discuss the stones and that damned imagined curse, which hadn't been the point of their visit.

What *had* been the point of their visit—who she and Lilah knew in common—had produced little fruit.

"What's with the grumpy attitude?"

Lilah's question was as tart as ripe lemons and he toyed briefly with ignoring it. He was saved by a lifelong drubbing of manners that had him taking the question seriously. "I deal in facts. And as part of those facts I've got two dead bodies. Speculating on a bunch of hokum about the jewels at the center of this issue was a waste of time."

"I'm sorry you feel that way."

"Are you? Because you and my mother were awfully content to wax on and on about the jewels and spent little time discussing who might be involved."

"Why does it matter? You've already put Steven on your short list. Just put someone on him to follow him and be done with it."

"I can't just have the man followed for no other reason other than he's an ass."

"Then go question him."

Reed knew Lilah's feelings on DeWinter ran deep and

held a complete absence of warmth, but he couldn't quite let the nonchalant comment slide. "On what grounds?"

"You've got a few questions. You're investigating a case and two dead men he was acquainted with. It can't be that hard."

"It's not hard."

Her gaze never left the road as Reed navigated them onto the highway into downtown. "Then why not just go do it?"

"We don't know how all the players are connected. If I go after him now and tip him off to the fact that I think he's involved, he might rabbit."

"Steven doesn't rabbit. He cooks it, but he's not a man to back down. Believe me."

Although he was always aware of what Lilah had been through, it still amazed him—that visceral punch of anger that slammed into him every time he got a real sense of how the man had hurt her.

"That may be so, but I need to play this right."

"Then use me."

The urge to stare at her hit him hard, but the thick late-afternoon traffic kept him from turning his head. "Excuse me?"

"Use me. We'll go to one of his restaurants and draw him out. It is Restaurant Week. He's sure to be preening over his special menu."

Reed took in Lilah's words, still not quite believing what she had suggested. His gut had told him it was a bad idea to draw his mother into his case, but he'd needed the help and the extra pair of trusted eyes she provided. It was so damn hard to penetrate the upper echelons of society. He'd seen it firsthand as a civilian and he knew it to be even more so as a member of the police force.

But to use Lilah in the same way?

She was the victim in his case, not some piece of bait to be dangled in front of her jerk of an ex.

Only, he'd stopped seeing her as a victim from the very first.

And while he'd been equally against her involvement from the beginning, the uniqueness of the situation and the possible players involved had clouded his judgment.

That was all.

"I can't do that. This is an official investigation."

"An investigation into my life. You said yourself you didn't have any leads."

"I did no—"

"Fine. Call it a stuck case without a lead. I can help you. I may hate Steven but I hate this situation even more. The faster we can finish it the better. And if he knows something, we'll mess with his head and draw him out."

"I don't want you going back there."

"I'm not crazy about it, either. But you'll be with me. There will be witnesses. And then we'll leave."

Something dark churned in his stomach. If he were a fanciful man, he'd say it was the taste of impending battle, but he wasn't fanciful.

He was practical.

And there was no way he was letting Lilah get within fifty feet of Steven DeWinter.

Lilah saw the moment Reed shut down. To his credit, he wasn't subtle about it. Oh no, his feelings were telegraphed loud and clear by the set of his jaw.

"I want this over, Reed. Let's jump-start the process of doing just that."

"No."

"Excuse me?"

"What didn't you understand?"

Lilah knew she had a stubborn streak a mile wide. Her partners teased her about it. Her mother had spent her formative years boring up under it. And it was the one personality trait she credited for keeping Steven from fully destroying her.

It also added a wee bit of irrationality to her personality every now and again.

"Fine, I'll do it myself."

Their exit came up on The Tollway and Lilah figured it was the quick turn—and the car that nearly sideswiped them for the exit first—that kept Reed from actually exploding in the driver's seat.

"Are you threatening a Dallas PD investigation?"

"Absolutely not."

"Because your flippant attitude toward my job and my responsibilities is beginning to grate."

The proverbial red flag floated between them, but Lilah refused to acquiesce. She *did* respect his role, damn it. She knew what he was capable of and she respected the job he had to do.

But this was her life.

"I'm a civilian. And as I'm one who has the ability to move about freely, you don't have a say."

"I'll tie you up myself. You're not to go near DeWinter."

"Ooh. Kinky."

"Lilah—"

"Look. Hear me out." She tugged on the small strand of hair that had come loose over her ear. It was obvious baiting him wasn't the best approach, so it was time to plead with his sense of reason. "Please."

He took the turn onto Dragon, the slowing of the car giving him a moment to look at her. She saw the banked fire in his gaze but heard the subtle willingness to hear her out. "Fine."

"Steven isn't a man who likes to put his brutality on display. He's far more comfortable keeping to the shadows. Nothing will happen to me if we go to his restaurant."

He pulled into a spot in front of Elegance and Lace and put the car in Park. When she saw he wasn't going to respond, she pressed on.

"He's also easily baited. I learned quickly what his cues and trigger points were. All I'm suggesting is that we bait the trap a bit tonight. See what he reacts to. You can ask all the questions and I'll read the signs. If he's not involved, his boredom will be more than evident. But if he *is* involved..."

She let the thought hang there, torn between hoping Steven DeWinter held the answers and fearful that all she was doing was poking a sleeping bear in his den.

"And if he's not?"

"Then dinner's on me."

Chapter 7

Reed took the short walk to Lilah's front door. He'd left her at the shop earlier, still skeptical about the evening's plans but unable to argue with her point of view.

DeWinter was the possible key to finding out how Robert Barrington and Charlie McCallum got involved in the break-in at Elegance and Lace. For starters, he knew both victims. When you added on that DeWinter, McCallum and Barrington were intimately involved with Lilah and Cassidy, the connections jingled a bit too loudly to be ignored.

In fact, they'd jingled loud enough that he'd scheduled some subtle backup should things go sideways and it become evident DeWinter wasn't just involved, but was the mastermind behind what was going on.

Thankfully, Jessie and her husband, Dave, loved to eat, so they'd jumped at the chance to take part. He'd managed to snag them a seating at the same time as he and Lilah, and they'd provide additional eyes and ears on the scene.

The Uptown town house rose three stories above him as he rang the bell, its heavy echo audible from the other side of the door.

He liked this area—always had—and was surprised to realize how it suited Lilah. Several homes were connected, then each set of connections were nestled in rows.

A tight community.

He imagined people knew their neighbors—and their comings and goings. He'd already seen the community watch sign when he'd entered through the front gate that closed off the larger property.

Lilah's blond hair was visible through the frosted panes on either side of the door and he heard several locks flip over before the door swung wide.

And nearly lost his breath at the vision that stood on the other side.

The messy knot at her nape was gone, replaced by an elegant updo that showed off her neck and toned shoulders. A silky black dress clung to her like a second skin and it took him a long moment to remember to speak.

Focus on the job, Graystone. "Hi."

"Hey." Her gaze drifted over him, head to toe, before settling on his. "You ready?"

"I can't come in?"

"Why?"

"I'd like to see your place."

The comment was out before he could check it and he knew he'd better reel it back in. This was work. But before he could brush off the request, she'd also stepped away from the door, gesturing him in. "Sure. Of course. We've got some time. I'll give you a tour."

She moved through the house, pointing out various rooms as she walked. The subtle pops of color in each room were clearly her—bright, vivid impressions that reached out and grabbed the senses.

Just like her.

While each room offered fascinating insight into Lilah Castle, he couldn't deny his equal fascination with the woman herself. His gaze continued to roam over the long length of her legs, perched on another impressive set of heels, or the delicate stretch of her slim neck from just beneath her ear to the curve of her shoulder.

But it was their arrival at the kitchen that spoke volumes. Her slender frame telegraphed a sense of happiness and peace. Reed couldn't explain exactly how he knew that other than he did.

Just like her professional workspace, the kitchen gleamed, the marble counters shined to a high gloss. A Sub-Zero refrigerator stood on the far wall, followed by a top-of-the-line gas stove.

"You spared no expense."

"The kitchen's mine. All mine. And it simply doesn't make sense to work with lesser tools, either at work or at home." She let out a small sigh. "That was the one lesson Steven taught me I was willing to take along."

The mention of DeWinter stilled him, any sense of playfulness vanishing at the reality of what they were about to do. "We don't have to do this, Lilah. I can find another way in. Heck, I can bring one of my team members with me and we can go tomorrow. We'll make it look like a date."

"It won't be the same."

He ran a lone finger down the length of her arm, the chill he found there breaking his heart. "It's asking questions, nothing more."

"If he's in this, he needs to understand we know. That I know. I need to do this. To look into his eyes and see if he was responsible for even more evil in my life."

Reed hesitated, the evidence of her hatred like a dark, living thing roiling in the kitchen, pushing out the sunlight and happiness. "Will you ever tell me the full story of what he did to you?"

"Someday. Maybe." She shrugged, the normally warm brown of her eyes going flat. "It's really not a very interesting story. A cautionary tale, maybe, but far from interesting."

"I'm interested."

"Well, I'm not."

Lilah folded and refolded her hands in her lap. The drive to Steven's flagship restaurant, Portia, wasn't far from her home, but the ride seemed to last forever. She'd struggled with something to say since shutting Reed down in her kitchen and so far, she'd managed to come up with a dopey comment about the summer heat.

Of course it was hot. It was August. In Texas.

Moron.

Worse, she was inept. Clumsy. Gauche.

Reed Graystone probably dated supermodels. Or women who looked like them at a bare minimum. Yet he was here with her. No one would believe it. Or understand why they were together. Steven would see right through it.

The words and thoughts kept drifting through her mind, one worse than the next, a shocking reminder of how easy it was to go back to that place. The one that suggested how worthless she was.

It took her a minute to register the large hand that had enfolded on top of hers.

"Lilah. We're here."

"What?"

Reed dropped her hand and waved off the valet, pointing toward a spot on the far side of the lot. He navigated them to the opening and it was only when he had the car in Park once more that his hand enveloped hers.

"You okay?"

"Yes." *No.*

"Let me rephrase the question. Do you want to go home?"

"No." *Yes.*

"Look at me." The warm gray of his eyes drew her in, going a long way toward calming her nerves and the hateful words scrambling through her mind like errant pinballs.

Errant zombies, more like. Ravages of a former life.

Her former life.

On a deep breath, she fought to frame up her strange and rambling thoughts in the hard-won perspective she'd worked for so desperately over the past few years.

She wasn't clumsy and gauche, no matter how many times Steven had tried to make her feel that way.

And what the hell did it matter what Reed's dates looked like in the past? He was here with her. Dressed up to go out with *her*.

Whatever madness her subconscious could cook up didn't matter because Steven wasn't going to suspect anything.

Because Steven thought of no one but himself. Ever.

"Whatever you're thinking, it's not true."

"It's not true that Steven had the outside of the restaurant repainted?"

His smile was gentle. "I meant the other thing that you were thinking. The one that had your skin as pale as a boiled potato."

"I never—"

Before she could say anything else, his mouth came down on hers, effectively silencing whatever she was about to say.

Liquid need coursed through her like the most potent of drugs at the immediate fire that leaped between them. Despite the cool temperature of the car, she thought she was on the verge of burning up. Hot, glorious flames licked at every inch of her skin, out of control as they kept pace with the increasing urgency of his mouth.

With nothing to do but follow him into the blaze, she shifted so he had even easier access to her mouth and lifted a hand to the back of his head. His thick, glossy hair was warmed by his body heat, and she reveled in the smooth texture.

The angle of the car prevented them from moving flush against each other, but he did shift to free her from the seat belt, then settled his hand over her hip. His fingertips seemed to melt her flesh, his touch over the thin strap of her thong as effective as a branding iron.

Fear and anger, anxiety and nerves—all faded under the power of his mouth.

His touch.

His taste.

And it was only when he pulled away, dark churning clouds filling his gaze, that Lilah realized he'd not only inflamed her, making her want and need in a way she'd never known, but he'd done something even more important. More precious.

He'd silenced the ugly, hateful words.

The Duke sat in the back of his car and barked out instructions to Alex. He'd planned to dine at Portia tonight, but he wasn't going inside now. Not with the woman and the police cozied up together like a besotted couple.

He'd almost missed them. His hand had been on the door and he was nearly out of the car when something familiar had caught his attention.

Hidden behind the blackened window, he instructed Alex to beg off his business dinner. Some mysterious illness from a recent trip overseas would do nicely.

Alex made the requisite call and the Duke watched as the woman disappeared into the restaurant. The cop's hand was low on her back, suggesting an intimacy the Duke was unaware of, as the cop followed her through the door.

This was an interesting turn of events.

He'd kept an eye on the police, dependent on his contacts inside the precinct to stay aware and informed. They hadn't failed him yet.

Of course, this little tête-à-tête was unexpected.

"It's done, sir."

"Thank you, Alex. I'd like to add a little surprise to the good detective's brakes before we go."

"Sir?" Alex turned from the front, surprise etched clearly on his face. "Are you sure?"

"Quite."

The man nodded, his expression resigned. "Of course."

With the taste of her still lingering on his lips, Reed escorted Lilah to their table. He'd settled a proprietary hand on her lower back once he'd helped her from the car and since she hadn't yet shaken him off, he wasn't budging. The subtle trembling of her limbs had stilled and normal color had returned to her cheeks and he was grateful for both.

What he hadn't quite reconciled was the devastating need pumping through his system in hard, demanding bursts.

He wanted her. With a determination he'd not felt in, well, ever.

He just wanted *her*. Lilah.

And the very last thing she needed was this complication. Hell, they were inside her ass of an ex-husband's restaurant and all he could think of was stripping her naked.

Ignoring the demands of his body that refused to be sated, he accepted the inconvenience for what it was. He'd take a million unfulfilled moments to make sure that spark stayed present in her eyes and that warm wash of pink highlighted her cheeks.

Anything other than the mindless fear that had gripped her on the drive over.

The small nod as he passed Jessie and Dave—both already in place and appearing for all the world like two besotted teenagers—brought him back fully to the moment.

This was an op. He'd do well to remember that.

Their hostess had them seated, menus already presented, and then departed when Lilah finally smiled. "At least that was one lucky break."

"What was?"

"That hostess is new. She had no idea who I was."

"It's been a long time since you worked here."

"It has, but the restaurant community is small, especially at this level. Once people get in with a good place, they're loath to leave."

The comment gave him the opening he needed. "It's a hard life. Waiting on others. Giving them special moments. Memories."

"No harder than any other job."

"Oh, I don't know." He set his menu aside, his focus fully on Lilah. "It's a lot of work to prep for an event and then another round of work to bring it off. In this very short amount of time, I've seen that with you and your partners. There's not a lot of downtime in what you do. Not a lot of time for yourself."

"I like it." She shrugged. "I like making something others think is special. Something they'll remember and talk about. Dream about."

"And you? How many moments do you get to dream about?"

"Enough." A small smile hovered about her lips. "And I have to confess, this duck à l'orange is one of those dreams."

He glanced down at his menu. "The duck? Really?"

"Seriously. I hate to admit it because any thought of my ex-husband is firmly locked in the boiling-acid waters of disgust and loathing."

"Boiling-acid waters?"

"Oh yes." She nodded as she took a sip of sparkling water already poured. "They make a Dallas summer look downright frigid. But as I was saying, the duck is a trade secret. One I likely could conjure up if I worked at it hard enough."

"Have you tried it?"

"No. I'm too distracted to cook."

"Distracted?"

She took another sip, her gaze thoughtful. "I mean that in the best way. I think about cooking and then there's always something else to do. Some new sweet treat to try or an item I'm working on perfecting. I enjoy food but I love pastries."

"I think I'm going to have to call in Vice."

Her eyes narrowed, the twinkle vanishing from her chocolate gaze. "Vice?"

"I thought it earlier, but you've only proven it. You're a sugar pusher, and your pastries are more addictive than crack."

The light returned, even brighter than before, and Reed felt himself pulled along in the moment. "That's basically the nicest compliment you can give a baker."

"Is it a compliment when it's true?"

"It's lovely." She laid a hand over his, the warmth of her touch going a long way toward reinvigorating his memory of their time in the car. "Thank you."

"Well, good evening."

The fingers that were so warm on his tightened as they both looked up into the steel-blue gaze of Steven DeWinter. Reed shifted his hand, the subtle gesture of his palm enfolding Lilah's clearly not lost on her ex-husband. "Hello."

Steven ignored his greeting, his gaze steady on Lilah. Reed didn't miss the way DeWinter's eyes traveled over the pink streak in her hair, a slight sneer turning the edge of his lips. *Interesting.*

Reed gave her fingers a soft squeeze, willing his strength into her via touch. "I'm surprised to see you here. You've not done a Restaurant Week with us in many years."

"I thought it was time."

"That always was your problem, wasn't it?" Steven gestured a sommelier over, the man's movements swift and efficient as he rushed to the table. "Too much thinking."

Reed fought the urge to say anything, sensing DeWinter's subtle dig wasn't quite the right moment to step in. Especially when the color he feared would vanish rode high and bright on Lilah's cheeks.

"Yes, brains are such a devastating trait in a woman." Reed felt her shift before she ran a lone finger over his knuckles, her touch light. Playful. "Almost as bad as the will to use them."

Reed maintained an air of the bemused new boyfriend, his smile broad and his besotted gaze vague and unfocused as Lilah worked over DeWinter.

"Pierre. Please see that one of our best accompaniments is brought to the table this evening. My compliments."

"Thank you, Steven." Lilah nodded, her smile simple. Contrite, even.

"My pleasure." DeWinter shifted subtly in the narrow space between tables, his hands outstretched. "I'll leave you to it, then."

"One more thing. Please be sure to send the pastry chef out with dessert. I'd like to ask him a few questions."

"I'll just bet you do."

Lilah fought the adrenaline spiking through her system like frequency waves. Big to little and back up to big again. If she weren't sitting still, she'd have sworn she was on a roller coaster, her head was swimming with that small moment of victory.

"Well played, Miss Castle."

"Thank you." She nodded and reached for her wineglass, clinking it to the one Reed had already lifted high.

"I don't think we'll see him again."

"Hardly." She leaned forward, unable to keep the conspiratorial whisper from her voice. "Why do you think I asked for the pastry chef?"

"To compare notes?"

She smiled and knew several drops of cat's cream dripped from the corners of her lips. "Steven is the face of his restaurants. He refuses to allow any accolades to come to his staff, no matter how minor or well-intentioned."

"So you primed the pump."

"Exactly. I give the pastry chef no more than thirty seconds tableside before Steven makes his reappearance."

"You seem sure."

"I've lived it. Seriously, we could clock it with an egg timer."

She saw the moment something changed. Those broad

shoulders—even broader under the black cut of his sport jacket—stiffened and his lips compressed into a hard line.

"What?"

"Nothing."

"Seriously, Reed. What?"

He hesitated another moment, which only managed to up the curiosity quotient. She'd yet to see the man indecisive about anything.

"It's nothing."

"Come on. Please say it."

"What did you ever see in him?"

Although she'd brushed off inquiries about Steven when they'd stood in her kitchen, Lilah knew she owed Reed some explanation. Sitting smack inside enemy territory only made that point even more clear.

Settling her nerves with a deep breath, she opened the mental door she usually kept firmly closed.

"He was larger than life. And he was older than me, which I suspect added a bit to the glamour. And, this evening aside, he can be quite charming when he wants to be. No one gets to his level in the restaurant business without managing a combination of polish and ruthlessness. I guess all I saw was the polish."

"There are a lot of ruthless SOBs who don't abuse others. In fact, their spouses normally sit on the top of the list of those they don't abuse."

She warmed at his immediate defense. "True. So maybe a better way to put it is that I was enamored of the polish and it deafened me to my instincts. Especially once the startling reality of the person I'd joined myself to began to sink in."

"I'm glad you started listening."

"Me, too."

Lilah glanced around the restaurant. The vibrant hum of

diners surrounded them, creating a strange sort of cocoon in the midst of the noise and excitement. "It's a strange business. A tough one, too.

"The question you asked me earlier? About being on call during everyone else's personal moments? Those personal moments can turn on you in a heartbeat. It's so hard to keep a restaurant successful beyond your early halcyon days. And that's if you're lucky enough to even take off and have halcyon days."

"Do you miss it?"

"Not in the least. Maybe that was colored by Steven. It'd be silly to think it had no impact. But what Vi, Cassidy and I do? It's fulfilling on a different level. A deeper one. We create memories for someone that they will carry their whole lives. It's special. And it's a special thing to be a part of."

They sat in silence for the moment, as cocooned as she'd imagined. For a few brief seconds, Lilah allowed herself to forget the rubies. Forget about the secrets that had lain hidden in the shop. She even allowed herself to forget the pain of her past.

In that moment, she wanted to enjoy the company of an attractive, vibrant man. One who listened to her and seemed genuinely interested in what she had to say.

One who challenged her.

He had recognized from the start that she had a skittish air, yet he'd pushed and poked and prodded his way beneath her defenses.

It was humbling.

And exhilarating.

"Ms. Castle?" A large man in a chef's apron interrupted the moment. "I'm Wilhelm Brown. It's lovely to meet you."

Lilah thought the use of address needlessly formal—almost subservient—but smiled up at the pastry chef, his address likely engineered by Steven. "So lovely to meet you, Wilhelm. But please, it's Lilah. Are you responsible for this evening's trio?"

"Yes, ma'am."

The small trio of desserts had been laid out with their coffee service and she'd enjoyed tastes of each. "The coconut crème is exquisite."

"Thank you." The man nodded, his smile broad.

"The coconut is not exquisite. Not by a long shot."

Yep, she thought. *Could have clocked it with an egg timer.*

Lilah watched the smile fade from the pastry chef's face and knew the man wasn't long for Steven DeWinter's world. He'd likely be gone as soon as Restaurant Week was over.

She'd recently heard wind of an opening at one of the large hotels downtown. With a quick mental note to shoot Wilhelm's name over to the hiring manager, she focused her attention on Steven. And worked on providing Reed with the opening he needed to probe into Steven's recent activities.

"Nonsense, Steven. The coconut is divine. You never were a very good judge of sweet things."

She smiled once more at Wilhelm, giving him an opportunity to exit their ridiculous power play. "Thank you for sharing your creation this evening. It's divine."

Steven's distaste was more than evident but, furthering the image in her mind of a play, he said nothing until his pastry chef had departed for another table. "I expect the best in my kitchen. Anything less than that is an insult. To my guests and to me."

"Yes, well, bygones." She shot a brief glance at Reed before shifting gears. "Speaking of times past, I have some sad news to share. Did you hear about Robert and Charlie?"

"Who?"

Although Steven made a good show of it, his face

scrunching up, a finger to his chin in thought, Lilah saw the flash of awareness in his gaze before it was quickly banked.

"Cassidy's brother-in-law, Charlie McCallum. And her former fiancé, Robert Barrington."

"They never married?"

"No." Lilah shook her head, her eyes downcast before she lasered them straight back to Steven. "Some people know how to cut their losses before the marriage."

"I never knew them well beyond our relationship. I haven't kept up with either in some time."

"Still, it's a shame. Both passing and within a few days of each other."

"Hmm."

Lilah didn't dare look at Reed, but she sensed action before he spoke. "Both murdered, as a matter of fact. I can't believe you haven't heard the news."

"I've been busy. This is one of our biggest weeks of the year."

Reed reached for her hand once more, toying with her fingers. "Well, consider it a triumph. The food was exquisite."

Although his gaze could have cut glass, Steven had never been immune to praise of any kind. He nodded, his bow practically courtly, before he stepped away from the table. "I'll leave you both for the evening."

Lilah waited to speak until Steven was out of earshot but closed her mouth at Reed's subtle head shake. With a broad smile, he tightened their fingers. "A superb meal. I've so enjoyed this evening, darling."

"Did you enjoy the duck?"

"You mean the one on my plate?"

At his wink, she nodded, then made small talk until he'd finished the bill.

* * *

"You pegged it." Reed dropped into the driver's seat after walking Lilah to her side. "Every step of the way, you had him down cold."

"He's an ass."

"One you're well rid of."

Her dark gaze was inscrutable across the small width of the car, but her words were impossible to mistake. "Thank you. For tonight. For being there with me. I never could have done that without you."

"Don't underestimate yourself."

"No. I mean it. I didn't want to be there, but I never felt in danger." She laid a hand on his arm. "Thank you for making me feel safe."

He grinned at her, more pleased than he could have ever described at her words. "It's all part of the job, ma'am."

"You take serving and protecting awfully seriously."

"I do."

Reed knew her words were meant as a lighthearted riposte, but he quickly understood his answer held something more.

"I love what I do. What it means to right other's wrongs. To find justice. It took me a long time to understand what drove that or why it matters to me. But it *does* matter to me."

As you do, Lilah Castle.

The thought was wholly unexpected, but as he let the words—and more important, their meaning—drift through his mind as he pulled out of the restaurant parking lot, he knew them to be true.

"Did you get what you needed tonight?"

"I think so. But give me your impressions first."

"Where do I start?" She let out a small laugh. "Okay. First of all, he pretended not to know who I was talking about when I mentioned Robert and Charlie. Total bs and a dead giveaway."

"Yes." Reed added his agreement as he took the on-ramp to the highway. "Amateur move."

"Steven may be a lot of things, but he's not an amateur. So I'd say that was his first major mistake. And then his complete lack of reaction at the fact they were murdered. He missed the mark. It's one thing to pretend not to remember them. But it's a whole different matter to have absolutely no reaction to hearing they were murdered."

"Give you the detective's star, Castle. You've read my mind on both counts."

"He's scared."

Reed was intrigued at the diagnosis and pressed her. "Elaborate. What made you think that?"

"He's an arrogant ass, so it wasn't a shock that he tried to bluff his way through the discussion, pretending how busy he is. But I saw fear behind his gaze. Real fear. It's something I've never seen before."

"So how do you know what it is?"

"Because I saw it more than enough times in my own eyes. Night after night, I'd find some time to steal away to the bathroom, desperate to figure out what I'd done. Where I'd missed the mark. How I'd gotten myself involved with someone who had such a disregard for me. Such disdain. Was it something I'd done? Something I deserved?"

She stopped, the now-silent car full of the words and emotions and the years of pain she'd endured at the hands of that bastard.

Hands tight on the steering wheel, Reed fought his own rash of nerves and anger and upset. They'd had a good night—a productive night—and turning the car around to beat the hell out of Steven DeWinter wasn't a smart move.

But oh, how he wanted to.

He hadn't lied to Lilah. He took his job and his role as a protector of the city seriously. But there was little he wouldn't give for two minutes alone with Steven DeWinter.

One-on-one.

Red taillights lit up in the distance and he refocused on the road, the heavy traffic yet another example of the continued population growth of their fair city. He'd lived here all his life, and it was amazing to see how industry and prosperity had driven a boatload of new residents to Dallas.

So here they were, nine o'clock at night with a line of traffic waiting to get into downtown.

The light tap on his brakes did nothing to reduce his speed and Reed pressed his foot again, a spark of concern racing up his spine when he still felt no change in the car's velocity.

What?

He tapped again—harder this time—and still, his speed never wavered. And the red brake lights before them kept getting closer and closer.

Concern morphed into full-on panic as he ran through the images in his mirrors.

Left.

Center.

Right.

Damn, they were locked in, traffic on all sides. With a slam on the dashboard, he hit his flashers, willing the small symbol to give those around him some sense of his distress.

"Reed?" Lilah's voice matched the sudden racing of his heart. "What's going on?"

"I don't think we have any brakes."

"Oh my—" She broke off on a light cry as he narrowly swerved around a slowing car on their right.

"I need you to take my phone. Call a number for me."

Reed gritted his teeth as he kept his foot firmly off the brake and worked on navigating himself toward the far right across the five-lane highway. Their only hope was to hit an upcoming off-ramp with his foot off the gas, then find something hard to break their stop.

"Where is it?"

"Here. My pocket."

He felt her hand snake into his coat pocket, digging for the small device as he swerved around another car. Heavy honking filled the night and he immediately splayed his forearm across Lilah's shoulders as he took a hard right. "Hang on."

Another resounding round of horns let out, but whoever was on their right sensed some problem and slowed enough to let them over.

"I'll be damned," Lilah breathed on a strangled giggle. "No one ever gives an inch in this town."

"They sure as hell don't."

The exit sign was only a quarter mile away. The lack of pressure on the gas had slowed them some, but not nearly enough to miss the cars that had already slowed to the overwhelming traffic.

"What's the plan?"

"That ramp. The one before downtown. I want to coast up the exit and then we're going to have to take the wall."

"No! It's on your side."

"Which is why you need to call 911. Now."

He kept his focus solely on the road, swerving once again and bracing against the impact when he nicked a rear bumper on a slowing car in front of them. The heavy thud only reinforced the speed they were still going, but it slowed them slightly and cleared him for the exit ramp that was his goal.

Lilah maintained her calm, dialing Emergency Services and speaking immediately once they came on the line. She frantically whipped out instructions to their location and what had happened to them. He heard the 911 dispatcher's garbled voice through the phone, one string of words loud and clear.

We've got backup on the way.

Reed cleared the ramp, the slight incline slowing them even further, but one glance at the odometer and he knew it wasn't enough. One additional glance at the cars stopped in front of them at the off-ramp intersection and he knew he could no longer wait it out.

The back of his forearm still on Lilah's chest, Reed braced himself for impact and made a hard left turn into the highway retaining wall.

Chapter 8

Lilah fought the overwhelming urge to scream and instead focused on getting to Reed now that the air bags had deployed. The screech of metal had been unbearable—the entire crash happening as if in slow motion—and the subsequent explosion of the safety bags had only added to the sense of unreality.

With fumbling fingers, she managed to find the gearshift and slammed the car into Park. She had no idea if it mattered at this point but figured it couldn't hurt.

"Reed." When she got no answer, she tried once more. "Reed!"

"Hmm? Wh—" A hard moan accompanied his half-slurred question and she pushed at the heap of exploded nylon in their laps.

"Are you okay?"

With his head resting against the headrest, Reed turned toward her. His eyes had a dazed, unfocused look and Lilah could only send up a silent prayer when she heard the distinct sounds of sirens. "You okay?"

"I asked you first."

A bit of the haze dissipated from his eyes and his brows narrowed in hard lines. "You could have been killed."

"I think that was the whole idea."

Before either of them could say anything more, blue-and-red flashing lights were upon them and there were professionals dragging open her car door hollering in strong tones to gain her attention.

In the continued unreality of shouting and motion and action, she couldn't stop one lone thought from resounding over and over in her mind like a gong.

Reed had taken the wall for her.

Lilah heard them before she saw them. Two sets of frantic voices, followed by the calming presence of two deeper male baritones.

"Where is she?"

"We're here for Lilah Castle—"

The two demands wove over top of each other as Cassidy and Violet practically attacked the night-nurse station in their rush to see her.

She heard the murmured calm of the nurse and the directions to her bay.

And then Cassidy and Violet were there, flinging back the curtain and rushing to the side of her bed and both talking at once and crying like babies.

Lilah thought she was strong. She'd held it together from the moment Reed had realized something was wrong, all through the ride to the hospital and the poking and prodding of the doctors.

She'd even stayed calm as she asked after Reed, ques-

tioning everyone who came to see her for an update on
how he was doing.

But at the sight of her two best friends, tears she hadn't
even realized she held back opened with the force of a
dam breaking.

"Oh. Oh no. It's okay." Cassidy had her first, pulling her
close in a tight hug. Violet sat on the other side of the bed
and Lilah felt herself pulled into a tight melding of arms
and heads and murmured assurances that all would be well.

The three of them rode out the storm and a few minutes later it was Tucker's warm voice that penetrated their
sodden circle.

He leaned over Cassidy and pressed a kiss to Lilah's
head. "How are you doing, Champ?"

"If that's a *Rocky* reference, I'd say it's apt. I feel like I
went about ten rounds with Apollo Creed."

"Air bag?" Max asked, his supportive wince suggesting he'd done a tango or two of his own with an air bag.

"I never expected they'd hit so hard. Like a ginormous
fist slamming into me all at once everywhere." Lilah could
still feel the moment of impact, the odd juxtaposition of the
air bag's power along with its ability to cushion the blow.

"What happened?" Violet's soft touch smoothed several
strands of hair behind her ear before she went into general
mode. "And how?"

"Did you get any information on Reed?"

"Nothing yet," Max said. "Let me go make a few inquiries."

Tucker dropped a lingering kiss on Cassidy's head. "I'll
go give Max a hand. I think the three of you need a few
more minutes."

They watched the men go before Violet shifted straight
into inquisition mode. "Seriously, Lilah. What happened?
Was it drunk driving?"

Lilah shook her head and tried to figure out where to start. She'd given the nursing staff her friends' numbers to come get her, but she knew the details hadn't been shared. "I was on a date with Reed. At Portia."

At the mention of Steven's restaurant, Cassidy squeezed her hand. "Why did you go back there?"

But it was Violet who honed in on the matter at hand. "A date?"

"A pretend date." Lilah gave her a pointed stare before shifting toward Cassidy. "And we went to Portia because I had to. Steven played the gallant host with a free bottle of wine for our table, but Reed didn't drink a drop. He was on the clock."

"So it was just an accident?" Violet pressed.

Lilah hesitated, unsure of how to proceed. The past week had taken a toll on all of them and what was a danger to one was a danger to all.

"Lilah?" Violet pressed once more.

"Reed's brake lines were cut."

Violet and Cassidy went still, their gentle stares frozen in place.

"We obviously need to find out more, but Reed didn't realize it at first and it was only once we were on Central and he needed to slow down that he realized he couldn't."

"Who does something like this?" Cassidy spoke first, disbelief layered beneath each word. "To you? And to a cop? Who does this?"

"Someone who wants me out of the way."

Reed pushed one arm through his shirt, wincing hard at the stiffness in his body. Every muscle ached and he felt as if he'd gone up against a gorilla.

A gorilla with iron fists.

He'd checked out okay, with the instruction to main-line aspirin for the next few days and to come back immediately if he felt dizziness or any shortness of breath.

He'd felt neither until he imagined Lilah, lying broken beyond help from the crash.

Or what the crash could have been if he hadn't gotten them off the highway.

"Graystone."

Tucker Buchanan and Max Baldwin stood at the entrance to his room. "Gentlemen."

"Cassidy and Violet are with Lilah," Max said. "We thought we'd find you and find out what's really going on. What the hell are you doing dating someone you're supposed to be protecting?"

"While I'm quite sure Miss Castle can decide who she spends her personal time with, we weren't technically on a date."

Even if it gave every indication of being one, Reed decided to keep that thought to himself.

"So where were you? You're both dressed up." Tucker had seemed like the cooler head when they'd first met and his calmer tone and observant gaze only reinforced his straight man to Max's "punch first, ask questions later" approach to situations. "It looks like a date."

"We went to DeWinter's restaurant. There's some suspicion he's involved in this case and Lilah thought this would be a way to suss him out. Pretending it was a date was designed to get DeWinter's ire up."

"DeWinter, as in her ass of an ex-husband?" Tucker asked.

"One and the same."

"And the crash?" Max demanded.

Reed sighed. There really was no other way to tell it other than quick and clean, like tearing off a Band-Aid.

"My brake lines were cut. Or they felt cut. We'll know more tomorrow."

Whatever Max had already lined up as a retort faded at the evidence of what Reed and Lilah had been through that evening. "Cut?"

"It had to have happened while we were at dinner. The car was fine before that. And after—"

"You were at Portia, right?" At Reed's nod, Tucker continued, "With your car parked in a public lot with valets running all over managing cars."

"We parked ourselves at the back of the lot. Lilah had some hesitation when we pulled in and I skipped the valet to spare her the embarrassment if she wanted to leave."

Tucker shook his head. "Still. The parking lot's not that big. How could no one have noticed someone messing with your brake lines?"

"All I know is that someone got to them." He barked the response, not surprised when the bigger thought underneath rose up to slap at him. Someone got to Lilah, even under his protection.

"Mr. Graystone." A young doctor, obviously consigned to the late shift, poked her head around the doorway. "I've left your completed paperwork at the desk. You're free to leave with your friends."

He nodded his appreciation, then stood and reached for his sport coat. The fabric was covered with the fine dusting of talc that came from the air-bag deployment and he briefly toyed with stuffing it in the garbage. "I'd like to go see Lilah."

"If Cassidy and Violet will let you through." Tucker pointed toward the hallway. "They had her surrounded like a human phalanx when we left."

"Graystone. One thing." Max stopped him. "Do you think DeWinter did this?"

Reed had been over and over it in his mind and he still hadn't come to any conclusions. He'd confirm with Jessie in the morning, but they'd kept a pretty solid eye on DeWinter all through dinner. The man had made it his business to float around the restaurant or stand guard over his open kitchen. At no time did Reed remember DeWinter disappearing for an extended period.

Add on the sense he got Steven DeWinter didn't like getting his hands dirty and Reed had trouble pointing the finger squarely on the man.

Of course, he had denied any memory of Robert Barrington and Charlie McCallum and had shown even less concern at the news both men were murdered.

"I really don't know."

Tucker glanced toward the door, his voice low. "We've increased our surveillance over Elegance and Lace, and Cassidy's mentioned more than once how I hover closer than her shadow. I'll attach myself to her if that's what it takes, but I'm still concerned it's not enough."

"At least she talks to you." Max's disgust would have been evident even without the subtle sneer. "Violet seems to get a particular joy out of snubbing me."

"I can get protection detail put on the office. We've already got uniforms driving by several times a day, but after tonight—" Reed broke off before pushing on. "After tonight the department's going to take an even larger interest in this matter than they already are."

Max shifted from foot to foot in the doorway, that small sneer still riding his features. The man was frustrated, Reed realized as he took in the pent-up energy.

And he likely cared far more than he wanted to let on.

"I'll keep you both updated. Make sure you know what you're dealing with."

Max nodded, the acknowledgment of his contributions

going a long way toward stilling the nervous motions. "We'll do the same."

They were good guys, Reed thought.

He'd done his homework on them when he first caught the case. Both were in their early thirties, friends since they'd been in the military.

Where they had architectural abilities in spades—and a new business venture in the private sector as further proof of those abilities—Reed's digging had turned up some time on active duty, as well.

Apparently Buchanan and Baldwin were particularly adept at blowing things up.

The thought briefly jingled that they'd likely know their way around a car's undercarriage, but he quickly dismissed it.

Although they'd held back a few key details at first— namely, their suspicions that something was housed in the concrete beneath Elegance and Lace—they'd been on the up-and-up since Robert Barrington's attempted kidnapping of Cassidy.

To assume they'd set everything up to their own advantage didn't play with any of the events since. Still, he'd have Jessie run a few more background checks on both of them. What they had done before the service. Any juvenile record, for instance, or anything to raise a red flag.

For no other reason, it would complete the file and turn away the suspicions of anyone else who might take a look.

And based on the cut brake lines, he was proof positive the department mechanic was going to find tomorrow morning, Reed knew he'd better have a full and complete file ready to review with his lieutenant.

The Duke refilled his bourbon and reviewed the details Trey had shared with him upon returning from the crime scene. He bumped up Trey's on-scene report with the text message he'd received from his police department contact, only to find the same answer. By all accounts, the woman and the cop had walked away from the scene.

If they were unscathed was a different matter, but they had walked.

He ignored the strange sense of relief at that fact and focused instead on the matter at hand.

It had been four days and he still didn't have the rubies. Four days that they lay in the possession of others, mere miles from him.

Out of his reach.

It was inexcusable.

With the methodological precision he prided himself on, he worked his way through the matter from the start. The information that had come to his attention via Mc-Callum and Barrington.

Prior to that, the introduction made at DeWinter's insistence.

And prior to even that, the small rumblings that had traveled in elite Dallas circles for years of crown jewels smuggled here from Great Britain after World War Two.

He'd hunted down the appraiser, Gunnar Davidson, who'd claimed to have seen the jewels decades before, and he'd befriended the man. With Gunnar now one of the city's finest jewelers, the Duke had purchased copious amounts of pieces from the man, lining Davidson's pockets with a sizable investment.

And then he'd used that trust to gain the information he truly wanted. A late-night drunken confession that confirmed the truth of the tale before he disposed of the man with a poison that mimicked a heart attack.

Gunnar had sung, telling a tale of rubies of immeasurable beauty. Nearly flawless in their perfection and passed down through history since the Renaissance.

They even carried their name from the period.

The Renaissance Stones.

Along with the name, they'd carried a supposed curse. The Duke had enjoyed that aspect of the story but paid it little attention.

Curses were for fairy tales and Halloween stories. He was far too practical to pay them any mind.

What he also knew was that things of rare and priceless beauty were worth killing for.

Perhaps that was the difference between those who believed in curses and those who didn't.

He poured himself another finger of bourbon and let that thought take root. Those who wanted to assign supernatural happenings to inanimate objects did so because of the fear those objects elicited. But it was humans who created the fear, not the object.

And there were those who were more than comfortable preying on that fear, using it to their advantage.

Take the man who'd discovered the jewel in the seventeenth century. The poor sot had made the grave mistake of showing it off. Here he had a stone of immeasurable value and beauty and he'd passed it around like some prize.

The Duke shook his head at the vanity as he finished off his drink.

He'd learned early that showing off one's most prized possessions led to greed and envy in others. Which meant it was better to enjoy them in private.

Always better.

But since the Renaissance Stone's original owner wasn't possessed of the same self-control, he'd shown the jewel to a Dutch merchant, one of the key movers and shakers in the Dutch East India Company. The Dutchman had killed for the stone and had then taken it home.

Where he made the same damn mistake.

Idiots, the entire lot of them.

"Darling!"

The soft words drifted down the hallway toward his sitting room. He'd been ignoring his wife of late, and still, she smiled and preened over him, happy to welcome him home.

He'd chosen well there. And she was one jewel he was delighted to show off as often as possible.

He stowed the phone he used for his personal business in his desk drawer, locked it away from prying eyes and stood. He left the empty glass on the blotter, sure in the knowledge the staff would pick it up in the morning.

They took care of him.

His wife took care of him.

Little did any of them know how he took care of everything else.

Lilah opened her front door, barely stifling a yawn as she stepped through the entryway and reached for the alarm keypad. Max had dropped them off with no small degree of reticence, but Lilah had been appreciative of the help.

The help and the fact that Violet or Cassidy hadn't been their driver.

She loved her friends, but their questions about Reed had grown a bit much. Especially as she was still trying to get her head fully wrapped around her feelings.

Reed had insisted on staying with her, and she waited for him to close and lock the door before she reset the alarm.

"You're quick with that thing."

"I like to feel protected."

He nodded, nearly asleep on his feet. She'd seen him pass on the pain medication, so she could only assume he was horribly uncomfortable and aching, as well.

"Thanks for seeing me home. Violet was ready to lock me up in her house and I wanted to sleep in my own bed."

"Consider this door-to-door service."

"Can I get you anything?"

"A large round of aspirin would be great."

"Come on."

She sensed his pain more than saw it, his gait stiff and heavy as he climbed the stairs behind her. Her three-story townhome had always seemed lovely and modern, but at the sheer exhaustion overtaking both of them she'd have gladly killed for something small—and all on one story—like Cassidy's East Dallas bungalow.

Several small lights glowed when they reached the second-floor landing, setting off a mix of shadows as they moved toward the kitchen. Even with the horrible events of the evening, she couldn't stop the small measure of calm that stole over her at the comforts of home.

"Sit down and I'll get the aspirin and some water." She pointed him toward her kitchen table before moving to the cabinets to snag two bottles of water and the economy-size container of aspirin.

Her heart stilled as she came back to the table. Reed was unmoving, his large frame bent over and his gaze dull on the top of the table. He still held his suit jacket—the piece looked as if it would never be clean—over his arm and she could see a large hole gaping at the seam of his shirt where the sleeve met the material that draped the body.

She jiggled the bottle so as not to come up behind him. "How many?"

"Can I have the whole thing?" His smile was gentle,

but she saw the distinct note of humor in his eyes, and for the first time since he'd walked into her bay at the emergency room, she relaxed.

They were okay.

"Why don't we start with three?"

"Three it is."

He made quick work of the pills and the water, then seemed to notice the coat on his lap. "I should have left this behind."

"I was thinking the same thing. You have any sentimental attachment to it?"

At the small shake of his head, she reached for it, their fingers brushing at the contact. Ignoring the searing heat that always seemed present between them, she took the coat and marched it toward her garbage can. "We'll file this one away as the one thing this evening managed to kill."

"Lilah. I'm sorry."

She turned at that, the evidence her joke missed the mark stamped across the tired lines of his face in genuine distress. "No. I'm sorry. Gallows humor has always been a personal specialty and I need to remember not everyone agrees. Violet hates it."

"You have reason to joke about death often?"

"Often enough." She shrugged, surprised when the next words followed. "My father died when I was a kid. One day he was fine and the next he had an accident at work. A large TV monitor fell on him, of all things."

"A TV?"

She saw Reed processing the information and quickly pressed on. Why she'd even started this she had no idea, but now that it was out she knew she needed to finish.

"The idea of it seems so strange now. We don't have appliances that large anymore, especially not TVs and office equipment. But he was preparing for a presentation and they'd pushed several TVs into the conference room and he pushed the large cart the wrong way. The cart caught on the carpet and the size of the TV and the angle that it fell on his head—" She shrugged, the pointlessness of it all still a senseless waste twenty years later. "He never woke up."

"How did you deal with it?"

"The same way you deal with anything, I guess. You soldier on. One foot in front of the other, day after day. My mom bore the brunt, as you'd imagine, but it was just the two of us. And after a long while we found our new normal. A life without him."

"It doesn't mean it's easy."

"No. It doesn't." She glanced around the room, the toasted-almond colors of her mother's kitchen taking over her memories as her more modern setup faded from view. "After he died is when I started baking."

"Oh?"

"My mom was sad all the time and I always had a few hours after school before she got home from work. I started baking box cakes because they were easy and I thought something sweet would make her smile. Then I graduated to decorating whatever I made. And then I got really adventurous and threw away the box."

"Rebel."

She smiled at that. "You could say that. I think she was just happy I stayed out of trouble. She used to take whatever I made into work and after a while I started getting feedback from her coworkers. And then I got a request to make cupcakes for one of the women's kids. And it sort of steamrolled from there."

Those days were such a distant memory, but it amazed Lilah how quickly she could take herself back there. The sadness and the fear something would happen to her mom.

She'd worn it like a cloak, that fear that something random and unexpected would happen and then she'd be alone.

The baking had been an unexpected gift. When she focused on the whirling beaters or measuring ingredients or a particularly tricky decorating technique, she got lost in the moment, her restless mind settling as she worked through the challenge.

Those days had saved her. It had taken a long time to understand that, but she knew it now.

"It's like you said earlier. You made something special for someone else. You gave them a memory."

"I guess I did."

The small light she kept on the edge of the kitchen counter spilled over them in soft golds. Even with the muted colors, she could see the dark gray of Reed's irises. The shade was so compelling, just like the man.

He leaned toward her, his large body blocking out some of the light. She saw the small smile ghost his lips before he whispered against her ear, "Now I really do need to call Vice."

"Why's that?" She heard the breathy response and delighted in the raw emotion that coursed between them.

"You've clearly been a sugar pusher a lot longer than I realized."

"I do have a lot of satisfied clients."

His breath whispered over the shell of her ear before he ran his lips down the line of her jaw. "Besotted fools, just like me."

As he finished the journey from ear to jaw, Lilah turned and met his lips with hers. The warmth of his mouth enveloped hers, the sweet moment punctuating a roller coaster of an evening.

And as she allowed the moments to swirl out like the

finest threads of spun sugar, Lilah let loose on the tight reins of emotion she normally kept in check.

Here, in this moment, she was safe.

Chapter 9

Reed came awake to the hard, heavy pounding of his phone alarm. He reached for it automatically, nearly crying out at the pain that seemed to shimmy outward from his chest to his back before it ricocheted around to his ribs.

Awareness slammed into him even harder than the pain and he switched off his phone, then flopped onto the pillow.

The car. The cut brake lines. DeWinter.

And Lilah.

His jumbled thoughts over the accident cleared as the feel of her flooded him in a hard wave of sense memories. The light scent of her hair, a perpetual vanilla that was either her natural perfume or the result of her endless hours in the kitchen. The press of her lips, soft and solid at the same time. And under it all, a warm compassion and loyalty that was touching.

She wasn't afraid to hold her own or toss out a sarcastic remark, but she was unfailingly loyal. And she'd been sweet and kind to his mother, asking questions and waiting for the answers with genuine interest.

She was a contradiction. A slim pixie and a lush, dynamic woman. A rich treat that teased the senses and made a man want more—want all—after one single taste.

And he'd woken up thinking about her.

Snagging his phone off the end table, he dialed the precinct. He knew he was a bit early to get his lieutenant, but he wanted to leave a message and get the ball rolling on the review of the car.

He dialed Jessie next and had to bear up under her grumbles at the early hour.

"C'mon, Jess, it's seven."

"Yes, it's seven. And you kept me out last night until past eleven. Dave and I are an old married couple now."

"I was up a hell of a lot later." He quickly caught her up on the crash and his suspicions about her car.

Jessie's sleepy tone and grouchy voice vanished. "Are you okay?"

"Bruised like I went several rounds in a ring, but I'm fine. We're both fine."

"I'm heading in now. I'll start digging into the car and will meet you at nine at the impound lot. Do you need me to pick you up?"

"Lilah will drive me in."

"Lilah?"

Reed heard the interest at roughly the same decibel level of a train whistle. "I'm at her place. I didn't want her here alone last night."

"Very sensible of you."

"That's me."

"Reed Graystone. Exemplary model of the Dallas PD. His willingness to protect and serve is a 24/7 job."

"I'll see you at nine."

He disconnected the call before Jessie could get any further licks in.

Despite the pain, he lifted himself out of bed and stood. He waited a moment, taking stock of his various aches. His ribs hurt less than they had the night before, but his shoulders screamed in tightness and he rolled them several times to work out the painful kinks.

Resigned, he knew there was nothing to be done for it except loads more aspirin and movement. As a first step, he slipped into his clothes from the night before. Everything was filthy, with the lingering talc from the air bag embedded in every fiber.

He made a mental note to trash the rest of the outfit when he got home and opened the bedroom door intent on snagging more aspirin and a cab home.

But when he opened the bedroom door, the distinct smell of pancakes and coffee wafted toward him. He padded toward the kitchen and waited, fascinated by the sight that greeted him.

Lilah stood at the counter, her hair piled on her head in a messy knot. She wore an old SMU T-shirt and a small pair of shorts. He gave himself a moment to let his gaze travel over that small, compact body and the trim legs before moving fully into the kitchen.

Pain aside, Reed had one lone thought as he reached for a coffee mug.

He was fairly sure he'd died and gone to heaven.

Steven DeWinter groaned into his Egyptian-cotton sheets as the phone screamed from his bedside. He'd inhaled half a bottle of whiskey when he got home, a persistent mix of irritation and frustration dogging him since Lilah and her damn date had left Portia.

And now his mouth was cotton, his ears were ringing and he still hadn't worked off the irritation and frustration.

"What?"

"DeWinter."

The Duke's harsh tone echoed through the phone and Steven scrambled to a sitting position, pain swimming before his eyes. "Yes."

"Are you aware of who was inside your restaurant last night?"

"What felt like half of Dallas, but I suspect you mean my ex-wife."

"Your ex-wife and a cop."

A cop?

He was tempted to ask the Duke where he'd gotten his information, but Steven held the question. The man had his finger on the pulse of everything and questioning how he'd come by his information was futile.

"There's no way that guy was a cop. He was some besotted jerk who couldn't stop staring at her and rubbing her hand."

"Your belief or lack thereof doesn't change the truth. They were there to question you."

Steven rubbed the base of his neck, desperately wishing for an IV of Advil. "I barely saw them. They had a meal, we made small talk. That's all."

"Did that small talk involve Robert's and Charlie's recent deaths?"

Still, it's a shame. Both passing and within a few days of each other.

Steven's hand stilled, the memory of their discussion coming back to him.

Both murdered, as a matter of fact. I can't believe you haven't heard the news.

He had heard the news, of course. And still, he'd pretended he hadn't. But if Lilah's date was a cop, he'd likely garnered a second glance with the weak lie.

Damn woman.

"Well, then, I'll take that as a yes on the small talk."

"It was casual conversation."

When the Duke spoke next, Steven knew his protests had fallen on deaf ears. "What's done is done. I have a new project for you. A way to clean up your mess, as it were."

"Of course."

"I'll meet you at our usual spot. Ten o'clock."

The phone went dead and Steven rubbed at his neck once more. The early-morning light hit his eyes like ice picks, but he ignored it and headed for the shower.

Whatever pain he felt now would be a cakewalk compared to the Duke's ire if he missed the meeting.

Lilah scooped her second helping of strawberries and blueberries out of a small bowl before setting it next to the empty serving plate. She and Reed had managed an entire batch of pancakes, and while she'd like to lay the majority of the blame on him, she'd held her own.

And was still a little hungry.

"Those were amazing."

"Thanks."

Reed took the last bite on his plate. "I'm serious. It's like you're the love child of Betty Crocker and the Pillsbury Doughboy."

She couldn't hold back the laugh, even as a thick morass of pancakes rumbled in her stomach. "Thanks. I think."

The domesticity of the moment wasn't lost on her, especially as she asked the next question. "Do you want me to run you home before I take you to the precinct?"

"That works and then you can just go on from there.

I'll catch a cab from home and have work set up a loaner car this morning."

"I don't mind taking you in."

He reached for her plate, stacking it on his and then on the empty serving tray. "You're only going to add to the interest."

"I'm dropping you off, not perching on the edge of your desk to sing show tunes."

"And wouldn't that be a sight?"

She knew it was small of her, but she couldn't quite hold back the delight at his sudden awkwardness. For some reason, he was embarrassed and she found it completely adorable.

He flipped the water on in the sink and began rinsing the dishes.

"You don't have to do that."

"You cooked. It's the least I can do."

The offer was so sweet she decided not to argue and dug into her berries. As the cool, sweet fruit slid over her tongue, she contemplated her next move. "How would anyone at the precinct even know I was there? I presume there's a parking lot for me to drop you off."

"I spoke with Jessie this morning. I need to meet her at the impound lot at nine."

Aha, Lilah thought as she scooped up her last blueberry. *The plot thickens.* "So she'll see me."

"Yes."

"She's the one who was positioned in the restaurant last night?"

"With her husband, Dave."

"So she saw our little show, then."

His voice was flat, his eyes on the dishes as he scrubbed the plates. "Yes."

"The googly eyes. The hand-holding. The whispered giggles."

"Yes."

"So how'd we do?"

He did glance over at that. "How'd we do at what?"

"Convincing her we're besotted."

"She did suggest this morning that I'm a full-service officer. Eager to protect and serve 24/7."

Lilah crossed the few steps from the table to the sink, dropping her bowl into his wet hands. Pleased he was distracted, she took a cue from his ministrations the previous evening. Moving up onto her tiptoes, she pressed her lips to his ear and blew a warm breath along the lobe. "Perhaps we need to keep up the show."

"What if it's not a show?"

Need whipped through her like a storm at the raw fire she saw flashing in his gaze. When had this gone past a game?

And when had they both begun to want each other so much?

She knew sexual attraction. Had enjoyed it a time or two in her life, even before Steven. And while her dating life hadn't been all that much to write home about, she'd dated a few times since her divorce. Tentative steps toward normalcy that never fully panned out but weren't a complete waste of time, either.

But this...*this* was different.

More intense. More needy. More *dramatic*.

It seemed like a silly word, yet as she tried it on, Lilah realized it fit.

They were in the middle of some serious drama and she knew that could heighten feelings of need or desire. Cassidy had worried about it with Tucker, wondering if the intensity of their circumstances had forced their feelings.

Cassidy now knew that wasn't the case—and Lilah and Violet had known it from the start—but her friend had still worried.

And now in the light of her own attraction, Lilah was forced to wonder the same thing.

With Reed's words still hovering between them, she gave him the only thing she had.

The truth.

"If it's just a show, then when it's over we'll take our bows and go our separate ways."

"So tell me about Jessie."

At Lilah's request, Reed navigated the drive to the impound lot. Between driving an unfamiliar car, the early-morning traffic and a fair amount of stiffness from the night before, his eyes were firmly on the road. Which meant he had plenty of opportunity to hear the question underneath the question.

"She's one of my oldest friends."

"And you both ended up on the force. Partners?"

"Sort of. My most recent partner retired about two months ago and I'm still trying different people on. Our lieutenant has paired us up on a few cases to see if our friendship can extend to a proper working relationship."

"Is it hard to find the right person?"

"I wouldn't call it hard, but it does take some getting used to. Different styles and ways of working. Different attitudes to the job. It's just something you know when you know."

"That's how we felt about Gabby. When we started the business, we were interested in having some sort of catering offering. I can do limited catering with appetizers and the like, but not a full-on meal."

"Let me guess. Your appetizers normally have layers

and layers of puff pastry. The sort Baldwin eats until they come out his ears."

He caught her smile from the corner of his eye. "You'd be correct. If I can wrap it in dough, I'm a happy gal. Beyond that, I'm relatively useless."

"And a lot of couples want to feed their guests more than appetizers."

"Oftentimes, yes." Like a dog with a bone, Lilah returned directly to the matter at hand. "What's it like working with a woman?"

"Not that much different from working with a man."

"Really? Because I found working with men in the kitchen a vastly different experience than what I have now."

"Your useless ex-husband doesn't count."

"Beyond Steven. Men bring a different energy and different thought process. I don't mean it in a battle-of-the-sexes way, but it's a different working relationship."

Recognizing her point, Reed thought about the past two months and the jobs he and Jessie had partnered on. They knew each other so well it had been easy to fall back on the comfort of their friendship, but now that he gave it some thought, he had to admit she challenged him in different ways.

"She doesn't let me skate on anything. She's dogged as we pursue leads."

"I can't see you slacking."

"No, but she does see things differently. Is quicker to pick up on motivations than I am."

"How long have you been friends?"

Amused at her insistence, he thought about one of his oldest friends. "I told you about my dual life."

"What? You're Dallas's version of the Dark Knight?"

"Not quite." He wanted to smile at the joke, but their

impending highway exit had a shot of adrenaline skittering down his spine. Although it wasn't the same exit as the previous evening, it was humbling to know the memory wasn't far from the surface.

Pleased to have something else to focus on as he cleared the ramp, he continued his story. "Jessie was the first friend I made at my new school after my mom married Tripp. Overnight I went from having friends in a shabbier part of town to being the new kid at a school full of the city's wealthiest progeny."

"That must have been a shock."

"Kids are kids, so I knew a bit of what to expect, but yeah, it was a shock."

"And Jessie?"

"She was a bit of a rebel. Always ready to defend the underdog. She's terrifyingly brilliant and usually three steps ahead of everyone else. She pegged me for the class bully's latest target if she didn't step in and help, taking me under her wing."

"I'm always amazed how perceptive some kids are. Did she succeed?"

"She did. I made friends pretty quickly and then once I got involved in sports, it became even easier. But she remained my friend. First and best, as I've always thought of her." He took the last turn for the city's impound lot and couldn't resist finishing off the story. "She was right about the bully, too."

"Oh? Did he threaten to meet you after the last bell to fight in the schoolyard?"

"Nope."

"Toilet paper your house?"

Reed snagged a spot and put the car in Park. "Not that, either."

"What happened, then?"

"The bully ended up getting kicked out of our rather pristine private school for cheating a year later."

"Teachers are pretty serious about that stuff."

"Especially when the cheater's the meanest girl in school who delights in creating misery as often as possible."

He couldn't hide his own smile when Lilah's mouth dropped, her deep brown eyes widening in surprise. "Your class bully was a girl?"

"Yep. Piper Tremain. She never did get over her wicked ways, either."

"Some people never learn. There are a few delinquents in my class that you hear about from time to time."

"Well, Jessie arrested ours last year. Seemed that she was involved in a high-level embezzlement ring in one of the banks downtown."

"Wow. You just never know."

"You don't." Reed glanced out the window, the subject of his story stepping from her car. Her jaunty wave matched the speculative grin that spread quickly across her face. "Jessie's the one who cracked the case."

"How?"

"Remember how I mentioned she was three steps ahead of everyone else?"

"Sure."

"The moment she heard Piper Tremain had gotten a job at the bank, our Jessie started keeping a tickler file of anything suspicious."

"She knew."

"She sure did."

As preparation went, Reed figured his childhood story was a poor substitute for reality, but there really was no way to describe the whirling dervish that was Jessie Baxter

Hurley. The woman moved ninety miles an hour and wasn't happy unless her mouth was running at a speed to match.

"So you're Lilah. I heard you had quite an evening last night."

"You could say that."

Jessie's face turned serious and Reed recognized the anger that leaped into her gaze. He'd been on the receiving end of that look more times in his life than he could count and he knew it never boded well when her eyes narrowed into small slits. That light of battle had him abstractly wishing for the antacids sitting in his impounded car. "The Dallas PD doesn't take that sort of thing lightly. We've already requested the security tapes from the restaurant and I've got several team members working any of the feeds from the local street cameras. We're going to find out who did this."

"I believe you will." Lilah hesitated before she pointed toward the large chain-link fence that surrounded the lot. "Do you mind if I take a look?"

Reed couldn't hide his surprise at her interest. "Are you sure?"

"Positive. I need to see what we're up against."

"You know what you're up against. A nameless, faceless threat with one agenda."

Lilah shook her head, the early-morning sun catching the strands of gold in her hair. "I want to see the evidence. There can't be any question in my mind."

"Question about what?"

"When this threat comes knocking again, I won't hesitate to protect myself."

Jessie shifted into protector mode, her stance on immediate alert. She'd remained silent up to now, but Reed already knew what ran through his partner's mind and he quickly spoke up. "You can't make threats like that in front of cops."

"I'm not making threats. I'm stating facts. Less than a week ago my best friend thought she could deal with her ex-fiancé and it nearly cost her her life. I want to be damn sure I remember this moment so I don't make the same mistake."

"You think DeWinter did this?"

"No." She stilled, her gaze roving over the vast array of cars in the lot. Her warm brown gaze went bleak as it stopped on their mangled wreck, located just inside the gated entrance. "But I think he knows who did."

"Which is why we'll handle it." Jessie finally spoke up, her normally jovial voice brooking no argument.

Lilah's gaze never wavered from the car. "Don't mistake my meaning. I've never been a big fan of guns and I'm not going to start now. But there are other ways to stay safe, namely, with security and watchfulness. What I'm saying is that I won't let my guard down. And I'm not going to treat this like something I can manage on my own."

The hard lines of Jessie's mouth softened, her smile returning. "We *will* protect you."

Lilah's smile was sincere, gentle even, but Reed saw the refusal to believe settle over her like a thick winter cloak. "I know you mean that and I genuinely believe you will do everything in your power to protect us. But there are monsters that lurk in the dark and this monster has waited a long time. You think a few more weeks matters one way or the other?"

Chapter 10

Monsters.

With faces or without, Lilah had spent her life dealing with those threats that lurked in the shadows, waiting to devour you with sharp teeth.

Her father's death had been first. He'd simply been doing his job, providing for his family, when something dark and dangerous had leaped up and taken his life.

Steven had come next. As clichéd as it was, the man had been the proverbial wolf in sheep's clothing. Her only problem had been ignoring the teeth that had snapped at her in warning, hidden beneath the layers of wool.

Well, she'd be damned if she'd be unprepared—*or* unrealistic—this time. Whatever threat loomed, waiting to snatch her, was in for a nasty surprise. She was never going to be a victim again and she wasn't going to quiver in fear, simply waiting for the threat that stalked them to make its next move.

They'd plan. She, Violet and Cassidy, along with Tucker and Max. They'd figure out how to tackle what lurked in the shadows and they were going to dismantle it.

Was it a network of people? Someone acting alone? Based on the number of individuals already involved, she leaned toward a network, yet the whole job had the distinct markings of someone leading the charge and pulling the strings.

But who?

She needed to get into the shop but made a game-time decision to hit up Gabby for some coffee. A glance at the clock and a quick calculation on a tray of strawberries that still needed dipping and she estimated she could spare a good half hour. Since her friend had a perpetual pot going in her kitchen, Lilah decided to take a few minutes to try to settle.

The bright sign for Taste the Moment beckoned her as she turned onto Slocum, and Lilah was glad she'd made the quick detour. A fellow business owner in the Design District, Gabby had turned an old decorator's warehouse into a lavish kitchen operation.

She used about half the space to cater, and had then set up what was basically a second kitchen where she taught cooking classes and held wine tastings. The mixed use had served her well, as it meant she had a steady stream of people sampling her work and able to recommend her for catering services.

It also meant the woman slept little, hence the perpetual pot of coffee.

Gabby waved at her from the front window and opened the door. "What's up with y—" Her friend broke off as she opened the front door. "What happened?"

Lilah knew it was petty, but her first thought was that she must look like a train wreck, and how could she have gone out of the house looking like that with Reed? Before she could muster a second thought, Gabby had her pulled in tight for a hug.

"What happened?"

"Gab—"

Those strong arms relinquished her from the python squeeze, but Gabby's dark eyes remained sharp. "You look upset."

"I had a bad night."

"Bad memories?"

"More like a bad memory that made a return visit."

Gabby waved her in, the morning heat already oppressive, then locked the door behind her. "Let's go sit down."

In moments, the two of them were at a small table Gabby kept in her large kitchen, steaming mugs of coffee in front of them. Lilah caught her up on the night before, all the way up to her impressions at the impound lot.

"My cousin Ramon manages the paperwork for the lot. Want me to look into this with him?"

Lilah smiled and tried to conjure up if she'd met Ramon at the Sanchez family's previous year's Cinco party and couldn't quite summon up a face. "Reed's promised to keep me informed."

"Reed, is it?" Gabby's eyes held wide-eyed innocence as she stared over the rim of her mug, and Lilah wasn't buying it for a moment.

"Thanks, by the way. All that Detective Yummy stuff got me in trouble yesterday."

"A bit of fun with an attractive man." Gabby laid down her mug. "And how'd it get you in trouble?"

Lilah stared into her own mug as she recognized her hasty words. "I might have gotten a bit jealous."

"Of who?"

"You."

"Me?"

"Um, yeah. You're gorgeous."

"Oh, baby doll." Gabby shook her head before she stood to snag the pot off the warmer. "That man only has eyes for you."

Lilah wanted to argue, but the distinct sensation of his breath wavering over her earlobe filled her thoughts as a delicious shiver raced down her spine.

"Yeah. Well. Um."

"Well, um nothing." Gabby set down the mugs before taking her hands. "You deserve happiness. And if it came in this most unlikely way, reach out and take it. Make it yours."

Was it that easy?

She knew she was jaded. Knew the years of her marriage had done damage and left scars that she still didn't know the full extent of.

Even knowing that, she knew she wanted more. Wanted all. She'd spent her life believing she could find someone to love. Someone who loved her fully and who wanted to be with her.

Was Reed Graystone that man?

"I don't know, Gab. He's working this case. We've had a few heated moments, but that's just it. They're only moments. Likely stolen ones."

Gabriella resumed her stance at her chef's station, a large cutting board full of several heads of lettuce. "You buying this bs you're busy peddling or is it just for my benefit?"

"It's not—" At the dark look, she amended, "Okay. It is a little bit. But you can't say I'm totally off the mark. He's a cop, for Pete's sake. He deals with dangerous situations all the time. I, on the other hand, am the noob who's battling lingering fear and self-doubt, coupled with a massive problem that's landed in our laps."

"I think you're underestimating both of you. Oh, and letting Steven DeWinter continue messing with your head."

"That's low."

"Which is why I said it." Gabby sliced neatly through a large head of lettuce. "The man did enough damage and you've done a lot of work healing yourself. Just because he's involved in this, don't let that make you forget all that hard work. He doesn't matter anymore."

"No, he doesn't."

An image of Steven hovering over their table the night before flashed before her eyes. He loved playing the big man. Using his imposing height and physical breadth to intimidate and take over a situation.

She'd held her cool and stayed calm.

And Reed had been a rock, taking it all in with a wry sense of place that had managed to calm her and intrigue all at once. With him across the table, she'd managed to distance herself from the Steven she knew and feared in her heart. Instead of seeing him as the instrument of her pain, she'd seen the truth.

He was a bully.

"So promise me you'll think about it."

"I will." At Gab's pointed stare, Lilah breathed renewed life into the promise. "Honest, I will."

"Good. Now get over here and help me with these. I've got to get three bags of carrots shredded for this salad."

"Taskmaster."

"You bet."

She hip bumped Gabriella after washing her hands at the sink. "I'll help you on one condition."

"What's that?"

"After we finish, you come over and help me dip five dozen chocolate-covered strawberries."

"Deal. Maybe if I'm lucky, your detective will show up while I'm there."

Reed had already taken Jessie's ribbing the entire way to the station about his new "love interest," but when she was still offering up small jabs as they sat at his desk reviewing traffic-cam footage, he lost his cool.

"I can have the LT reassign you."

"Irritation isn't a reason to get someone reassigned."

"It will be if I hog-tie you to your desk and duct-tape your mouth."

"Empty threats."

Reed leveled a dark eye on her as he flipped to the next piece of footage. "Watch me."

Her mouth was open before she snapped it closed and leaned toward the laptop centered between them. "There. Rewind it."

"Where?" He toggled the footage backward, frame by frame, until she jabbed at the screen.

"There!"

He slowed the program, then enlarged the frame to see what he could make out. Sure enough, a dark shadow hovered toward his car, then disappeared from view as he was presumably managing the cuts to the brake lines that their mechanic discovered that morning.

Within moments, the figure disappeared, falling out of frame.

"Is it the valet?" Jessie asked.

"He didn't come from the direction of the valet stand."

She rewound and they watched the intruder move in frame from the far side of the parking lot. "No, definitely not the valet. And I know we don't have cameras for the corner of the lot because I've asked. It's a dead zone."

"Nothing even from a distance?"

"Nope. Nothing." Jessie rewound once more, then hit Pause after watching the man walk back into frame. "Time stamp says 8:02."

Reed scratched the time on his notepad, thinking through the previous evening. Their reservations had been at eight; at two after, they'd barely been seated. And within moments, DeWinter had joined them at the table.

"It can't be DeWinter."

Jessie tapped at the keys. "My gut tells me he's involved."

"Mine, too, but consider this. He didn't even know we would be in the restaurant until we were seated. Lilah confirmed he looked surprised to see us and I could see it with my own eyes."

"Dave and I saw it, too. He hadn't expected the pleasure of your company."

"So who cut the brakes?"

"Whoever DeWinter's working with."

Reed followed the thought but again, he came up with a dead end. "I'm not seeing it. If DeWinter didn't know we were there, how could he have alerted someone he was working with?"

"So you were tailed."

Reed shot her a dirty look, unable to fully fight the immediate affront at her words. "I would have known."

"Seriously? You're besotted with your passenger and you're paying attention to who might be following you."

"I'm still a cop, Jessie. I know how to manage my surroundings and how to manage an op."

When she said nothing, Reed took the silence as a good thing. He damn well knew when he was being followed and he also knew good and well that they weren't on their way to the restaurant.

So who knew they were there?

"Speaking of managing, where are you on the Barrington paperwork? We still have no idea who signed him out for his bail."

"I've been working on it. The papers are routed to, like, six different places."

"So what are you waiting for?"

He knew he was being a world-class jerk, but the case increasingly felt as if it was closing in on them. His sore ribs and stiff neck and shoulders only reinforced the concern.

With one last glance at Jessie before she disappeared from the squad room, he returned to the video footage from Portia. Reed toggled through the footage, unable to read the face on the dark shadow that hunkered down in front of his car.

Even with the lack of defining characteristics, he knew the man was acting on the orders of another. Although they'd yet to come up with a full psych profile of the killer—or killers—everything they'd amassed so far suggested a mastermind who was plotting behind the scenes. McCallum and Barrington had obviously gotten greedy, but their deaths indicated they'd not worked alone.

Add on the fact that something went down in the parking lot of DeWinter's restaurant even as the man couldn't have known they were headed in and his conviction they were dealing with more people only increased.

Which meant the threat could be anyone.

And if he didn't snag a lead soon, there was no way he could ensure the safety of Lilah and her friends.

Gabby's words continued to keep her company as morning drifted steadily toward lunch. Lilah had finished her strawberries and sent them off to their final destination with one of her contractors and now had a traditional chiffon to whip up for a bridal shower.

Stilling her roiling thoughts, Lilah conjured up an image of the bride-to-be, an older woman who had finally found her forever love in her fifties. Her friends had wanted something simple but elegant and they'd settled on a bright, summery lemon chiffon with an array of butter cookies on the side. She already had the cookies in the oven and was now foaming the egg whites for the meringue that would fold into the batter.

Reed hadn't shown up all morning and while she knew he was busy, she hadn't quite shaken the nerves that had her on high alert.

When he was around, she felt calmer. Protected. And it was cozy to have him in her kitchen.

"I'm running to the Hilton for a consult." Violet raced into the room, her slender frame in high gear as she beelined for the industrial refrigerator. "Do you have the samples you wanted me to run over?"

"All packaged up in the baker's box. Top shelf."

Violet had them down and was nearly back out the door when she stopped and turned on a hard heel. "Are you doing okay today?"

"Sure." Lilah fought the urge to touch her hair and wondered what she could possibly be channeling this morning. First Gabby, now Vi.

She'd put on a smile, damn it. Why wasn't it working?

The whirling dervish that had invaded her kitchen vanished, replaced by an ocean of warmth and compassion. Violet snagged a stool and pulled it up to the counter. "Want to talk?"

"You sound like Gabby." At Violet's confused look, Lilah added, "I stopped there this morning for coffee. My head was sort of jumbled and it seemed like the right place to stop."

"She's good at managing drama. We all are, come to think of it."

"All in a day's work."

"Which brings me back to my original question. Are you doing okay? Last night was a big deal. I know you like to manage your kitchen, but we could bring Pearl in for some extra hours to help out. The business is doing better than we ever imagined and we can manage additional team when we need it."

Pearl was her most reliable contractor and the fact Lilah was even considering Violet's offer had her backing away from the counter, the protest forming on her lips. "No way. I can handle this."

"It's not about handling it, Lilah. It's about acknowledging you were in a major accident last night and you might need some time to feel one hundred percent."

"I'm fine. I'd rather be working, anyway."

"Yes, but—"

Lilah cut her off, the bigger reality of the previous evening tearing the words from her chest in a hard rush. "We can't put someone else in danger!"

"I...I mean, we—" Violet stopped, her brisk tone fading. "You're right. We have a responsibility to others."

"What about our brides?"

The nerves she couldn't fully quell dive-bombed her stomach in hard, choppy bursts. The problems with the shop and the gems had seemed so isolated and insular. But what if?

"Do you think someone would hurt them? Would actually find a way to sabotage our business to get to us?"

Although it was silly, Lilah imagined the words floating between them like heavy bubbles, lumbering along waiting to pop. "I don't know what to think. Especially after last night."

"We need a plan. And a way to manage this. If only—"

Violet stopped, but Lilah knew what was underneath the words. *If only Max Baldwin hadn't snatched the handful of jewels.* The original cache would be gone and they'd be safe.

"We can't go back, Vi."

"No." Violet shook her head. "No, we can't. But we can do something other than sit here waiting for the other shoe to drop. I'll host tonight. Let's get the guys together and we can figure out a game plan."

"Which reminds me. In the craziness of last night I forgot to tell you the new information. Reed's mother thinks the rubies are the famed Renaissance Stones. We should add that to the list of information."

"I read something about them. It was quickly, in passing, like a list of some of the world's most famously mined stones, but I passed it over." Violet dragged out her phone and tapped herself a message. "I'll look them up as soon as I get done with my appointment."

"I can do it."

Violet grinned at that. "I know you. It took you a day to remember the supposed name of the jewels. Are you really going to give up your afternoon of baking solitude to hunt around on the computer?"

"You know me so well."

Violet's green eyes twinkled with humor before she added a quick wink. "I know. And now we have one more clue as we figure out what to do with the rubies."

Lilah shifted and the ruby stored in her shoe rubbed against her toe like a punctuation point to Vi's comment. She knew she needed to leave it at home. Locked up in the safe in her bedroom. But without it, she felt bereft.

Naked.

For some reason she couldn't define, the ruby had become something of a talisman. And holding on to it gave her the illusive feeling of power. As if she had a bargaining chip.

Something to fight with.

At that very thought, she knew she'd put a bit too much faith in her own abilities to protect the rubies—or the one she had control over.

Violet was right. They had to find a way to move the jewels into safer territory, and then figure out a way to ensure the ones who wanted the stones didn't see them as a threat any longer.

Imagining herself some battle-ready negotiator wasn't smart or safe. And she'd spent far too long working to be both to give it up now. She'd arrange another safe-deposit box in the morning and then they'd work on getting the stones returned. It was the only way.

"Do you want Reed involved?"

"Of course. We've got nothing to hide and the more we work with the police the sooner we can get this behind us." Violet glanced at her watch and leaped up, snagging the box off the counter. "I need to go. Follow me out and lock up behind me."

Steven guzzled his second cup of coffee and ignored the screaming pain in his temples. Despite four aspirin and the second cup since arriving at the small café, he wasn't having any luck shaking the hangover.

Damned Lilah.

The woman made him crazy. Always had. And here he'd spent the past four years believing himself over her. Well rid of her, more like.

How humbling to realize he'd achieved neither.

The espresso was hot on his tongue—and a poor imitation of what they served in Italy—but it would have to do as he mapped out his strategy. He had until three o'clock tomorrow. And then he was to meet the Duke a block away from Elegance and Lace, the ruby in hand.

Why the Duke seemed convinced the women even had the stones in their possession was ludicrous, but he'd follow the man's orders. All Steven needed to do was entice her to give it up and the Duke promised he'd handle the rest.

The whole plan smacked of lunacy and Steven had had the fleeting thought—more than once—to head off to his Vegas location for a few days. He was a businessman, after all. A position the Duke respected. The man would surely understand his need to attend to his business.

He'd get away for a few days. Play the tables. Visit with Darla—Didi?—whatever her name was, after she finished up her burlesque show at the hotel.

Just clear his head.

That was all he needed and then he'd figure out how to handle this damn thing.

He slugged down half the espresso, an image of Robert's and Charlie's eager faces chatting him up about the rubies.

"Who knows what's there, man? Josephine Beauregard's father was the jeweler to the Queen." Charlie giggled as he slammed a hand on the table in one of the private rooms at Portia. *"The freaking Queen of England!"*

"What Charlie means is that we don't know how big the score is. The rubies are a sure thing, as are the fake crown jewels. Beyond that, who knows what else was smuggled out of England?" Robert had remained calm, but Steven had seen his tell. Excitement had hovered behind Robert's eyes, snapping with impatience to have his hands on the score. *"We just need you to help us make the connection."*

"Word has it there's an interested buyer." Charlie warmed to the topic. *"Like Robbie here says, it's a sure thing."*

A sure thing.

There was no such thing.

He'd hunted for one all his life and every time he thought he got close, it vanished, replaced with people who gave him a hard time. Wanted too much—no, *demanded* too much.

Like Lilah.

She'd been perfect at first. Fresh and sweet, that blond hair like a halo around her head. He'd been enamored from the start, determined to have her all to himself. And oh, how he'd had her.

She'd been an unexpected fireball, full of as much passion in the bedroom as she showed in the kitchen.

And he'd been hooked. Lilah. His drug. Sweeter than any pastry and more decadent than the finest wine. The first few months were intoxicating. Portia had taken off like a rocket and they were riding the wave together.

A packed house every night, Dallas's elite filling the tables. She'd helped further cement that, table after table ordering her desserts.

Then the press had gotten wind of their relationship and it took off to another level. Society invites. Parties. They were the freaking crème, and he'd finally arrived.

And then she'd gone and gotten cocky, suggesting what he should serve. Getting testy about her dessert menu, claiming she knew better what should be offered up each night.

He knew his menu.

Knew his vision for Portia.

And he refused to settle.

On a small sigh, he drained the last of the espresso and

briefly toyed with ordering a third before resisting the urge. He needed to plan, and a layer of jitters on top of the headache wouldn't help.

Lilah hadn't been able to handle him and the moods that came on him when he created. He well knew she wasn't going to invite him into her kitchen with open arms.

So he needed to figure out his way in.

Refreshed at the challenge, he let Vegas fade from his mind. He'd do this and find out what Lilah was doing with a cop, of all things. He dropped an insulting tip for the crappy espresso and walked out of the café.

The noon sun nearly blinded him as he walked toward his car, an image forming in his mind. As the vision took shape, his steps lightened for the first time that day.

His problem of an ex-wife was in for quite a surprise.

Chapter 11

"**D**o they always argue like this?" Reed's voice was low, audible only to her, as they both kept their attention firmly on Violet and Max.

"*Always* seems like a stretch since they haven't known each other that long, but..." Lilah hesitated, running through all the previous times she'd been in both their company. "Well. Yes, they do."

"It's fascinating and a bit daunting, all at the same time."

"That's because it's the verbal equivalent of foreplay." Cassidy murmured the words from across the coffee table, the twinkle in her eyes evidence she hadn't missed their discussion.

Laughter welled in Lilah's throat and she reached for her glass of Chardonnay to keep the giggles at bay.

Violet and Max *were* a sight.

They'd all arrived at Violet's for light hors d'oeuvres, cocktails and an elaborate crime scene re-creation.

"Where'd you get the whiteboard, Vi?" Cassidy piped up from the rich leather couch that separated the kitchen from the living room. Violet and Max quieted, Cassidy's question like the bell at the end of a prize-fight round.

"Our storage closet."

"We have a whiteboard?" Cassidy's eyes widened. "At our shop?"

"Yes, we have a whiteboard."

Amusement tinged both their words, but it was Violet's long-suffering sigh that had them all smiling. Their acute businesswoman was surrounded by creators and Lilah knew they drove her nuts.

The city's lights filtered through the window of Violet's high-rise apartment. Lilah loved this place, the city spread out before them. As someone who had lived in Dallas her entire life, it was fascinating to see how the city had changed and grown, and Violet's building was just one more example of Dallas's progress.

Floor-to-ceiling glass rimmed half the apartment, the exterior giving way to exquisite views of downtown.

Reed had again chosen a nonalcoholic drink and he settled the soda on the coffee table before leaping up and crossing to the whiteboard, his patience clearly at an end.

Lilah gave him considerable credit for the spry moves, even as she noticed the distinct stiffness in his back. For a man who'd spent the previous night getting bandaged in the emergency room, he had retained a remarkable sense of nimble grace. "Do you mind if I write down a few things?"

"Of course not."

He made a quick map, placing X's at various points and a small bulleted list of notes beneath.

"You look like you're teaching class, Graystone." Max tossed the good-natured jab before shoveling in a beef crostini.

"Of a sort." Reed turned around and capped the dry-erase marker. "We have a lot of leads, but once you dig underneath them, what looks like a connection seems like a dead end. What we need to figure out is where there's a real connection."

"But we have one. Steven."

Lilah fought the knee-jerk nausea that swam in her stomach at Violet's reminder, frustrated that even after talking about the man for two days he could still reduce her to jelly.

"Yes, but how?" Reed asked. "He's a connection to Robert and Charlie, but we've pretty much ruled out his involvement in last night's violence."

"Why would you rule him out?" Tucker spoke up from beside Cassidy. He'd been quiet up to now, taking in the discussion.

"The timing just isn't plausible."

Reed had shared his thoughts with her earlier and Lilah had to admit it made sense. The time stamp on the video footage he and Jessie had reviewed made it virtually impossible Steven had ordered the cut brake lines.

"But if it's not Steven, then who?" Violet crossed in front of the board and tapped a fingernail against her glass of wine. "He's the only logical connection."

"Maybe not." Reed walked everyone through some of the other theories he'd tried on her over the past few days. Jessie had already discovered the death certificate on the gem appraiser and Reed had added the man's details to the other information they knew on the whiteboard.

The working assumption was that the man had talked at some point in the past fifty years.

Beyond that lone fact, Lilah couldn't see any other connection beyond Steven.

So what was hidden beneath the surface?

There had to be something there, in the soup of words Reed had scratched on the whiteboard. Threads between the disparate information that would lead them to their answers if they only tugged on the right one.

Lilah listened to the arguments with half an ear as her thoughts drifted to Steven.

Where they thought they'd had answers, she now knew all they had was a loose thread.

She knew it was petty to feel disappointed he didn't appear to be involved in their accident. No matter what she thought about him—or what emotional scars still lingered—the fact remained that it was a long stretch from bully to killer. He was a man who did his damage in private, where he felt powerful and in control. Would he really risk his cushy life for something with such dire consequences as murder?

But even as she tried to convince herself not to be disappointed Steven wasn't at fault, something stopped her.

Lingering anger over three lost years of her life?

Was she so petty that she'd allowed Steven to remove any sense of compassion? Had his slow and steady decimation of her self-esteem also eroded her belief that people were fundamentally good?

And that an individual was innocent until proven guilty?

Hell, in her mind she'd already hung Steven by the noose of his vanity and small personality, assuming he had added killer to his less-than-stellar résumé.

And what did that make her?

Suffocating fingers clawed at her throat and she excused herself to the restroom. Maintaining even strides, she had no interest in tipping off the rest of them that she was in the middle of a meltdown over the horrifying realization that her soul was still as damaged as ever.

But damn it all.

Damn, damn, *damn*.

Steven. Why did it always come back to Steven?

Violet had left a small light on in her spare bedroom and Lilah slipped inside. She could still hear them arguing and was grateful everyone was distracted by the discussion at hand.

A few minutes.

That was all she needed to get her raging thoughts under control. To get the roiling storm of memories back in the bottle, the stopper of her iron will trapping them tight inside.

She'd healed. She had moved past the abuse and the bruises and the damn heartbreak. She'd begun to believe in herself again. In her ability to make decisions and believe they were the right ones for her future.

And in a few short days, all that time and effort had vanished as if it had never been.

"Would you like a refill?" Violet stood in the doorway, the Chardonnay in her hand, the contents catching the light of the small bedside lamp she'd left on earlier.

Lilah stared down at her empty glass. "How'd you know?"

"Reasonable hunch. You said restroom but you took your glass with you." Violet refilled her wine, then followed with her own. "Want to talk about it?"

"Isn't that all we've been doing is talking about it?"

"I suppose." The edge of the mattress depressed as Violet sat down next to her. "But sometimes it's the things we're not saying that cause the problem."

"I'll give you one good guess what I'm not saying."

"Steven DeWinter. The gift that keeps on giving." Violet took a sip before exhaling on a huge sigh. "Bastard."

"Yeah."

"What did Reed think of him last night?"

"He didn't say much, but his cop's eyes spoke volumes."

"That man doesn't miss much."

Lilah thought about his steady view of the restaurant the night before. Like a predator, he appeared unaffected by his surroundings, yet she knew he saw everything.

Watched everyone.

And could pounce with lethal force at a moment's notice.

"I'm sure he spent the entire time wondering how I could be stupid enough to mix myself up with Steven."

"If you believe that, then I think you're sorely underestimating Reed."

"How couldn't he?"

"I think the real question is how could you? The man's done nothing but defend you and believe in you. And if my powers of intuition and an ability to sense sexual tension are any indication, he's already in way over his head with you."

Lilah diligently ignored the image of her and Reed wrapped up in each other, focusing on the matter at hand.

"He got a taste of my jerk of an ex-husband last night. How could he possibly see me as anything but some dumb woman, taken in by a preening peacock?"

Violet remained still, her steady green gaze considering. "Do you remember last year? When I forgot that big spring booking and the couple went somewhere else."

Stymied by the change in topic, Lilah could only nod. "Yeah. Sure."

"I cost us a six-figure affair. We'd have likely cleared about twenty thousand to our bottom line."

"It was a mistake."

Lilah's eyes were sharp. Unflinching. "Yes. Exactly. It was a mistake. Clearly, you're capable of recognizing them."

"This isn't the same."

"While I won't argue the emotional impact of what you dealt with is far more severe, the fundamental concept of a mistake is just that. Something unintentional."

Lilah wanted to argue the point but—as usual—Violet had wrapped whatever she was saying in a nice neat bow. Crafty and cunning, that was their Violet.

"It's not the same."

"Suit yourself." Violet took a small sip of her wine before she spoke once more. But where Lilah braced herself for another round of arguing, Violet knocked her sideways.

"You said Reed doesn't miss much."

"No, not that I've seen."

"Me, neither. And what I've observed is that he certainly doesn't miss you."

The protest sprang to Lilah's lips with the speed of a bullet. "It's not something either of us can act on."

"Why not? And if you tell me it's because he's a cop, I'm taking the wine away."

Lilah smiled at that, the threat swift and immediate. "You don't play fair."

"Forget fair. You've got an opportunity for something wonderful. Don't run from it."

"I'm not running."

"You're making excuses and it's the same thing."

"But what if—" Lilah stopped, her earlier thoughts rising up in a cacophony of mental noise. "I have baggage. And while I know that hardly makes me unique, it's baggage that interferes with his case."

"Because your ex-husband is a suspect?"

"Because I *want* my ex-husband to be a suspect."

Violet stared at her wine before she turned, a small smile ghosting her lips. "I can usually interpret Lilah-speak, but you need to give me a bit more here. Because try as I might, I really don't follow you."

"Steven's in this. I can feel it. But all evidence suggests he wasn't at fault for last night."

"You don't know that. And even if he wasn't responsible for the act or for deciding to have you killed, it doesn't mean he's innocent. The man knows what's going on. He practically told you that when he pretended not to know or care Robert and Charlie were murdered."

"But he couldn't have ordered the hit on us. And there's a part of me that wants it to be him so Reed can wrap this up, nice and tight. What kind of person does that make me?"

"Human." Violet's sharp answer brought her up short and Lilah could only stop for a moment and stare.

Even as she knew it was hardly fair to condemn anyone, her friend's ability to hold up a mirror was refreshing. The guilt receded like a wave going back out to sea.

"People make their own choices, Lilah. If Steven's in this, and by all accounts he is, he's done this to himself."

"I know." Lilah nodded, a forced laugh bubbling in her throat. "My ex-husband certainly is the gift that keeps on giving."

Violet was about to pat Lilah's arm when she stopped, her eyes widening. "That's it."

"What?"

"It's not his involvement so much as his connection. Maybe Steven's been the conduit all along. Cassidy thought it was Robert but maybe it's been Steven as the connection to whomever is the one behind the scenes leading all this."

"It fits."

It did fit and Lilah opened her mind to that possibility.

And to the reality that her past with her husband had little to do with the very real problem they faced now. Steven knew Robert and Charlie and he had access to any number of the city's movers and shakers. Not everyone amassed wealth in a way that was honest and aboveboard and, knowing her ex-husband as she did, recognized that could be rather intoxicating.

And if some lingering part of her wanted to pin all their problems on Steven, forcing him to serve out the rest of his life in a cage, his golden-boy reputation ruined beyond repair?

Maybe it was time to accept the emotion and move on.

"Reed will get to the bottom of this." Violet's conviction was the final balm she needed to reset her expectations.

"You really think it's only human to want to see my ex-golden-boy-jerkwad get his comeuppance?"

Violet nodded, a gleam lighting her vivid green eyes. "Hell, yes. A good comeuppance is all that jerkwad will ever deserve."

Reed navigated the last few blocks to Lilah's house. She'd kept up a steady stream of chatter on the short drive, but he had the distinct sense her heart wasn't in it. She'd flitted from topic to topic, seemingly unable to stick to anything.

The evening at Violet's had been equally confusing. Despite three hours of going over any and all connections the six of them could think of—including a dissection of how close Steven DeWinter was with Robert Barrington and Charlie McCallum—they weren't much further along than when they'd begun. He did manage to capture a few notes he wanted to follow up on, but nothing felt all that solid.

Their landlady, Jo, was still in the hospital, but Cassidy's latest information was that she was being moved to a rehabilitation facility the next day. He thought he'd take some time to gently question Jo and Max's grandfather and see if he could get any further on the jeweler who'd appraised the rubies before they were buried.

Beyond that, he didn't have much.

"You doing okay?"

"Sure." Her tone bordered on a squeak and Reed had another layer of reinforcement that something had shaken her.

"You and Violet were gone for a while. Please don't tell me the two of you were cooking up a new scheme to draw this problem out?"

"Our vigilante days are over. Cassidy learned that lesson the hard way and it was a warning to us all."

"I'm glad to hear it. Unless you count the ruby you still carry around as a genuine vigilante move."

"That's a bargaining chip." He caught her smile from the corner of his eye as he turned the corner for her block. "And you'll be pleased to know I was just thinking earlier that it's time to get it in a safety deposit box and out of my shoe."

"Hallelujah."

All he got for his efforts were her rolled eyes, but Reed was pleased to see them on firmer footing. He let the moment hang another few beats before pressing her once more. "Did something else upset you?"

"No."

He pulled up to Lilah's home, that lingering sense something was wrong only reinforced by her leap out of the car.

"I'll see you tomorrow, then."

"I'll walk you up."

"It's not—" She broke off at his steady stare and nodded. "Thanks."

The night was quiet, the oppressive August air surrounding them like a thick, wet blanket. He remembered nights like this when he was on patrol, trying to manage tempers when the stifling heat only added to a domestic dispute or a fight between rivals.

Those days that had seemed endless, he remembered now, when all he wanted was a shot at the detective's test and to prove himself.

Reed followed Lilah to her door, the skills he'd honed over the past fifteen years jingling loud and clear that she was upset about something.

"Mind if I come in for a cup of coffee?"

She fumbled her key before fitting it in the lock. "Sure."

The door swung open and she made quick work of the alarm, disarming it, then resetting it once they were both inside. He didn't miss the slight tremble of her fingers once more as she tapped in the long code, the system flipping to green as she hit the armed button.

Although he knew the direction, he followed behind her as she wended her way through the darkened house, flipping on lights as she went. "Different lights are on than last night."

"Well, sure. I can't have the timers go on at the same time or in the same place. What's the point of having them, then? All anyone would need to do was watch the timers for a few days and they'd still know I was gone."

Intrigued, he couldn't resist pressing her. "Who's watching?"

"You never know."

Small traces of fear echoed beneath her words and—not for the first time—Reed cursed Steven DeWinter. Although he suspected she and her mother had formed a protective circle around each other after her father died, DeWinter was the one responsible for turning awareness of one's surroundings to fear.

"How'd you get away?"

"Excuse me?" She turned from where she measured

coffee at the counter, her eyes wary, like a mouse watching a large cat.

"Steven. The jerk you married. How'd you get away?"

"Why are you asking about him?"

"Because I can only assume Steven DeWinter is the reason you have lights all over your home set on varying timers to foil would-be intruders. And I can only guess he's the reason you lock your home up tighter than the entrance to a gold mine. And, finally, I can deduce from both that he's the reason that layer of wary fear fills your warm brown eyes no matter how hard you try to hide it."

He ran a lone finger down her shoulder, intrigued by the solid strength in that small frame. "So strong, yet so afraid. Why?"

The slight tremor he'd seen in her fingers shifted to a full-on tremble as she measured the coffee. "I don't want to discuss it."

"Are you sure? Because I suspect that's exactly what you discussed with Violet tonight when you both disappeared."

Lilah flipped the switch on the coffeemaker, anger rapidly replacing the fear. "You've no right to ask me this."

"We've moved well past rights." He touched her once more, unable to resist.

And in that moment, he realized how desperately he wanted her to come to him.

Willingly.

Lilah warred with herself. She knew it was dangerous to accept what Reed offered. Steven may have shattered her sense of self, but the man before her had the ability to crush her, heart and soul.

She knew it as clearly as she drew breath.

Reed Graystone had the power to simply destroy her.

And still, she wanted him. Wanted what he offered. Wanted the safety and the sheer exhilaration of being in his arms.

"You still don't have the right to ask me these questions."

"Oh, I don't know." His gray gaze was speculative in the subdued glow of the lights that hung over her sink. "I think it's killing you to keep it in and who better to tell than a cop?"

Who better?

And then his arms were open and she was launching herself into them, the thick, steady beat of his heart thudding beneath her ear.

Why had she resisted?

Especially when safety felt so damn good.

They stood there for a moment, aware yet quiet, before Lilah summoned up the words. The usual pain of the memories was muted somehow, as if they couldn't swipe at her while she stood in the protective circle of his arms.

"It was Las Vegas."

His arms tightened, but he said nothing, just waited for her to continue.

"Steven had the opportunity to build a property in one of the new hotels in Vegas. It was all he could talk about, week after week, the plans and the menu. I was careful to show only my excitement, encouraging him in each and every conversation, and he responded in kind. I had my husband back."

While her time with Steven had remained vivid in her mind, those last weeks were especially sharp. The late nights, talking over his new restaurant. His palpable excitement and her feeling that they might have returned to common ground.

That she might have rediscovered the man she'd fallen in love with.

"It was thrilling. I thought I might finally have my marriage on track."

"But it wasn't."

Lilah lifted her head from his chest and stared into those compelling eyes, so full of understanding and compassion. She'd feared censure.

Had feared pity even more.

But all she saw was understanding and acceptance.

"No. It wasn't. I was supposed to accompany him to Vegas for one of the last construction meetings before the restaurant opened and I caught a massive bug. Flu, chills, all of it."

"Let me guess. He wasn't very understanding."

"No." Lilah shook her head as her mind summoned the moments, that last night the stuff of nightmares. She was already weak, her body rebelling as it fought off a virus.

And then she'd had to fight the one man in the world who should love her. Respect her. Revere her.

"It started with a small shove, up against the counter as I reached for a tissue. I was miserable, already crying, and my nose was running extra hard because of the flu. He just kept screaming at me. How I didn't understand. How I was jealous, sabotaging his moment."

"Despite the fact that you were visibly ill."

"Yes." She nodded, the lingering shame of the moment—of staying far too long in a situation that was toxic—rising up to swamp her. With deep breaths, she reminded herself that she was okay. That she'd gotten away.

That she was safe.

"What happened, Lilah?"

"He finally pushed too hard. Slammed me into the counter as the discussion rose to a fever pitch. I cracked two ribs on the thick marble I'd chosen myself for our kitchen."

"Why didn't you have him arrested?"

"I tried. He had several slick lawyers and I...didn't."

"And he didn't come after you?"

"I had one ace in my pocket that kept him from succeeding. Two, actually." Lilah smiled now, the image of her two best friends the beacon of light that saw her through. "They're both pretty connected in town, between Cassidy's father and Violet's parents. Violet suggested that it would be a simple matter of spreading a few rumors about his business and his behavior. The police might not listen but gossipmongers certainly would."

"Social destruction. I can see where that would be a bigger threat than jail time."

"Exactly."

"And he's left you alone?"

"Until he walked up to our table at Portia, I haven't seen him since that night." Through very careful maneuvering, she acknowledged to herself, but the point was still fact. She and Steven had gone their separate ways. Their divorce was handled through lawyers and she'd spent the ensuing years doing her level best to forget she'd ever met Steven DeWinter.

Her hands still lay on his shoulders, the thick muscles under her fingertips strong and solid. He was a good man. An honorable one. And he made her forget to be scared.

For both those reasons, she owed Reed Graystone a debt of gratitude.

But it was the man before her who stirred something else. Something more.

Lifting on her tiptoes, she pressed a soft kiss to his lips. "Stay."

Chapter 12

Reed was still struggling with his feelings toward Steven DeWinter, the evidence of what the violent bastard had done to Lilah sending him into a murderous rage, when her words finally penetrated the thick haze of anger.

"What?"

"You and me, Detective." She smiled before pressing another kiss on him. "Together."

His body was already strung to the breaking point, the temptation of her slender frame a torment he'd been unable to resist for days.

But the rest...

"Are you sure?"

"Absolutely."

"I pushed you tonight. Asked questions I know you didn't want to answer."

The soft light in her eyes faded, replaced with a wariness that broke his heart. "If you don't want to—"

He held firm, unwilling to let her squirm away the moment the conversation moved into choppy waters. "Don't mistake my words. It's not about wanting. It's about respecting where you've been and what you need."

"I thought I made what I needed more than clear. I have had sex since my divorce. I'm not some china doll who's going to shatter the moment we get naked."

The anger—that rash burst of fire she was so good at laying down—hit him and he ignored it. "I wasn't suggesting you were. But I'm not some caveman jerk who only wants to get you naked."

"I know."

"Then believe me when I tell you I want you."

She sighed before softening her tone. "Then why are you thinking so much?"

"Because when you come to my bed, I don't want you thinking about another man." He pressed a soft kiss on her lips, gentle in the moment even as his body screamed mercilessly for release.

Had he ever wanted a woman like this?

The need to protect warred with the need to ravish and he fought to keep both in check.

He wanted her, yes. But to admit he needed her?

That suggested a speed and a progression to what was between them that had moved far too fast and had tilted his world on its axis way too far.

Yet hadn't it?

He was a cop. He had a cop's instincts and a cop's sense of awareness.

So how could he continue fooling himself, pretending he didn't want her? Or worse, pretending he didn't have feelings for her?

Because he did.

This little slip of a thing who brimmed with fire and passion and something wholly unidentifiable—yet uniquely appealing—had blindsided him, turning his ordered world on its ear.

"I can promise you, you're the only one I've been able to think of." Reed opened his arms once more and she moved willingly into them.

"On that we're agreed."

"Then let's take the moment. There's enough bad in the world. I want to reach for something good."

Lilah stepped away and extended her hand. "Something better than good. Something wonderful."

Reed never broke contact, his hands on her the entire walk up to her bedroom. Lilah was torn between reveling in the delicious feel of his touch and stopping every few feet to draw him close for a kiss.

The intermittent stops had a second benefit—they'd managed to strip each other of nearly every piece of clothing. Soft light spilled from her bedroom as the two of them closed the last few feet to the doorway.

"That was a productive trip." His hands skimmed over her bare skin, lighting sparks wherever he touched.

"I'll say." She allowed herself a moment to simply explore, the hard planes of his chest firm beneath her palms.

Had she ever experienced anything like this?

The urgency to take—to consume—was a palpable thing, but it was only a part of what they shared. What they gave to each other.

Along with pure, unadulterated joy in the moment.

She lifted her lips to his, their breaths mingling on a lilting sigh. His shoulders were thick with muscle and she ran her hands over that warm flesh, enjoying the hard strength underneath as their mouths joined and rejoined, lazy even as urgency built moment by moment.

When he pressed his lips to her throat, she let her head tilt back, another soft sigh rising to her lips. The warmth of his mouth set off a fresh wave of need, cratering low in her belly.

Was this what it felt like to be cherished? To be treated as if you were something precious?

His mouth drifted from her neck as he pressed kisses in a line across her collarbone. With increasingly clever hands, he worked his way down her torso before his fingers skimmed over the sensitive skin of her stomach. Another wave of sparks lit her skin, a potent reminder of what was still to come.

Lilah tried to keep up—wanted to savor each and every sensation—but they were fast rolling up into one overarching conflagration. His hands were seemingly everywhere at once, a gentle caress followed by more insistent strokes against her flesh, teasing her.

Tempting her.

But it was his whispered words against her skin that engaged her mind as fully in the moment as her body.

Murmured words like *beautiful* and *amazing* and *entrancing* fell from his lips as he pressed kiss after kiss and Lilah felt herself fall a little harder—a little swifter—into the moment.

Into him.

Oh, how she wanted this man.

Reed Graystone, who had swooped into her life at one of its worst moments and who'd managed to turn those moments into something precious and fine.

Overwhelmed by the moment and anxious to show him the same pleasure, Lilah settled her hands on his lower back and pulled him toward her, walking them toward her bed.

The mattress hit her midthigh and Reed let out a slight

oof as they hit the barrier of the bed. "I nearly squashed you."

"Give it your best shot, Ace."

She tugged once more, tumbling him just enough so he fell onto her, his hard body nestled firmly against hers.

"Lilah. I'm too heavy."

"Oh, I don't know." She wiggled underneath him, pleased when the evidence of his arousal only grew more... *evidential.* "Why, Detective. That's quite a weapon you have there."

As jokes went, it was pretty lame, but the goofy, lop-sided grin that greeted her at the words did something funny to her heart.

"Any cop worth his weight knows how to use his weapon."

Brushing off the altogether gooey sensation that filled her stomach, sending a sharp wave of nerves streaming through her system, she hunted for a pithy response.

And avoided frowning when her voice came out slightly strangled and hoarse, her words anything but breezy. "Well, I certainly hope so."

He pressed another kiss to her lips before murmuring, "Me, too."

As the butterflies in her stomach eased, Lilah was satisfied they'd returned to common ground. She ran a hand over his chest, one lazy finger shifting lower between their joined bodies. "But just to be sure, I should probably check things out."

"Leaving no stone unturned?"

"Just like a good detective I know taught me."

His eyebrows lifted, amusement sparking deep in his gray eyes. "If that's the case, then you surely know the importance of strong interrogation tactics."

"I suppo—" A hard cry of pleasure interrupted her

words as his fingers brushed the most sensitive of flesh. On a hard moan, she tried desperately to focus on his words, but was lost as his thumb pressed down on a particularly sensitive spot.

"What was that you were saying?" He whispered the words, his fingers flicking once more against her core, the amusement in his gaze turning decidedly wicked. "You were complimenting my interrogation tactics?"

"Wh—"

Lilah tried to focus—she knew there was some response required—but all she managed was a hard, dark moan, drawn from what felt like the depths of her soul. She could barely contain a coherent thought as his hands continued their magnificent torture.

And as those eyes continued to devour her, hot with need and desire and...*expectation*?

Of her? Of them? Of what could be between them? The questions swirled, fading in the face of the increasing demands of her body.

"Reed!"

His name tore from her lips on another hard exhalation as her world shattered into a million tiny fragments, one more beautiful than the next. His hands never left her body, but they did slow, his ministrations soft as he pressed her to the full depths of her orgasm.

And then she heard it, as she slowly came back to herself. Her name—just her name—whispered over and over. "Lilah."

"I. Um." She gripped his shoulders, trying to make sense of what had just happened.

She hadn't lied before. She'd had sex since her divorce—not a ton of it, but not exactly a full-on dry spell, either—but nothing had prepared her for this.

Nothing in her entire life had prepared her for this.

For him.

And as her thoughts still jumbled, flitting here and there, unable to settle, one rose to the forefront.

"You." She lifted a hand to his cheek, the softness she saw there nearly her undoing. "You gave that to me."

"Yes."

"It was beautiful. Amazing."

"It was breathtaking to watch."

"But you're—" Lilah broke off, not sure of what she wanted to say. There was nothing to be embarrassed by and she *wasn't* embarrassed.

But she was unnerved.

"You've given me a bit of a head start on the evening."

"Lilah." His humor vanished, replaced with something richer yet darker. A subtle anger that he couldn't quite suppress. "We're sharing pleasure with each other. There's no score. No timekeeper. And I'm not in any rush."

"I know. I know." And she *did* know. So why was she suddenly so clumsy with what she wanted to say?

It wasn't Steven. He'd been churned up in her thoughts lately, but he wasn't the reason for her hesitation.

"So what's wrong?" Reed asked.

How did she explain it? This strange sense that she was going to mess everything up.

"Lilah?"

Her body still hummed with the aftereffects of Reed's touch, yet here she was, thinking about her bad marriage anyway.

Her failure.

Would it ever go away? Especially at moments of great joy or triumph or accomplishment, it was always there. Taunting from the background, chewing away bits of her happiness.

"Look. I'm sorry. It's great. Better than great."

"Nope." He shifted them to their sides, his hands firm on her hip to keep her from moving. As if he was calming a frightened animal, he held her still yet never made her feel trapped. "That's not an answer."

"Sounded like one to me."

Despite the gentle concern that skimmed his brow in light lines, she again saw the subtle amusement in his gaze, as well. "What's the matter?"

"Nothing." *Everything.*

When had he come to matter so much? And how had she even let him in? And how the hell was she going to make room for him to stay?

That was if he even wanted to stay.

It was sex. *Just* sex.

Her body still tingled with the just sex and they hadn't even fully gotten to the just sex.

Although she knew she still needed to do a lot of work on her emotions, she *had* moved on from Steven. She'd built a life and a business she was proud of.

So why couldn't she shake the inner sense that she'd somehow walked into a trap? That all this time she'd spent avoiding entanglements and commitment had led her here anyway?

Straight to Reed.

The desire to run was strong—too strong—even as the rational part of her mind screamed at her not to screw this up.

She'd never find another man as good as Reed. None as wonderful as him, either.

So why was she so insistent on messing this up?

His hand caressed her hip with the same swift strokes he'd used to bring her to orgasm. "I'm not going anywhere."

"What if I asked you to?"

He hesitated a moment and she saw surprise replace amusement before his eyes narrowed deliberately. For a man who wore a damn solid poker face, she was shocked to realize how much he usually veiled in those pools of gray.

And maybe even more shocked to realize he let her see behind that veil.

"If you asked me to leave, I would."

"Oh."

"Do you want me to leave?"

"I want—" She broke off when his fingers ran the length of her hip, over her ribs before coming to rest on her breast.

His hand stilled, but stayed firm against her flesh. "You were saying?"

"Right." Lilah fought the urge to grit her teeth and kept her voice perfectly normal. "Where would you go?"

"Downstairs." His thumb rubbed lightly against one taut nipple, the sensation shooting a renewed wave of need rocketing through her body. "That's a comfortable bed you have in your spare room."

She actually gritted her teeth and focused on her point. On *the* point.

She had a point, didn't she?

"Is it? I've never slept on it."

His thumb teased her flesh once more, even as his expression remained somber.

"It's soft." He added his forefinger to the exquisite torture, the thick, roughened pad of his fingertip tracing the underside of her breast. "Lush."

Lilah nearly gasped at the subtle contact. His touch was a torment and the infernal man damn well knew it.

So why wasn't she asking him to leave?

"You know what else is soft?"

His whisper floated toward her, pulling her from the abyss of her dark thoughts. "The pillows?"

"You."

The same hand tormenting her moved to her face, and as he cupped her cheek, Lilah knew the first moments of real panic.

Even as her fears calmed at his gentle touch.

"You're with me. Right here with me. And if you don't want to go any further, we won't. But I won't have another man in this bed with us."

"It's not like that." When she sensed his skepticism, she rushed on, "It's really not that. It's just that... I mean—" Stopping, she forced her thoughts to coalesce into something remotely coherent.

"I don't want to mess this up. And I'm horribly afraid I might do just that."

"It's not possible."

She knew it was possible, but the reassurance he didn't believe her was oh, so seductive. "How do you know?"

"Because being with you is better than anything I could have ever imagined."

"You haven't been with me yet." She laid her palm over his hand, where it still lay pressed to her cheek. "I mean, the opening act isn't a full performance."

"You really are something." He shook his head before pressing a soft kiss to her lips.

"No, I'm not. I'm damaged."

"No." He pressed one more kiss to her lips before lifting his head. "You're perfect. You just don't believe it."

The words seemed to float on the air above them, hovering like wispy clouds that drifted in lazy arcs across the sky.

"I'm not perfect."

"You are to me. Isn't that really all that matters?"

A soft sigh escaped her lips and Reed gave her a moment. He wanted her—desperately—but he wanted her to come to him even more.

"I didn't bring anyone else into this room. Not intentionally. But those feelings—" She broke off and he gave her the space to gather herself. "Those feelings don't just go away. Of not being enough. Or wondering what you did wrong. Intimacy only heightens that piece."

A bone-deep anger flashed through him, stunning him with all the swiftness of a battle-ax. "Did he—"

"No." Her hand tightened over his and she squeezed, before taking his hand in hers, linking their fingers. "Steven never raped me. He was an ass and an abuser, but he never did that. I'm lucky."

Reed wasn't sure that was quite the term he'd select, but the proof she hadn't suffered through a violation of that sort went a long way toward calming him.

She squeezed his hand once more, the gesture one of sweet reassurance.

"So I can say I'm lucky I got out and moved on with my life, but there's also a sense of failure. A feeling I should have known better. That doesn't just go away, Reed." Her voice lowered. "How I wish it did."

With sudden clarity, he remembered stray comments his mother would make every now and again. Even after meeting and marrying Tripp, she'd carried memories of her time years before. "A big part of me would like to brush it off. Tell you it's not your fault and then because of that, *poof*, it goes away. I know it doesn't. I saw my mother live with it and I see it in my work."

"Your mom?"

"Sure. She made a bad choice with my father and got me in the bargain. That's an awfully large consequence."

"She's crazy about you!"

The ready defense was sweet and Reed marveled at

her immediate leap. "And I'm crazy about her. It doesn't change the fact that she spent nearly a decade and a half as a single mother. My father was never in the picture. He beat it and ran the moment he found out the girl he'd been seeing a few weeks was pregnant."

"She loves you."

"Of course she does." Images of his mother through the years—even her use of "Reed Edward" when she was riled—filled his mind's eye and he knew he was lucky. Knew they were both lucky in how things had worked out. "And I love her. But that doesn't mean pain and hurt simply vanish."

"No, I guess they don't." Her lids lowered, shuttering the rich dark depths of her eyes.

The soft light in the room was low, a small lamp on the corner of her dresser obviously left on from one of her timers, and Reed enjoyed the soft glow as it painted her face. With gentle motions, he laid a fingertip beneath her chin, tilting her face toward his.

"You know, for people who haven't known each other long, we've certainly shared quite a few moments. Why do you think that is?"

She swallowed hard, her gaze never wavering. "Gabriella would be fanciful enough to call it fate."

"What would you call it?"

"Right. Just right."

"Me, too."

A small smile lit the corners of her lips, matched by a lilt of her eyebrow. "You know, it's all well and good to put names on things, but I prefer to think of myself as a woman of action."

"Oh?"

"Oh yes." Her hand slid between their bodies, quick as a whip, and Reed felt the jolt down to his soul.

He pressed his lips to hers, murmuring against that witchy smile. "Why don't you tell me about that?"

"Maybe I can show you instead."

Reed knew there were still things to discuss. The big things that couples who cared about each other discussed and worked through and managed.

Together.

But for now they were together. And it was enough.

Lilah pressed on his shoulders, pushing him onto his back with gentle pressure. He moved with her, more than willing to let her set the pace.

Her hands roamed over his skin, her touch strong. Not for the first time, he admired the simple strength in her hands—a strength earned through hard work and effort. With questing fingers of his own, he ran lazy strokes down her rib cage, the slender bones in contrast to her soft skin.

For several long moments, they stayed that way, enjoying the moment, alive with the simple pleasure of the other's touch.

So it was with no small shock to his system when she changed the game, running her hands down his chest and quickly following with her mouth. The soft, tender flesh of her lips laid a trail of kisses, followed by a torturous lap of her tongue. Over his chest and down his rib cage before she ran her tongue along the line of muscle over his hips.

And then he was helpless to her as she moved even lower. His breath exploded as she took him into her mouth, that glorious, wet heat enveloping him fully.

"Lilah." Her name whispered from his lips on another hard exhale.

Rather than respond, she simply used his reaction to fuel her own, amping up the exquisite torture another level. The moment was the most erotic of his life—a true giving of pleasure—and as that thought pierced the veil of sheer, unadulterated enjoyment, it was also the one that kept him from fully going over the edge.

With trembling fingers, he reached for her shoulders, willing her to join him to completion.

"With me—" The words ripped from his throat as she sinuously slid up his body. "Here with me."

"One minute."

That same sinuous glide of her body had her draping over him, the press of her breasts against his stomach muscles tightening his body to the point of pain. He dimly registered the echo of her end-table drawer as she pulled it out and the light crinkle of a packet.

The realization that she'd grabbed a condom did little to calm the fire in his blood, even as it dimly registered that he'd nearly forgotten any protection at all. As she slid her way toward him, he closed his fingers over hers. "Let me."

"Be quick." She nipped his ear as she handed over the packet and he did his best to oblige around the light tremor of his fingers. She continued to tease with her hands and lips as he worked the condom over straining flesh, her touch making it that much harder to focus on his task.

"Vixen."

Before she could respond, he had her hips in a firm grip, guiding her over his straining erection. She took him in, setting an immediate rhythm that dared him to keep up.

Reed matched her movements, his breath growing as ragged as they pushed each other to the limit. Like a race no one could lose so long as they crossed the finish line, they pressed on and on, bodies straining as each sought fulfillment in the other.

Pleasure as he'd never known coursed through him and he reached a hand up to her neck to pull her down for a kiss. His gaze caught on her, the room's soft light painting her skin, and in that moment he knew the most desperate sort of need.

Understood the desire that drove sailors to the rocks.

He wanted. And whatever he'd imagined—whatever he'd desired—was nothing compared to the reality of making love to Lilah.

The shift in her breathing and the tightening of her body around his let him know she was close, and as he heard her cry, he watched the pleasure suffuse her features.

And then he followed her, a willing participant straight over the cliff.

The mug appeared first through the shower door, followed by Reed's sloe-eyed gaze. "Morning."

He handed her the coffee through the open shower door, careful to keep it just outside of the spray, and she had the fleeting thought that she'd like to stay right here, in the shower with this man, for the rest of her life.

There were those who called Texas a little slice of heaven, but up until the previous night, she'd never believed them. Now she had a glorious, loose-limbed lethargy suffusing her muscles and a gorgeous man bringing her coffee, suggesting those wise souls had been right all along.

"What's that look for?" Reed's gaze finished its lazy perusal of her body, already eliciting a series of shivers on the journey.

"I'm wondering if I can stay here forever."

"The water might get a bit cold."

"I don't think I'd care."

She took a sip before he set the mug on the counter, then stepped into the shower with her, pulling her into his arms. "I'll keep you warm."

"See. A perfect plan."

"I bet I can make it more perfect." His lips trailed over her throat, his hands already reaching for the soap dispenser she had embedded in the wall. As his slick hands roamed over her body, Lilah felt that same glorious slide into pleasure overtake her once more.

And as she allowed herself to be carried away, Lilah knew she teetered on the edge of something special.

Something big.

Something that felt a lot like love.

Lilah danced around her workspace on light feet. Her night with Reed had exceeded every single fantasy she'd had about the man and even a few she hadn't managed to think up yet.

He was strong. Sexy. And shockingly adept in bed. And last night he'd been hers.

A hard sigh rose up in her chest as she dragged open the fridge to pull out several cartons of eggs. She could still feel him. His hands on her body and his mouth crushed to hers. Those amazing moments when he pushed her on, demanding all she could give and then coaxing forth even more.

More pleasure. More joy. Just *more*.

She could admit to herself now that she'd stumbled a bit on her drive to work, her thoughts from the shower buzzing in her mind. Love. Need. Affection. Desire. All had their place, but it was the love part that had her twisted up.

Was she in love?

Was it even possible?

She and Reed had spent an amazing night with each other—and a morning that had only cemented how good they were together—but that didn't mean it was love. After dissecting it in true Lilah Castle fashion, she'd finally decided she didn't care if it was love or not-quite-love because she hadn't felt this amazing in, oh, about *ever*.

The dancing continued as she did a sort of soft-shoe to the counter. She'd spent the morning creating rows of gum-paste flowers for the two base layers of a cake for their wedding that weekend and was over the moon with how they'd turned out. Every flourish had seemed more pronounced—more artful—and she knew the bride and groom would be pleased.

Now she'd shift gears to the third layer and an elaborate vine design that would complement the flowers.

Music pounded from her speakers as she worked, Pink's rebel voice bringing a smile to her lips as she did several shimmies behind the counter.

Damn, but she felt good.

Prime, as if she'd exercised *and* eaten healthy, only she hadn't had to bother with either.

Lilah smiled and mentally corrected herself. She might not have gone on one of the eight-day veggie cleanses Vi was always trying to push on her, but she sure had gotten a workout.

The buzzing doorbell penetrated her thoughts and she mentally ticked off the deliveries scheduled for the afternoon. Flipping off the mixer, she kept up the dancing, softshoeing her way toward the back door.

And opened it to find Steven on the other side.

Chapter 13

Lilah took a hard step back before she registered the mistake. She should have slammed and locked the door and instead, Steven was already inside.

"Lilah." He nodded—actually *nodded*, as if she were one of his subjects—before moving fully into the kitchen.

His speculative gaze drifted around the room, landing on various areas as he walked. He ran a finger over the stainless-steel countertop, pulled open several drawers and firmly snapped off the music when he reached the music dock.

"That's better."

He hated music in his kitchen. Had always claimed it was an unnecessary distraction, but she'd suspected it was something more. He wasn't good at managing stress or distraction and she'd always seen his aversion to music as a further sign of how difficult he found interference of any kind.

In the silence, her anxiety clicked up several more notches and she fought the twin urges to run and stand her ground. Reluctantly opting for the latter, she pressed for answers. "What do you want?"

"Nice welcome."

"You're not welcome. Here. Or in my life."

"Yet you're the one who came to Portia the other night, flaunting a new guy in my face."

His words were like a hard slap as she reflected on the evening from his vantage point. Her trip with Reed to the restaurant had been designed to suss out information, but she could understand how it might have looked differently to Steven.

"It was Restaurant Week and my date selected Portia. I didn't know until we drove up."

The excuse was smooth, but she heard the tremors underneath the words and forced herself to take calm, even breaths.

She would *not* cower before him.

He stopped at the counter and before she could register his motions, dipped a finger into the bowl of coconut cream.

"Don't—"

"It's okay." He shrugged, then dipped a finger once more. He'd already ruined it by touching the filling at all, but the second dip was designed as pure insult and she well knew it. "You never did get coconut quite right."

"Some people can't appreciate the complexity of the flavors."

The insult registered, his gaze turning dark. Menacing. And Lilah began to rethink the urge to run.

Forcing a bravado she didn't feel, she mustered up a dark stare. "What do you want?"

"I want to talk to you."

"So talk." *Then get out.*

"Little tart-tongued Lilah. You always did think your-self above everyone else in the kitchen." He stepped away from the counter, his gaze flicking over the bowl before skipping back to her like a skimming stone. "How silly of you."

The words were designed to put her in her place, but it was the dismissive attitude toward her work and her kitchen that did the real damage.

Of all the things she remembered, it was those moments the most. The bruises had healed, vanished as if they'd never been, save for the memories. But the dismissal of her work had lingered long after it should have.

"I have a question." Steven snagged one of the stools she kept in the kitchen for use while she worked and took a seat. The move was deceptively casual and she wasn't fooled for a moment.

Rather than acknowledge, she remained silent, waiting for him to continue.

"What were you doing in Portia the other night?"

"As I told you before. My date chose the restaurant and I didn't know until we drove up."

"Wrong answer." His low voice sent a hard shiver through her and what had been uncomfortable up to now morphed into genuine panic.

The night before at Violet's, she'd struggled with her belief that Steven was involved with the rubies. But now, as he sat like a predatory beast in her kitchen, she was forced to rethink her instincts.

He *was* involved. She knew it with a sudden clarity that seemed to sharpen her vision.

She avoided glancing toward her office or the back door, but she mentally calculated the steps toward the main area of the shop. Violet and Cassidy were both out on consults, but if she could get to the front door she could run to the decorator who owned the shop two doors down.

And then she could call Reed.

Confirm what they both believed was true.

He'd maintained Steven couldn't have ordered the cut brake lines based on timing and they'd both let that piece of evidence cloud their thoughts on the bigger problem.

Steven was *in* this.

The ruby she kept stuffing in her shoe suddenly felt like a lead weight beneath her toes and she avoided the urge to shift from foot to foot. *Damn, damn, damn, why didn't I go to the bank first thing?*

"Little Lilah." Steven tsked. "What were you doing in Portia the other night with a cop?"

He knew?

The rabbit-quick beat of her heart flooded her bloodstream with adrenaline. What exactly was he into?

"What makes you so sure Reed's a cop?"

Steven cocked his head, his laser-sharp focus concentrated fully on her. The sensation was uncomfortable, his daring glare confrontational to the extreme.

His gaze bored into her like a drill and once more, she calculated how quickly she could get out of the building.

And knew she'd never make it.

Steven was too large—too fit—and he had a good foot on her, which meant his legs could carry him a heck of a lot faster than hers could.

She did calculate the distance to her knife drawer and debated the wisdom of trying to use one or distract him away from them. A bruise she could handle. A knife wound, likely not.

With that thought firmly in mind—and her body angled away from the knife drawer—she decided to gamble.

"What would you know of cops? What are you involved with?"

"The very same thing you are."

"I'm not involved in anything. Not intentionally." She hesitated, then decided to go for it. "Unlike our marriage."

"You never could handle me. You had no idea how to be a society wife."

"No, Steven. It's you who can't handle anyone. Anyone who disagrees with you. Or who has a talent or self-confidence or ability. You never understood that surrounding yourself with good people only made your good work even better."

"You know nothing. My restaurants flourish because of me. Why the hell do you think there were all those people at Portia the other night? Because of the damn sous chef?"

"He contributed to the evening."

"It's mine! They were there for me!" The response was so unexpected—so unnecessary and juvenile—that Lilah's jaw actually dropped at the outburst.

How had she never understood this?

This strange, stunted inability of his to accept he wasn't the center of the universe. She half expected him to stomp his feet next, like a frustrated toddler.

Only he didn't.

His large frame was off the stool and around the counter before she could blink, her chef's coat fisted beneath one large hand. "Where is it?"

"Where's what?"

Memories assailed her as the present shimmered into past and back again.

Steven was *here*. And he had her, his fists primed to hit her.

All her work—all her effort to avoid him—and it had still come to this.

Don't hit me. Don't scream at me. Don't hate me so much.

The thoughts pinged through her mind like errant pin-balls on a table, all striking and slamming into her mind.

And underneath it all, the lone word that had haunted her for over two horrible years.

Why?

"The ruby! Give it to me!"

"I don't have it!"

A hard slap hit her cheek, her head snapping with the force of motion. "Where. Is. It?"

"Nowhere!"

Tears ran freely down her face, the hot fire lighting up her cheek and mixing with the warmth of her tears as she braced for a second hit.

His hand never loosened on her coat, but his gaze did change. The challenge in the depths of his eyes faded, re-placed with something very much like resignation. The fear at his swift punishment shifted, morphing into a cold, clammy layer of terror that stole over the skin.

"I know you have it and I'm not going anywhere until you give it to me." His hand tightened on her chef's coat, the twist of the thick material nearly cutting off her ox-ygen as he began to stroke her hair with his free hand. "Your choice."

She stilled, the stroke of his hand a far worse violation than the slap. Where Reed's hands had been soft and gentle the night before, full of reverence and warmth, Steven's were the opposite.

His touch was mild, but it veiled a terrible threat.

"You're in over your head, Lilah. Give it to me and I'll leave."

"Why won't you believe me?" She wanted to keep her calm—desperately wanted to control the situation—but her words came out on a harsh, strangled sob. "I don't have it."

"Just like before. I gave you the chance to tell me you were with a cop and you lied. Years ago, I gave you a chance to give me honest feedback on the restaurant and you lied, suggesting improvements just for spite. And now you're lying about this." The fingers in her hair twisted, dragging pain to her scalp with swift punishment. "Tell me now!"

She was already on her tiptoes, instinctively giving herself the height to keep her airflow open beneath his fist, but the pain in her scalp was so all consuming, she kicked out.

Her foot connected with his shin, her already-loose shoe flying off as the toe of her Croc hit on an odd angle.

Although she couldn't see what was happening, the heavy *thwap* of the shoe hitting the floor was immediately followed by a light tinkle of something solid hitting the concrete. Steven's attention shifted to the floor, a dark smile filling his face.

"That's convenient."

"You can't have it. You need to get as far away from this as fast as you can. It's dangerous."

The hand at her throat loosened enough for her to take free breaths, but he still hadn't fully let go. "No. You're the one who needs to stay away from this. Where are the other ones?"

"I don't have them."

But of course he'd want the others.

The fear for herself was nothing compared to the fear for Violet and Cassidy that suddenly swamped her.

"Where are they?"

"Hidden. I hid them."

"More like your partners in crime hid them. One for each of you, no doubt." He cocked his head, his gaze considering before he let go completely and bent to pick up the ruby.

The same thoughts that had drifted through her mind earlier—from running to snagging a knife from the drawer—filled her once more but she stayed still.

Unmoving.

"Take off your other shoe."

"I don't have them."

"Off."

Lilah kicked off the other shoe, the empty toe reinforcing her words.

"You can't fight this. It's so much bigger than you think it is. Get with your gal pals and get their stones, too. Get whatever you stole and get ready to turn it over."

"We didn't steal anything."

"You can't fight this." Steven turned the ruby over in his hands. "I wouldn't even try."

He vanished as quickly as he'd arrived, the air still thick and heavy with his presence. Her gaze skittered around the room, pulsing in time with the erratic beats of her heart, taking in impressions and sensations, unable to settle.

Her shoes, both lying on their sides where they'd fallen.

The empty stool where he'd sat, taunting her.

And the bowl of coconut-cream filling, now ruined by his touch.

Just the way she was.

She could run—could pretend she was normal and over him—but she'd never be free of the threat.

Or her inability to rise above the fear.

She knew she needed to call for help. Violet and Cassidy would be there in a heartbeat. Gabby was two blocks away.

And Reed.

She shook her head as a wave of chills gripped her. She

couldn't call Reed. Not now. Not with the mark of Steven's hand still lighting up her cheek in raw streaks of fire.

She'd failed.

The monster had come to her door and she hadn't been strong enough to fight him off.

The back door beckoned and she knew she needed to lock it, but her legs shook, her muscles going to water as she sank to the cool floor. Steven might come back. He wanted the other rubies.

He *would* come back.

So she needed to plan. Needed to figure out a way to keep Cassidy and Violet safe. A plan was all she needed.

And as the tears rolled down her face, Lilah curled into herself, her arms wrapped around her knees, and desperately tried to think of one.

Reed fielded a series of questions from his lieutenant as he caught the man up to speed. Despite spending the morning with his thoughts full of Lilah, he'd managed to dig deeper into the history of the gem appraiser and had also made time for a conversation with Max Baldwin Senior.

He'd wrapped up both into his latest report to Granger.

"Cut brake lines?" His LT eyed him above his laptop. "An oldie but goodie."

"Afraid so."

"And Miss Castle is okay?"

"Yes, she's fine. The hospital cleared her after it happened."

"And you?" Granger's gaze never wavered.

"I'm fine. A few bruises but I've had worse."

Granger nodded and exhaled on a small harrumph before returning his focus to Reed's report. "Weddings?"

Reed had worked with Tom Granger long enough to know when a question was rhetorical and he was curious to see how the man worked through the meaning that hovered beneath his words.

"How did three women who plan weddings get in the middle of something like this? It's a strange juxtaposition, don't you think?"

"How so?"

"Priceless gems in the floor? The secreted crown jewels? And now they won't give them to you?"

"They belong to the landlady fair and square. The provenance on the gems is clear about that." Reed fought the slight sensation that crawled up his spine as he thought about Lilah's current "storage" of the ruby in her possession. "The women have them secured."

"Have you called MI5?" Granger snapped the lid of his laptop. "Let them know what's possibly hitting the black market."

"You want their jurisdiction on this?"

"I think it's time."

"Tom. With all due respect, this isn't a smash and grab. Whoever wants these jewels wants them for some personal purpose. Do we really want to involve foreign jurisdiction?"

"I don't think we can afford to ignore it. Word gets out on this and the Dallas PD is sitting on its next fifty years of embarrassment."

"I don't follow you."

"Hell, Reed. We've been known as the city that killed Kennedy for half a century. You want to add the bumbling idiots who messed up major British artifacts to that list?"

Steven turned off Dragon and cut down Cole, the large black SUV idling at the corner, facing Riverfront, exactly where he expected. The whole neighborhood still had several dodgy edges and Steven wondered what Lilah possibly saw in the area.

Hell, he'd seen himself as a pioneer when he opened Portia in the newly burgeoning Uptown area over a decade ago and that hadn't been half as seedy as where Lilah and her friends chose to run a wedding business.

Amateurs.

Once he'd actually held the ruby—and the damn thing was huge—he'd briefly pondered heading in the opposite direction, but a deal was a deal.

And a deal with a slimeball like the Duke was only going to end one way if he reneged on his side. Charlie and Robert must have learned that one the hard way and he had no interest in following their footsteps.

Nope.

Much as he was enamored of the heavy weight in his pocket, he'd dutifully turn it over and give the Duke instructions on how to secure the other two gems. Lilah had refused to tell him where they were, which meant Cassidy and Violet both had to have them.

The three of them were freaking inseparable and there was no way they'd not find the beautiful symmetry in splitting the hoard up between them.

Amateurs.

The word rang through his mind once more as he snagged the door handle, a blast of cool air hitting him as he hopped up into the SUV.

The Duke was settled in the plush interior, his black Armani seeming to fade into the car's rich leather. "Thanks for the ride. I've got it."

"And?"

The word hung there and, not for the first time, Steven cursed Charlie and Robert for this asinine plan. He'd known of the Duke, of course. No one who managed a small business in Dallas was above paying the requisite protection to ensure their establishment thrived and flourished.

But it was virtually impossible to determine who the man was. Hell, it had taken him over a year to even get in the man's good graces to secure a face-to-face meeting. And had he been surprised to realize the Duke was a well-respected man about town. A regular patron of Portia, as a matter of fact.

Steven had filed the information away, knowing full well it was idiocy to mention it to anyone. Men like the Duke didn't get into positions of power by tolerating gossip. Their base of power depended on it.

"Well, Mr. DeWinter?"

"Take a look." He pulled the ruby from his pocket, the surface cool in his hand. He had a flash—nothing more substantial than that—of blood and fire as he handed over the gem.

A strange sort of half smile lit the Duke's face as he turned the ruby over in his hands. "It's magnificent. Legendary."

"If you're into that sort of thing."

The Duke lifted his gaze from the stone. "You believe this is the only one in Miss Castle's possession."

"Yeah. She's thick as thieves with the other two. If there are three stones then they have three guardians."

"Interesting."

Steven didn't think it was all that interesting—Lilah never had been able to think for herself unless her two sidekicks gave their opinions—but he opted to say nothing.

Silence descended in the car and Steven sought for something to say. "We missed you the other night. Should I have your table ready this evening?"

"No, not tonight. I have plans with my wife."

Steven shrugged, admittedly relieved. They'd spent

too much time in each other's company the past few days and he'd like a night to relax. He always kept a few tables open and if the man changed his mind, he could accommodate, but it was a relief to think he wouldn't have to be *on* this evening.

"Alex." The Duke's lone word rang out as he nodded to his driver. "We're ready."

Steven reached for his seat belt, intending to buckle up for the short drive to Portia. The thick strap was still in his hand when his door opened, his body flying through the air as he was dragged from the car.

"Wait!"

He hit the concrete with a thud, pain radiating through his arms as he landed hard on his wrists, gravel and grease coating his hands.

What the hell?

One of the large men he'd seen with the Duke before stood over him, his huge, meaty body practically shutting out the sun as he filled Steven's vision.

Run.

The word pulsed in his mind, struggling for purchase amid the confusion and unreality of the moment.

He did what he was asked to do. Delivered the ruby just as he promised.

Run.

"Thank you, Mr. DeWinter." The Duke's face filled the open car door, a gun in his hand.

Steven scrambled backward, pain radiating from his wrists in hard waves as his feet scrabbled to find purchase on the hot concrete. Was something broken?

Run.

The mental admonition came too late as pain exploded in his neck, the bullet's impact throwing him backward into concrete and gravel.

* * *

The tears had stopped but Lilah still hadn't left her position on the floor of her kitchen. The hard concrete grew even harder against her butt as she rocked and rocked, her problem racing through her mind with the sheer force of a tornado.

How was she going to keep Violet and Cassidy safe?

Where could they go? How would they escape?

She could bargain herself. Call Steven back and tell him she had the other jewels. Or better, she'd trick Cassidy and Vi into giving her theirs and could bring them to Steven.

Or whomever he was working for.

She'd explain there were only three stones. Would tell whomever hid behind this problem that they were the famed Renaissance Stones of legend and now he had all of them.

She'd *fix* this.

She knew how to deal with monsters.

Even as she thought it, the censure rose up in her mind. *Yeah, right*, she knew how to deal with monsters. Like with today's pitiful excuse for bravado as she simpered the moment Steven looked sideways at her.

She didn't slay monsters, she was slayed by them.

Defeated.

Just as it had before, her conscience whispered for her to call Reed, but she ignored it once more.

He deserved better than this. Better than a woman who couldn't even keep a priceless gem in her shoe.

The hard snap of the back door had her sitting upright, the noise rocketing through her with the force of an arrow.

He's back.

Hands shaking, she quickly got to her feet and moved in determined steps toward the knife drawer. She wouldn't cower this time. Wouldn't…

Hot summer air blasted through the door but no one followed.

The knife drawer still beckoned and she'd taken two quiet steps backward when she heard a long, low whimper.

What?

She raced to the door, her bare feet slapping on concrete when she stopped hard at the entrance. And found Steven sprawled over the steps, blood covering his neck and chest.

"Steven!"

His eyelids fluttered as he looked up at her, a hard croak escaping his lips. "Help—"

Shock and confusion danced across her mind as some other small corner simply moved into action. She bent, her hands beneath his shoulders as she half dragged him in while he pushed with his feet. The slick concrete floor helped, but the movement was hard enough that he cried in pain as she settled him inside the door.

Towels lined the counter but all were dirty with the day's work. Dragging off her chef's coat, she wadded it up, inside out, and kneeled next to him. She pressed the coarse material to the base of his neck, the flesh torn and bloody.

His legs flailed and she whispered nonsense as she pressed the coat to his neck, her other hand firm on his chest. "Hold still. Shh."

"Over. It's not over."

"Shh. Don't say—"

His hand snaked out, gripping her wrist, the movement firm. Unlike before, there was a determination in the motion instead of violence. "Lilah."

She stilled at his urgency and gave him a moment to speak.

"You're—" He took a hard breath, dragging in air in a hard wheeze. She kept the pressure firm against his body but struggled to figure out what to do next when the white cloth rapidly turned red with blood.

"They're coming for you. For all of you."

"Who?"

"The Du—"

"Lilah!" Thick footsteps filled the air behind her as Reed moved into her field of vision. Relief coursed through her as she kept her hands firm on Steven. He continued to kick out, his legs restless, and it took every ounce of strength to keep the pressure on his wound.

Ignoring Reed, she stared down at her ex-husband. The man who'd terrorized her, even up to that very day, suddenly seemed small when faced with the results of violence. "Who, Steven? Who did this?"

"Tripp."

"What?" Reed dropped to his knees on the other side of Steven's body. "Who?"

"Lange."

Chapter 14

The edge of his phone cut into his palm as Reed called in for backup. Nausea and fear swam in his stomach, mixing like thick concrete.

He couldn't settle—couldn't stem his thoughts—as his mind worked to process what he'd seen.

Steven DeWinter dying on the floor.

Lilah covered in blood.

His stepfather named as the culprit.

"He said Tripp Lange." Lilah stood opposite him, Steven's body separating them like a chasm.

"Yes."

"Your stepfather."

"Yes."

Fear for his mother's safety warred with the agony of staring at Lilah covered in blood.

"Reed—" She broke off and took two steps around Steven before Reed held up his hand.

"Don't. Stay there."

Her lush brown eyes, so full of emotion that very morning, were empty. A bright slash of red lit up her cheek, the raw fire of it filling him with anger, but still he pressed on with his observation.

Pink rimmed her eyelids, and the whites of her eyes had streaks of red. "What happened?"

"He— I mean—" She stopped. "Am I in trouble?"

He boarded up his emotions and focused on the moment. "I asked you what happened."

"He came here. Before."

"When?"

"Earlier. He wanted the ruby. He threatened me." Reed listened as Lilah recounted her experience from earlier that afternoon. The taunting violence as Steven pressed her for the ruby.

"When was this?"

"A while ago? I don't know." Her gaze skipped to a clock mounted near the door, confusion marring her features. "Not that long ago. Violet had an appointment at three."

Reed glanced at the clock, the evidence only a half hour had passed confirming the shock he sensed was rapidly taking over her body.

The urge to go to her was strong, but still, he kept his distance.

Get it out. Ask the questions. Do the job.

"Why didn't you call me? Call anyone?"

"I…" Her gaze drifted toward the body. She didn't blink, her voice fading as she processed the moment. "I couldn't."

Pain lanced through his chest but still he kept on. "Did you shoot him?"

The question snapped her head back with blunt force. "Me!"

"He's lying there in your arms."

"He left. Steven left. Before. He hurt me. Threatened me. Then took the ruby when it fell out of my shoe."

Her words were mechanical, her voice like the manufactured voice on his cell phone. There was no inflection—no warmth—as she recounted facts and information.

"Reed?" Her shoulders were stiff beneath the tank top she wore, bloody streaks marring the pale pink material.

Pain lanced through him once more as he took in the evidence of what she'd been through. Of what she'd survived.

On a hard moan of pain, he dragged her around De-Winter's body and into his arms.

Jessie provided a steady stream of information over his car speaker as Reed drove hell for leather to his mother's. They'd sent a patrol car on ahead and Jessie confirmed his mother was ensconced in the back of the cruiser.

"She's pissed, Reed."

"Too bad."

"She's apparently taken a strip off Anderson's scalp."

"He can handle it."

The late-afternoon traffic had him jammed down Mockingbird and he slammed his hands on the wheel in frustration.

Tripp?

Tripp was responsible?

"You want to tell me why your mother's in a police cruiser on this fine summer afternoon?"

"No."

"Reed?" He'd known Jessie forever and it killed him to say nothing, but how could he? He'd known Tripp equally as long and his stepfather was a criminal.

A murderer.

"I need to talk to her is all."

"What's going on with you?"

"Jess. Please. Please give me this."

Whether it was their years of friendship or something in his voice, Reed didn't know, but she eased off the questions. "I'll let you go. CSI just arrived at the bridal shop."

The phone clicked off and he let the quiet sink over him. Through him.

He had to get to his mother. Had to make sure she was safe and then he'd try to figure out what she knew.

Did she know?

Did she know she was married to a murderer? A criminal who likely had deep fingers in the Dallas PD?

Who was involved? His LT? Jessie? Half the freaking department? Was that why he was assigned to the women of Elegance and Lace? So Tripp could keep an eye on everything?

Reed thought through the morning of the previous week when he'd caught the case. Dispatch had made the call, sending him out to pick up information.

No one had seemed particularly interested in his management of the case, and until the night of the cut brake lines, he'd filed his reports and avoided any unnecessary questions from the brass.

So who knew?

There was no way it was coincidence.

He'd bet every last breath in his body, someone had arranged for him to get this case.

To keep Tripp informed? One step ahead of the cops?

He made the turn onto his mother's street, the cruiser visible halfway down the block. Fortunately, Anderson hadn't turned on the lights, but the police vehicle still stood out like a stain.

Because there was a stain. A stain on Dallas. And one on his family.

Did his mother know?

Reed knew he was jumping to conclusions—Steven DeWinter wasn't exactly a perfect witness—but the determination in his gaze and the words he uttered before dying suggested they pay attention.

And then there was Lilah.

Had she really tried to deal with all of it on her own?

He hadn't waited around long, the bone-deep need to get to his mother and ensure she was safe overtaking the moment. As soon as backup had arrived at Elegance and Lace, he'd split. But he knew Lilah had battled DeWinter once. And he also knew—with absolute clarity—the red mark painting her cheek had come from the bastard.

Yet she hadn't called him. Even after the night they'd spent together, she'd obviously tried to handle it on her own, forgoing his safety and solace.

His protection.

He pulled behind the cruiser and leaped out. His mother pointed her finger at him, her face set in angry lines. The uniform assigned to pick up Diana got out to greet Reed and he could hear his mother's voice through the open door.

"She's a little upset."

"I'm sorry you got stuck bearing the heat."

"No problem, Detective. What else can I do?"

Reed gave his mother another pointed glance. "Would you mind staying for a few minutes? I'm concerned there's a threat that's been made against her. As you can see, she doesn't want to believe it, but I'd like another pair of eyes as I try to talk some sense into her."

"Of course."

Satisfied he had help should Tripp decide to come straight to his wife, Reed approached the cruiser and opened the door.

Where did he even begin?

"Hi, Mom."

"Reed Edward—"

He lifted a hand to cut her off. "Hear me out. Please hear me out."

The anger faded in full, replaced with a wash of concern. "What is it?"

"Come here." He dragged her from the car and enfolded her in his arms. Hers banded around his waist in an immediate show of support.

She was okay. Untouched.

Now it was his job to make sure she stayed that way.

Violet and Cassidy huddled beside her on the oversize couches in the main area of the shop, their soothing words mixing in with intermittent exclamations of shock and surprise.

"I don't believe he had the audacity to come here like that." Violet had said the same numerous times, in various ways, since she'd returned to see their business was once again upside down.

"I'm so sorry we weren't here." Cassidy patted her knee, her voice soft. "That you had to deal with that alone."

"I'm such a fool. I didn't check the back door. I just assumed he was a delivery. It's my fault."

"There's no fault." Cassidy's gentle pats shifted to a full-on side-armed hug. "He was an intruder. You trusted that whomever you greeted was there as part of your business."

Whatever blame she wanted to assign herself, Lilah knew it was nothing compared to the tragedy of Steven's choices.

She wanted to be surprised. Knew she *should* be surprised. But the evidence Steven had gotten himself involved in something so dark and devious wasn't nearly as shocking as it should be.

The thought grew even less shocking when she married it up with the Charlie McCallum and Robert Barrington connection.

Had they all been that blind?

She'd struggled for years, even after leaving her marriage, questioning herself on how she could have been taken in by Steven. She knew Cassidy had battled similar questions after finding out about Robert's connection to the attempted theft of the rubies.

The need to soothe and reassure had come on swift feet and she and Violet had both assured Cassidy that the guilt lay with Robert.

But was that all?

How had they missed something so fundamentally flawed?

Images of Reed rose up in her mind's eye. His self-assurance and the clear, unmistakable qualities in him that proved he did what was right.

He was a good man. An honorable one.

And she'd ignored that honor in favor of hiding behind her own personal misery.

The knowledge of how that hurt him had stamped itself across his face and branded the air around him in a wash of pain and disappointment. And the only person she could blame for that oversight was herself.

The hum of activity swirled around them. Reed's partner, Jessie, had been on and off her phone intermittently throughout the past hour. Although she'd avoided asking about Reed's mother, Lilah had overheard Jessie giving the assurance that Diana had been picked up by a police cruiser.

His mother was safe.

Even though she was married to a monster of her own. Proof she'd never really be safe again.

Lilah eyed Jessie once more, backlit by the afternoon

sun, the woman's position near the front door and the cell phone glued to her ear ensuring she'd likely not hear the next part of the conversation.

"He's not going to stop at this."

"He who?" Violet asked.

"Tripp. Reed's stepfather. He wants the stones you both have."

"But we don't have them. They're hidden." Cassidy's gaze drifted toward the door, where one of the uniforms had stepped in to talk to Jessie. "Locked away."

"But we have access to them." Violet's voice was quiet when she spoke. "And that's all he needs. Someone with access."

"So we go to plan B," Cassidy said. "Make a show of it. Take them to the police and ask the Dallas PD to do a huge press conference."

Lilah eyed Jessie's position at the door once more before she leaned forward. "You don't think the Dallas PD is in this?"

Cassidy followed Lilah's gaze. "Her?"

"I don't think she's in it," Lilah mused as she considered the childhood connection Reed had shared with her. "But someone. There's no way it's a coincidence Reed was put on this case."

"Lilah has a point. There's been way too much coincidence already and it would be a seriously bad move to ignore that now." Violet tapped her lips. "But what if we can use that to our advantage?"

"Oh no—"

"How so?"

Cassidy's protest was immediate, while Lilah leaned forward, eager to hear Vi's ideas.

"Absolutely not." Cassidy kept her tone low, but the push

back was as loud as crashing symbols. "We tried this once already and look where it got us."

"This is different."

"How, Violet? Because from where I'm sitting, it doesn't look all that different from a week ago when you convinced me to drag my ex-fiancé out of hiding to play a game of 'what does the jerky ex know?'"

"Cass—" Lilah stopped, the idea of the three of them not in sync on something more than a little jarring.

"No, I mean it." Cassidy maintained the low, steady voice, but even in the quiet, the icy tone was more than evident. "We put ourselves in danger. *I* put myself in danger. I'm not going to watch either of you do that."

"But what if the police are behind this?" Violet asked.

"Then we give up the stones to a bunch of people who should be driven for justice instead of greed. But at least the stones will be out of our hands and away from us, where they can't do any more harm."

"You don't believe that." Lilah looked at Cassidy, then Violet. "Tell me you really don't believe that."

"Holding on to them isn't helping us." Cassidy didn't bother to hide her frustration. "The man who died in your arms today is proof positive of that."

They were tight. A unit. And even they couldn't come to an agreement on how to handle the situation. With that foremost in her mind, Lilah pressed on, the bleak truth at odds with the bright summer sun that filled the shop. "If we don't put ourselves into a position of strength, Steven isn't going to be the last one to die."

Tears streamed down his mother's face, intermittently interspersed with muttered streaks of curse words that would make a sailor blush. "Rat bastard."

"Mom. I know this is hard to believe—"

"It's unthinkable." Diana sniffed hard into a fresh tissue. "And it can't be my husband. I'd have known. I would know. What you're claiming is just not possible."

It had been like this for the past hour, heights of anger followed by deep disbelief, just before another wave of anger crested, swamping her. A pendulum of rage and disappointment so deep he wasn't entirely sure a person could recover.

They were in his apartment, the only place he could think of after he picked her up, the clean beige walls encasing them in a tomb of misery and disillusionment.

And grief.

Underneath it all was bone-deep grief for the loss of her marriage and, worse, the loss of the man she believed was her husband.

"He gives to charity. He has a good heart, Reed. I've seen it." A fresh wash of tears coated her face. "I've seen it with my own two eyes. Just last week we were at a picnic and he held Judy Stickley's grandson on his lap. He'd played with a baby. How can that man be a monster?"

"I don't know, Mom. Honest I don't. But I can't disregard what DeWinter said. He'd have no reason to lie. Especially at that point. No reason at all to accuse an innocent man."

"But—" His mother broke off, acknowledgment registering somewhere beneath the bleakness of her gaze.

He'd brought this to her. Delivered it to her damn front door, practically wrapped up in a bow.

"I have to talk to him."

"You can't. You can't go anywhere near him."

"Reed Ed—"

He cut her off before she could continue. "You can't go to him. He's wanted in the shooting deaths of three people and that's all I can connect right now. He's possibly got connections deep inside the Dallas Police Department. He's a danger and until I can get to the root of this, you can't go anywhere near him."

"He's my husband."

At the clear determination in her words, Reed leaned forward and grabbed his mother's hands tight in his own. The image of what Tripp was capable of—the bodies already recovered and the sight of Steven DeWinter bleeding out on Lilah's kitchen floor—put ice in his veins.

"You have to promise me you won't try to contact him."

Whatever grief had come up to now had been bad, but the shock in her eyes—those eyes so like his own—was forged in pure, hard steel.

"I...I won't."

"I mean it, Mom. You will get your day. I will see to it that he answers for his crimes and that he answers to you. But you can't try to get that for yourself. Please promise me you won't try to get that for yourself."

He saw the sparks of rebellion vanish as her shoulders slumped. He'd like to think himself fanciful to believe he saw grief and regret there, but he knew too well—knew his mother too well—to think otherwise.

She'd already begun to process the truth and, with the determined heart she was known for, she would see this through. She'd accept the truth about Tripp and she'd accept the demise of her life.

He only hoped he could keep her safe and sound until her husband was forced to pay for his crimes.

Tripp Lange stepped through the back door, late-afternoon sun painting the kitchen in a warm yellow. Diana loved this time of day, when the sun began its descent and their evening was on its way.

He'd grown to love it, too.

Those gentle moments with his wife, when the fire in his mind quieted and he could focus on something other than the raw, blinding ambition that had driven him since childhood. He tossed his keys into the small bowl she kept near the door, then moved toward his office.

He'd meant to store the ruby at his other home, the compound a haven for his spoils, but he'd not been able to part with the stone. The feel of it in his hands and the strange, elemental tug on his soul had him holding on to it.

Hell, he'd gripped it nearly the entire drive home.

After finishing DeWinter, Alex had driven him to the compound. He'd meant to spend a few hours working through the next steps on the other two gems, but he'd been so enamored of the one DeWinter had secured, he'd gotten nothing done.

And then that subtle intrusion—the desire to see his wife and slake some of his excitement inside her body—had overtaken him and he'd headed home, the stone in hand.

"Diana!"

The house was large and he didn't expect an immediate answer, but it did begin to register she might not be home. With an abstract stroke of the ruby in his pocket, he headed for the second floor and their bedroom.

It wasn't unusual for her to be gone. Although she loved this time of day, her commitments frequently ran late, whatever latest charity project she was focused on taking up a large swath of time.

Larger than he liked, truth be told.

Still, he encouraged her work and the ready facade it provided him as husband to one of the city's most well-respected matrons.

He moved through another halo of light, this one from the large window that lit their foyer and second-floor landing before heading on to the bedroom. The light held a purity this time of day, he mused, as if it washed everything clean.

He wanted to feel clean. Renewed. Reborn, even.

The past few weeks had been more trying than he'd realized, but now that he had one of the stones in hand he knew the others would follow quickly. And then he'd rest. He'd give himself over to the natural rhythms of life and take a few months for himself. For him and Diana.

That desperate urgency to possess that drove him on would relax, its fangs retracting as it slithered away to a far corner of his soul, and would give him some rest for a while.

Maybe he'd close up the compound, he thought as he moved into the bedroom. Shut it down for a while and make a real point to stay at home, reveling in what he had.

Rest was good.

It was a sign a man knew how to enjoy the fruits of his labors.

He drifted into their bedroom, his tie undone, and stopped to stare at the bed, fully dressed as Diana liked to call it. It was one of her little quirks—something he loved about her—and he had always loved coming in to a made bed.

Do something productive every day, she'd often said. *Start with making the bed.*

She'd drummed it into Reed with military precision. Funny how the boy had taken that knowledge and turned it into a career. His stepson was one of the most productive souls he knew. He'd made detective—one of the Dallas PD's youngest—and he'd been maniacally focused on solving his cases.

Tripp respected him. Was proud of him. And used

Reed's knowledge of the city mercilessly toward his own gains.

Which made it that much more jarring his stepson had taken up with one of his victims.

Tripp removed his cuff links and set them down on the dresser, his gaze catching on the quick flash of light on his wife's side of the dresser.

Her wedding rings.

The six-carat diamond winked at him, along with the band of diamonds that she wore with it.

Like a waterfall coming to life after winter's ice, his blood rushed in his veins, pounding the panic alarm.

She never left home without her wedding set. And she wasn't home now.

The large ruby in his pocket seemed to mock him and he settled his hand over the stone, satisfying its demand for attention.

Where was Diana?

He left the room and was headed for the stairwell when his private phone rang. "Yes, Alex?"

"Sir. A Dallas police cruiser was seen in front of your house earlier this afternoon. I just got word from the captain."

"Yes?"

"Your stepson picked up your wife, sir."

"Where are they?"

"We've not triangulated yet, but chances are, his home." Alex waited, before adding, "Would you like me to go collect her, sir?"

"No."

"There is one other matter, sir."

Tripp sensed Alex's words before the man spoke. At his silence, Alex continued.

"It appears Mr. DeWinter survived the kill shot. At least

for some period of time. He made it to the bridal shop, sir. His body's there now."

"I'll meet you at the compound in an hour."

"I'll be waiting, sir."

The harsh winds of fury blew through him and he nearly threw the phone over the landing.

Nearly gave up his ever-present control.

His wife was gone.

And his stepson now knew exactly who he was.

Chapter 15

Reed paced Violet's living room, the lights of Dallas spread beneath them like diamonds, just as they had the night before. Only last night it had appeared as if the city was mapped with fairy lights, a bright jewel full of possibilities.

Tonight, it looked like an oasis of fool's gold, winking promises that were, in fact, lies.

"That was my grandfather." Max returned to the living room after stepping away to take a call. "They made it to my home in the Hill Country and the security I sent ahead met them there. They're safe."

"They're as safe as we can make them," Reed corrected.

Max frowned, then nodded his understanding before he took a seat next to Cassidy and Tucker.

Who knew how far Tripp Lange's influence extended? Hell, who even knew what the man's influence was? He'd begun digging but so far had turned up precious little.

Were they making a mistake?

His mother still doubted, and those doubts had made him question and requestion what he'd heard in Lilah's kitchen. Was DeWinter lying? Manipulating one final moment to his advantage against her?

Reed had turned it over and over, always coming back to the same conclusion. Why?

The man had nothing to gain by accusing an innocent. On the contrary, he had a chance to name his killer and seek some sort of justice, even if he wouldn't ultimately be the beneficiary.

His mother had protested being hidden away, of course. But in the end, he'd wheedled and cajoled, using the still-fragile state of the women's landlady, Mrs. Beauregard, and her need for attention and help. And then sent up a silent prayer of thanks for his mother's caring nature.

She still wanted to call Tripp—still might, he knew—but he'd also promised repeatedly he'd alert her to any news or updates.

And then he'd sent her on her way. Heartbroken and scared underneath the tearful bravado.

"Reed?"

Lilah's voice was tentative, her gaze wary as she laid a hand on his arm. "Come sit down. Let's talk through this."

"I'm good from here." He shrugged her off, then watched wariness turn to desolation.

"Of course."

He was being an ass and knew it, but he still hadn't reconciled her unwillingness to call him for help with the night they'd spent together. He had feelings for her. Had known it from the very start that there was something about her. Something special and warm and meant for only him.

He'd believed she felt the same.

And still, she'd avoided him at the moment she needed him the most. That wasn't a relationship. And it sure as hell wasn't love.

He turned his gaze toward the window as that little gem settled in his thoughts.

Love?

Was he in love with Lilah?

He loved his mother, of course. And up until that afternoon he'd held a genuine affection for his stepfather. But the love of a man for a woman? How was it possible he'd avoided entanglements his entire adult life, only to get caught in a trap the size of Texas?

Before he could further consider the irony his life had become, Violet took control of the room. "We need to figure out what to do with the other two rubies. Cassidy and I have them in separate safe-deposit boxes, but the events of the last week have proven someone won't rest until they have their hands on all the jewels."

"It's not someone. It's Tripp Lange." Reed turned from the window and faced the people he'd come to like and respect. "Tripp Lange. Dallas businessman. Purported family man. He's the one who won't stop until he has the jewels."

Violet nodded. "Tripp Lange."

"He also won't rest until he destroys you." Reed let his gaze travel around the room, to Max, then Cassidy, where she sat with Tucker's arm wrapped around her, then on to Violet, as he allowed that message to settle.

Finally he let his gaze linger on Lilah. She'd technically given up her ruby, but he had a sense that wouldn't matter. She was a pawn now, and if she could be used to manipulate her friends into giving up their jewels, Tripp would do it.

He might not know the depths of his stepfather's depravity, but he'd spent his formative years with the man. He'd then spent the next decade and a half watching Tripp continue building his business with ruthless efficiency.

Tripp had a soft spot for his mother and a sense of familial commitment, but none of it changed the fact he was a barracuda.

Reed just never realized that same sense of purpose and urgency and desire to win extended to illegal activities.

"You don't think your connection to him will change things?" Lilah pressed the question and he smiled at her sweet naïveté.

No matter what had happened, he wanted to believe she could keep that. Could still find it in her heart to give someone who most certainly didn't deserve it the benefit of the doubt.

"You can't think this is coincidence?"

"No, I don't." Lilah shook her head. "But what if it is? Don't we need to play that scenario out?"

"Three people are dead, each violently murdered when they stopped serving a purpose. I hardly think there's any other scenario to play out."

"Yet here you are. With good instincts you presumably got from your mother, also a person with good instincts. They've been married how long? Nearly twenty years?"

"Twenty next fall."

"So how does a person spend two decades with another and not know they're that vicious? A person doesn't just hide that. There's no way you can live that disciplined a life and not mess up."

Whether it was the question—one he'd asked himself all afternoon, after attempting to answer it for his mother over and over—or the sheer frustration at circumstances, he didn't know.

But before he could stop them, his words shot out with all the quiet lethal grace of bullets.

"You tell me, Lilah. You're the one who managed to marry a monster. How'd *you* see past it?"

Lilah wrapped her arms around her midsection, a bid for comfort and self-protection, before she dropped them, then stood to her full height.

Cassidy and Violet had begun talking angrily at once, but she needed to do this alone.

She needed to *stand* on her own.

Her gaze on Cassidy, then Violet, she said, "Would you mind giving us a moment?"

Everyone nodded or murmured their agreement, filing out of the living room and disappearing into Violet's study. Lilah knew their interest was high—and knew by the gentle pats on her arms and shoulders that her warriors wouldn't hesitate to come rushing back if she called them—but she stood firm.

And once she knew they were out of earshot—relatively—she turned her attention fully on Reed.

"That was uncalled for."

"After all that's happened, I'd say it was an appropriate reminder."

"I took you for stubborn and frustrating, but cruel never made the cut."

She saw the comment strike home—saw the acknowledgment in his stormy gaze—before he nodded. "I guess I never took you for someone who couldn't ask for help."

Lilah knew she'd misstepped earlier. She'd crawled into her shell and allowed the old fears—and her old life—to overpower her. But she knew damn well she didn't deserve to have that old life thrown in her face.

"I made a mistake, Reed. I was caught up in the moment and wasn't thinking."

"You didn't call me!"

The words spilled from his lips, layered in a sort of fierce anguish that clawed at her heart.

"I couldn't call you. After he invaded the kitchen and stole the ruby, I couldn't get off the floor. I kept trying to. I told myself over and over I needed to call you and tell you, but I couldn't move."

The stoic statue that had hovered at the windows all evening crossed the room in long strides. His hands were on her face, his fingers caressing her cheek that still stung from Steven's slap. "He put a mark on you. Hurt you. And still you didn't call me."

Those magnificent eyes that could flash from a liquid silver to a dark, storm-cloud gray were clear, shining with a layer of tears.

"I'm sorry. I can only tell you that at that moment I couldn't move. I simply couldn't come back to myself. I was so happy, dancing around the kitchen thinking about you. And then he was there and he wasn't you. Was nothing like you. And I froze."

His thumb brushed her cheek, the press of his finger a gentle caress over her bruise.

"It was like a slap, even before he laid a hand on me. A reminder that no matter how far I ran or how happy I tried to be, I'd never be free of him. And now—"

A hard sob exploded from her throat, one she wasn't even aware of holding.

"What is it?"

"I wished him dead. So many times over so many years. And now he is."

Tears she'd never have believed she had for Steven

DeWinter rose up and choked her throat before spilling over in a hot wash down her cheeks. "What does that make me?"

"A woman who wanted her captor out of her life where he could never hurt her again."

"No." She shook her head, pulling away from the gentle understanding that had replaced his anger. Understanding she didn't deserve. "I'm in the wrong. I wished for things that are unnatural. What he did to me was unnatural but wanting the death of another is no better."

"Lilah." He crooned her name as he pulled her close. She knew she should protest—should resist as some form of penance—but the feel of his arms was so wonderful as they banded around her. "Damn, but we're a pair."

"I'm messed up. You're rather dishy."

A hard laugh rumbled in his chest as he hugged her tighter. "I'll file that one away."

The hot tears continued to fall, staining his shirt with an ever-growing pool of wetness, and still he held her. Her rock. Her salvation.

And maybe—if she was truly lucky—her love.

Diana Graystone Lange lay in the small, darkened bedroom, staring at the ceiling and reflecting on her life. The Baldwin house wasn't huge, but it was state-of-the-art and Max Baldwin, grandfather to one of her son's friends, had already loaned her a laptop for her personal use.

The laptop now lay abandoned on a small desk across the room. She'd drafted several emails to Tripp, deleting each and every one after the cathartic words spilled forth from her fingers. Much as she wanted to hit Send, she respected Reed's parting words.

Respected even more the descriptions that still swam in her thoughts, of three dead bodies, all of whom were alive a week ago.

Was her husband responsible?

Had she overlooked something so fundamental in the man she'd chosen to make a life with?

Over and over, her tornadic thoughts ripped through her memories, churning up every experience—every moment—over the past twenty years. How had she been so stupid?

And where could he have done all these things?

At the heart of the matter, that was the question that stung the most. She lived with the man, for heaven's sake. Made a life with him, day in and day out. Where did he go to do these horrible, terrible acts? Because there was no way three bodies was the start of something.

Oh no, if anything, this was the end. Her son would see to it that this was the end of whatever choices Tripp had made over the years.

Her husband was a businessman and she'd accepted from the start that he'd have long stretches out of town or evenings full of commitments. Was it possible he'd filled those hours away from her with any manner of sins instead of coming home to her?

Instead of making a life with her?

It had taken her years to get over the poor choices in her early adulthood. Her one saving grace was that her misbegotten romance with Brad had given her Reed. Her beautiful baby boy, so bright and vibrant, the very best of herself and—she'd hoped—her inconvenienced ex-boyfriend.

And then Tripp had come along. Yes, he was older, but he had a gentleness about him that she fell in love with immediately. After fending for herself and her son for so long, she'd had someone to take care of her.

Of them.

She'd known fatherhood was likely not his first choice at that stage of his life, but Tripp had taken on his responsibilities to Reed, as well, and she'd loved him even more for it. It was Tripp who'd encouraged Reed's interest in the law, sending him to—

Diana sat up, realization striking with all the stealth of a high-plains rattler.

"It's dangerous, Tripp. Why would I want my son to become a cop?"

"It's his dream, darling. He's a bright boy and he has a desire to take care of others." Tripp laid a soft press of lips against her cheek. *"He's like you that way."*

"But a cop?"

"Not just a cop. A detective. He's going to be one of the Dallas PD's best and brightest. I'll see to it."

See to it?

That long-forgotten snippet of conversation mixed in her thoughts with all the weight of wet cement. She could still remember her concern for her son's safety when he'd decided to enter the police academy and all the horrors of what might happen to him in uniform.

Tripp had calmed her and promised her that he'd be fine. That he'd make detective soon enough, he'd said, so sure of it as their conversation had continued.

And Reed had. He'd become one of Dallas's youngest detectives, in fact, on the day he got his shield.

Had Tripp arranged it all along? Had his support hidden a deeper motivation? With Reed in place, Tripp had a ready set of eyes and ears inside local law enforcement.

And if he'd arranged for Reed's promotion, that also meant he had someone fairly high up on his payroll.

Lilah flipped through the cookbook at her kitchen table, willing page after page of brightly decorated cupcakes to calm her nerves. She and Reed had come to some sort of understanding at Violet's. They both still struggled with the decisions she'd made that day after Steven's visit, but they'd also committed to each other. To seeing through whatever was going on and working together as a team.

They'd even made love when they'd returned to her place. She'd insisted they wash clean—unwilling to have any taint of the day on either of them—and then she'd surrendered.

Warm and tender, she'd reveled in Reed's gentle touch, even as she hesitated. She wasn't some fragile doll, ready to break if she were mishandled with even the slightest roughness.

Nor did she want pity from her lover.

Which was an unfair thought to both of them.

Monumentally unfair.

The heavy pad of bare feet had her turning around, her insides leaping to attention at the half-naked man who stood in her kitchen. Long, lean muscles painted his neck, shoulders and arms, but it was the thin ridge of muscles that formed over his rib cage on down over his stomach, before disappearing into jeans, that nearly made her mouth water.

The man was absolute, physical perfection.

"A true baker's work is never done, I see."

"Just relaxing with some food porn."

"Excuse me?" His eyes widened, any traces of sleep vanishing at her word choice.

"Trust me. You know it when you see it."

"You'll have to tell me more." He pressed a kiss on her head before he took the seat next to her, dragging the book across the table.

"It's the way it's photographed and lit. All the dips and curves. Lighting the food as a highly desirable object."

"You seem to know it well."

"I've styled some food before, for photo shoots. It's

different than when you bake for others. The colors are more pronounced and the food is built for photographing, not eating."

"Fascinating." He closed the book and reached for her hand. "Just like you."

"I'm—" What was she? Tired? Irritated? Sad?

Try as she might, she hadn't been able to get a handle on any of it. So she'd sat here, methodically flipping pages and not really seeing anything.

"I'm not interesting. I'm actually rather one-dimensional. If it's not full of sugar, flour and eggs, I'm pretty much not interested."

He settled into his chair as if taking her measure and Lilah nearly choked on her tongue at the play of muscles across his chest.

Damn, but the man was lethal. Especially when you added in the warm smile, the fathomless gray eyes and the unwavering focus on protecting others.

"I think you're actually quite multidimensional. Yes, you're passionate about your work, but you're also a businesswoman. A friend. A family member." He broke off at that, his brow furrowing in a hard line. "Your mother. We need to get protection for her."

"She's out of the country."

"For how long?"

Lilah had briefly considered calling her mom and telling her about the events of the past week, but something held her back. They'd been so close when she was younger, before her father died. And after…well, after, their relationship had shifted and changed. The child had become the parent of sorts and they'd never fully returned to their old one.

That had only grown more true once she'd married Steven. He'd pushed her to avoid any relationships besides their marriage and she'd been too ashamed to tell her mother what she'd gotten herself into. On the rare occasions they did get together, their conversation had been stilted from disuse.

"She's on a month-long mission trip for her church to South America. She doesn't even know what's going on here."

"You should tell her. She deserves to know."

"Maybe. I don't know."

"How about making that maybe a yes. She's your mother."

"We're not close anymore. I love her," she rushed on, not wanting to make the relationship sound like a horrible one. Because it wasn't.

It simply wasn't what it used to be.

"But we're not close."

When he said nothing, a small spark lit under her skin. She knew it was irrational—hell, every thought in her head for the past twelve hours had been irrational—but the spark flamed anyway.

"You're awfully acquiescent."

His smile remained broad, just shy of cocky. "See. Add *vocabulary maven* to your list of multidimensional skills."

"No, I mean it. I tell you, I'm a bad daughter who won't even call her mother and you shrug it off like I'm infallible."

That same furrow returned, but this time it held confusion. "What's this about?"

"You tell me."

"I asked you first."

He stayed in that relaxed pose in the chair, looking for all the world like a male lion of the jungle. In control and calmly assessing all he surveyed.

It pissed her off.

"You saunter in here like you own the place. That bright smile that twinkles with laughter and freaking awareness of everyone, all the while you pity me and my circumstances."

"What—" He laid a hand on her arm, but she shrugged it off, pushing back her chair.

"You pity me! Even when we were having sex before, you took it slow and easy, brushing your fingers against the bruise on my cheek like I was some fragile doll who might break. I won't break! I'm not broken!"

"All evidence to the contrary."

He never moved from the chair, his expression as unwavering and calm as his voice.

Damn, the man is infuriating! "Don't sit there looking all superior at me."

"I'm not sure I'm sitting here doing anything but letting you get this out. So come on. Give me your best shot. I won't break, either, and I've got more than enough interest in you to still like you when it's done."

Whatever had been roiling and writhing like a coiled ball of snakes leaped out and struck.

"And there you go! You're acting all calm and rational and reasonable while I'm carrying on like a freaking shrew."

"A freaking shrew who makes food porn. I'm telling you, I'm interested."

"Stop it!"

The amusement that hadn't quite left his eyes vanished as he leaped up from his chair, crossing to her. He towered over her as she stood with her back to the counter and that same image of the lazy lion morphed into something far more dangerous and predatory.

"Stop what?"

She swallowed hard, the sudden reality of having him

leaning over her as sexy as it was overwhelming. "You show up here like you own the place. Like the day you walked into my shop, with your questions and your dark gaze roaming around the office and the kitchen. Judging it all. Judging my friends. Judging me."

"I was doing my job."

"Your job is to get evidence."

"My job is to figure out what happened. To dig under the surface and find answers." He brushed her cheek, his finger tracing Steven's mark. "And I don't pity you."

"You act like it."

"Since when are tender ministrations anything other than tender?"

"Since they made me feel like you think I'm fragile and broken."

"I don't think you're fragile and broken. I do think that you're crazy and these last few minutes only prove that." He moved in quickly, his mouth hot on hers. "Fortunately I seem to like crazy."

"Reed—" She pressed at his shoulders, the hard muscle there nearly her undoing.

"Shut up." His mouth covered hers once more, his tongue parting her lips. She met the assault, then moaned as his fingers flipped to the tie at her waist, dragging open the thin material of her robe. Hot and rough, his hands roamed over her skin, leaving her nerves in near-painful awareness.

His hands dipped to her waist and before she could register what he was doing, he had her in a tight grip and lifted her to the counter. The new position shifted the balance between them, placing her head above his as she leaned over him.

"Now who's in charge?" he whispered against her lips

before diving them both under with a hot, carnal flick of his tongue against hers.

She smiled against his mouth, before using her position to her advantage. "I am."

Kiss after kiss spun out, each hotter than the last. She ran her hands down his neck, her thumbs skimming the hard length of his collarbone, before she gripped the rounded strength of his shoulders.

That same image—of hard, leonine strength—again filled her mind's eye. Although Reed never fully looked unassuming and meek, he did manage to convey an air of quiet understanding and subtle masculinity when on the job.

But here. Now.

He was all masculine strength and predatory grace.

"If you're really in control, then you won't mind if I do this." His hands moved again, shifting from their grip on her hips to the tops of her thighs. With insistent motions, he parted them, then used his finger to trace her most sensitive folds.

"Reed!"

He caught the last part of her scream with his mouth, his hands never leaving her body. Hard, decadent waves of pleasure swamped her as he kept up his steady assault. Moments spun out as she rode the dark, dangerous waves.

And then the moment broke and she was flying, her hands flexing hard on his shoulders as she sought purchase against something. With someone.

With Reed.

Before she could catch her breath or even form a coherent thought, he dragged her against him. He'd lost the jeans he'd worn downstairs—where had they gone?— but had managed to snag a condom in the rush.

"You're prepared."

"With you, my love—" he pressed a hard kiss to her lips "—I'm eternally hopeful."

He made quick work of the condom and then pulled her against him, their bodies locked tight. She braced her hands on the counter, using the hard surface for leverage as he set a hard, driving rhythm for both of them.

As the world quickly rushed up to meet her, exploding through her body with the force of something more powerful than she ever could have imagined, recognition struck.

He'd called her *my love*.

And as she fell, Lilah knew she felt the same.

Chapter 16

Reed toyed with the idea that he'd died, but he figured heaven would be more comfortable than a solid hardwood floor and hell wouldn't involve a naked woman draped over him, deliciously warm and pliantly soft.

"Are you okay?"

"Hmm?"

Recognition rapidly returned and with it, an uncomfortable wave of embarrassment that he'd let Lilah push his buttons. With gentle hands, he tugged at her shoulders, shifting them to a seated position. His tailbone protested the movement against the solid floor beneath him and he chalked it up to penance for losing his temper.

"I'm good." A shy smile tipped up the corners of her lips. "And I like you when you're mad."

"You're good?"

"Better than good." She pressed a quick kiss to his lips before wiggling off his lap. "I'm a woman who just had sex in my kitchen."

"It's an experience."

"And, thanks to you, a new one, as well."

Reed was halfway to a standing position when her words stopped him. "New?"

"Hmm?" Lilah was halfway to the floor herself, retrieving her robe. "New what?"

"You've never had sex in the kitchen before?"

"No. Have you?"

He took a moment, pleased when she hit him with a swift smack to his shoulder.

"Clearly you need to dive into a rather large catalog of entries, Detective."

"My hesitation is because I can't recollect ever finding the kitchen counter all that enticing. So, yeah, it's a first for me, too."

She leaned up on tiptoe to press a quick kiss to his lips before she breezed out of the kitchen and Reed was left standing there, an oddly dazed feeling as if he'd just run sprints in the precinct's gym rushing through his veins and making him slightly light-headed.

Who'd have thought?

He had the great good fortune to initiate kitchen sex with the baker of his dreams.

Reed was still humming with his evening revelations from Lilah when he keyed into Jessie's hard stare from his passenger seat. "I can hear you thinking, Jess. What is it?"

"You still haven't told me why I sent a patrol car to pick up Diana G. I gave you space but I'm fast losing my patience since you won't share why."

"She wasn't picked up by patrol. She was put under their protection."

"Same thing."

"I think those who've been legitimately picked up would

beg to differ." He barely avoided the second swat to his arm that morning when he rushed on, "I needed to see her about something."

"What?"

"A personal matter."

He expected anger—had braced for it, in fact—so when he heard a hard sniff, he risked his focus on Central Expressway traffic to look at her. "Jess?"

She waved him off on a hard harrumph. "Nothing."

"It's not nothing. What's wrong?"

"We're partners and we've been friends longer than that. I can't believe you won't tell me what's going on."

Whatever mistrust had driven him since discovering his stepfather's identity disappeared in the face of her anguish. He had to tell her.

But he'd be damned if he was going to do it in a government-issue sedan that had possible listening devices embedded in the dash.

"No. I won't."

The next five minutes passed in perfect silence. He pulled into a small parking lot that housed a jeweler, a bakery and two real-estate agents. These strips were a fixture of Dallas living, usually half a block from a freeway entrance, and the stretch of storefronts normally housed any number of small businesses in and around the city.

He imagined Lilah, Cassidy and Violet here and realized they fit far better in the Design District than in a tiny, cramped shop. He'd thought it strange, on his first visit, to realize they had a bridal salon in the heart of the city's old Warehouse District. But as he'd observed what they'd built—from Lilah's state-of-the-art kitchen to Cassidy's workspace to Violet's efficient office setup—he realized they'd found a space that was perfect for their business.

Jessie was out of the car first and he followed her, pulling her to a small seating area one of the Realtors had set up in front of her office. "Come here."

"So you can ignore more of my questions."

"No. So I can tell you what's going on."

A distinct change morphed her features from hurt to curious, her inherent cop's nature quickly overtaking everything else. "Out here?"

"It's better than the car."

He waited until they were both seated, the car still parked several doors down, when he filled her in, confident there was no chance their conversation was bugged. He explained what he'd discovered since the break-in at Elegance and Lace, especially the news since DeWinter gave his deathbed confession.

The sullen features she'd worn in the car had vanished, replaced by a combination of disbelief and very real sadness. "Reed, it's not possible. You know the man. He's your stepfather, for Pete's sake. He can't be a murderer."

"Why not?"

"Because he's Tripp. Mr. Lange. Diana G.'s husband. You do realize your mother has impeccable taste and good sense. And she's no one's fool. How could your mother be married to an evil murderer for twenty years?"

"She's spent the entire night asking herself the same thing."

"I'm sorry. I just can't see it."

"I'm beginning to think that's the point."

He and Jess tossed ideas back and forth as they waited for the jeweler to arrive, the unreality of the conversation striking both of them more than a few times.

"There she is." Reed pointed to the old Cadillac that pulled into the parking space next to his sedan. "Maria Davidson."

With a cop's skill for compartmentalization, he and Jess

both pasted on smiles and headed for the woman as she stepped from her car. Although the vehicle might show its age, the granddaughter of Gunnar Davidson—believed appraiser of the Renaissance Stones—was as young and fresh as a Texas spring. She wore designer heels like a pro, along with perfect hair and makeup that would still look as impeccable at five o'clock when she walked out of the store.

"Excuse me? Miss Davidson."

A small layer of confusion skittered across her dark gaze as she took in both of them. "Yes?"

"Dallas PD, ma'am." He and Jessie held up their badges in unison. "We'd like a few moments of your time."

"Kitchen counter? I'm impressed." Violet reached over and squeezed Lilah's hand. "Although you now know I'm not coming over until you disinfect the whole damn room."

"Spoilsport." Gabriella elbowed Violet from her position on the other side of the conference table. "You think of Lysol and I'm thinking of juicy details. Spill 'em."

Lilah blushed, the heat rising in waves from the top of her chest to the top of her head. Why had she even started this discussion?

Because you're happy and you want to share, a little voice in her mind quickly rose up to admonish her.

"I say you should only share what you're comfortable sharing," Cassidy said from her side of the table as she organized a row of photos in front of her.

"Spoilsport," Gabby muttered again.

Cassidy shot her a pointed glare, before adding, "I also think that, as your best friends in the entire world, that means you should be comfortable sharing everything."

"That's more like it." Gabby nodded. "Leave no detail undescribed. Including just how broad Detective Yummy's shoulders actually are when you get his shirt off."

Lilah nearly choked on her coffee since that thought had run through her mind more than once. "Broad. Impressively so."

"I knew it." Gabby dropped her chin into her fist. "Cassidy gets the sexy architect and you get the sexy cop. And Violet's going to have the other sexy architect if said sexy architect has his way."

"I am not doing anything with the sexy architect."

Three pairs of eyes descended on Violet before Lilah pressed her. "So you do admit he's sexy."

"I'm not blind, Lilah. Max Baldwin is attractive."

"I knew it!" Cassidy slammed a hand on the table, scattering her carefully ordered photos. "I knew you had a thing for Max."

"Tart insults that border on nasty are not a thing."

"They are in every book and movie and second-grade crush," Gabby added.

"Well, this isn't a book or a movie and it sure as hell isn't second grade." Violet closed the subject with all the finesse of slamming a door. "It is, however, a major problem. We've got two weddings in the next two weekends and no way of knowing if the threat against us is going to manifest itself there."

"It can't," Cassidy protested. "What would someone have to gain?"

"A lavish, business-destroying way to take us out."

Lilah fought the urge to shake her head—cartoon-style—at Violet's ominous words. "You don't really think our brides are at risk? Their guests?"

"How can we know?" Violet said. "We have no idea how deep this goes. And Tripp Lange is a powerful man even without us understanding his underworld connections. A lot of people will do a lot of unpleasant things for the promise of a few thousand dollars."

Lilah digested Violet's words, the reality of what she suggested not as impossible as it seemed. "But it's a major event. Saturday night's at one of the city's largest hotels. Their security's already involved in the wedding overall, to make sure they're monitoring anyone coming or going who's had too much to drink."

"I can recruit some of my cousins to help out," Gabby offered. "And I'm not catering this, just helping you all with extra arms and legs, so I know what to keep watch for."

"It's a start." Cassidy tapped a finger on one of the photos. "Tucker and Max will help and I'm sure Reed will, too. We just need to see if he can add any help from the PD."

The events of the past week rushed through her mind's eye and Lilah hated the thought that settled with dark finality. "I'm not sure the Dallas PD is quite the friend we think they are."

Reed had given Jessie the lead as she explained the purpose of their visit to Maria Davidson. He'd sensed she would be more comfortable hearing the news from a woman, and Maria's quick agreement to talk had only verified his instinct was spot-on.

"My grandfather talked on occasion of magnificent stones he'd appraised years ago. I remember hearing the story as a kid, the idea of these large rubies brought here to Texas a fanciful story." The vestiges of memory lit up her dark eyes with wry humor. "I think they're one of the reasons I chose to follow my grandfather's footsteps into the business."

"Did he keep any records?"

Maria smiled, her dark gaze tinged with warm memories. "My grandfather was of the old school. He scribbled it on paper and dropped it into a filing cabinet. If you can call that records, you're more than welcome to take a look through what I've got."

Reed glanced around the small establishment, not sure where they'd keep fifty years of paperwork, but appreciated the offer all the same.

"May I ask why the sudden interest in this? My grandfather's been gone a few years and no one's asked before now. Hardly anyone ever asked while he was alive, either."

"Someone asked him about the stones?"

"I remember one of his good customers asked about them a few months before he passed away."

"Did your grandfather think anything of it?"

"Oh no. My grandfather had a soft spot for any client who regularly purchased their jewelry from Davidson's."

A small, cold feeling punched his gut, leaving icy edges in its wake. "Could you share the name of this client?"

"We don't normally—" Maria broke off, confusion warring with the knowledge she'd shared something that caught their attention. "I mean, it's confidential."

Ever the diplomat, Jessie offered up a small smile. "It's a basic investigation, Miss Davidson. All we're doing is checking some background details and asking questions."

"If you're sure?"

"Of course."

"I guess it's not a problem. I mean, it's no secret he shops here regularly for his wife." Maria hesitated, then rushed on, "Tripp Lange has been a good customer of Davidson's for years. He and my grandfather became friends, in fact."

Those icy edges spread through his gut in ever-expanding fractals. "We appreciate the help, Miss Davidson."

Reed avoided making any calls from the car, but used the late-morning hour as an excuse to stop for lunch. Jessie waited in line for sandwiches and Reed stepped outside the sub shop to call his mother.

"Reed. Are you okay?"

"I'm fine, Mom. How are you doing?"

"I'm good." She sighed, a hard choke clenching her voice. "Which is a lie. I'm not fine at all."

"I'm sorry, Mom. Really, I am. But I need to ask you something."

"Sure."

"Your jewelry through the years. The different gifts. Do you know where Tripp purchased them?"

"Davidson's. It's his favorite place. He's raved about the owner forever and was very saddened by his death a few years ago—" Diana broke off, before her voice sharpened, the hitch in her voice fading. "Why?"

"Davidson was the appraiser on the Renaissance Stones. He's the one Max and Mrs. B. hired to look at the rubies."

"Should I ask them?"

He toyed with the idea—Max Senior and Josephine Beauregard were well aware of what their actions nearly fifty years before had wrought—but still, he was hesitant. "I'd play it by ear. If they seem well enough to hear the information, you can say something, but I wouldn't push it."

"I understand."

His mother quieted and he knew she did understand. Whatever disappointment or disillusionment she might be feeling, his mother was inherently kind and thoughtful. She'd know if the time was right to share details with the octogenarians.

"He killed him, didn't he?"

"Mr. Davidson?" Reed waited, then continued, "It's a possibility. It's also a possibility the man simply died of old age. I'm looking into it."

"Beyond that, though. Tripp used him. For information on the rubies."

"We're moving forward on that assumption."

"Everything I own is tainted." Another layer of tears filled her voice. "Maybe it's a good thing you pulled me away from the house without any of my things. I'm not sure I want to see them anymore. How could I wear something that has blood on it?"

He didn't know.

Although he'd barely had time to breathe since finding DeWinter's bloody body the day before, Reed had wondered what lay ahead in his quiet moments. His mother had suffered a horrible deception and there was no way her husband was headed for a good ending. Reed was committed to getting answers—he could do no less—but the hunt for justice would hurt the one person who had supported him and loved him his entire life.

"We're going to get to the bottom of this. I'm going to get you answers."

"I know you are. That's the thing that keeps me going. That, and the fact that when this is all over, you're going to give me a daughter-in-law."

He nearly dropped the phone, both at his mother's words and at the sudden, enticing image they evoked. "What?"

"You heard me. You love Lilah. And if you're a smart man, you'll tell her and do something about it."

"I don't know, Mom."

"I do. I might be feeling awfully down about love right now, but it's not for lack of belief in it. You love her."

Of all the places Reed imagined he'd fall in love—or come to the actual realization he was *in* love—standing in front of a sandwich shop in a small strip mall wasn't it.

He waited, expecting a tightness in his throat or a hard ball of lead in his stomach, but neither came. Instead, a swift flutter of excitement seemed to lift his body a few inches off the ground as a wave of warmth spread through his chest.

"I do love her."

"I know, sweetie."

The knock on the back door had Lilah glancing up from the fondant she rolled out for the top layer of the weekend's wedding cake. Wiping her hands on a nearby towel, she went to the locked door. After a quick peek through the side window, she flung it open when Reed stood on the other side.

"I've missed you." He pulled her close, his lips against her ear.

"I've missed you, too."

He hung on extra tight, and while she loved the feel of his arms around her, Lilah sensed he was a bit off. "What is it?"

He closed the door, then followed her to her work area. "I talked to my mom a while ago."

"How's she doing?"

"She's hanging in there. She's sad and upset, but she's hanging in."

An image of the bright, vibrant woman who had fed her iced tea and desserts filled her thoughts. A woman who now lived with the betrayal of the one person she was supposed to trust and believe in above all others. "I'm so sorry she is going through this."

"Yeah."

He paced before the counter, his gaze on the fondant, before he moved on to the small trays of drying gumpaste flowers she'd finished up earlier after deciding she didn't have quite enough for the first two layers. "These are amazing. So lifelike."

"Thanks."

He continued to move around the counter, his attention fully captured on the flowers, and she nearly said something when he spoke. "What makes people get married?"

"Love."

The response was so immediate—so deeply felt—she almost caught herself off guard.

Was it possible? Even after all she'd been through, that she truly, deeply believed in love?

A tiny flicker of hope—something she'd feared long dead—sparked to life in her chest and Lilah knew the truth of it. She did believe in love. With her whole heart, she still believed you could love someone and they could love you back. Totally and completely.

Steven had taken that away from her—or he'd tried to—but that stubborn hope had remained, watching. Waiting.

Waiting for Reed.

He turned from where he paced at the counter, a caged animal making laps for no other reason than he couldn't sit still.

Only he did still.

And stared at her with a world of emotions swimming in the depths of those magnificent gray eyes.

"I love you."

That flame of hope that had lingered long after she'd believed it had died spread through her soul like wildfire. Reed Graystone loved her.

She stood before him, colorful stains on her apron and her hair in a messy twist. The tips of her fingers were green and purple, the same color as the flowers she'd created. Her feet were encased in the ugliest pair of orange Crocs she owned, broken in so completely that she saved them for the days she'd be standing for hours on end.

And still he loved her.

With startling clarity, she knew there was only one answer she could give in return.

"I love you, too."

Chapter 17

Tripp Lange paced his office at the compound, his thoughts a jumbled mess.

Diana had left him.

He'd tried her cell phone repeatedly, not once getting through as the phone continued flipping over to voice mail. When he'd finally checked one of his private software programs to trace her location, he'd come up empty-handed, as well. The phone was off, not transmitting at all, and the last place she'd used it had been from the house.

He'd briefly toyed with going to Reed's, but the risk was too great. He needed to deal with his stepson, but that required planning. If Diana was there—and he wasn't sure Reed would take such an obvious tack—Reed would never let him get to Diana.

And if she wasn't—

"Sir?" Alex stood in the doorway of his office.

"Yes?"

"I've not been able to confirm the officer that managed the removal of your wife from the house."

"Did you follow the usual channels?"

"Yes, sir."

Tripp paid well for that knowledge and he didn't appreciate the inability to get the answer to a simple question. "Has Trey kept watch on my stepson's apartment?"

"He has. Reed hasn't returned home yet."

"He's with the baker."

"Shall I tell Trey to shift his focus?"

Tripp ran through his options, his lingering anger over the lack of information from the police still filling his thoughts when it hit him.

"Jessie Baxter. Go pick her up."

"And if she's with her husband? Shall I bring him, too?"

He paid Alex well for his obedience, but Tripp still appreciated the man's willingness to ask. Alex was loyal—had been since he'd trained him fresh out of the old country—and he suddenly realized what a precious gift that loyalty really was.

Especially in light of the fact his wife obviously had none.

"Don't wait for him, but if he's there, subdue them both. Bring them to the new space out near Fair Park we used for Barrington."

"I'll alert you when I'm on my way with the package."

As Alex departed, Tripp mapped out how he'd get his stepson to the warehouse. He had the slightest moment of regret as he imagined killing Reed, but it couldn't be helped.

Lilah helped Violet finish drawing the curtains in Elegance and Lace before she turned back to take another glance at Reed. They'd both been quiet after their private declaration of love, their heads bent together for several long moments as the reality of what they'd found in each other sank in.

And then they'd returned to work, she in the kitchen, him taking calls in her office. It bore a simple sort of normalcy that was as enticing as it was calming.

Normally, in the days before a major event, her mind raced with all she had to complete. The details for the cake. The last-minute needs for any of the other desserts she was providing. And managing any contractors they were bringing on. For as big as the Kelley-Gardner nuptials were, the Elegance and Lace team was lean, the bride and groom opting to have much of the catering expenses rolled into the hotel.

Lilah kept waiting for that frenzied feeling to come, but all she felt was calm. And it was all because of Reed. And the fact they loved each other.

"I can rent a damn tux, you know." Max's voice boomed across the shop, breaking through that calm.

"We don't need you in the ballroom." Violet's voice was prim and proper, her green eyes glittering with all the warmth of steel.

"You need all the help you can get and you damn well know it."

Sensing Max and Violet had already gone a few rounds on this argument, Lilah abandoned her mental happy place and dived into the fray.

"Vi, you need to get that ginormous stick out of your very fine bum. Max is capable and willing to help. Put the man in a tux and shut up already."

"I need eyes and ears outside."

"Which the hotel's already providing." Lilah kept her voice calm, even as the urge to pop Violet one began to dig in with sharp claws. "I want more people we know and trust inside the ballroom."

"Perimeter, Lilah. We need a secured perimeter."

"And that's it." Cassidy wagged a finger at Violet. "Someone's been watching way too much TV."

"Why aren't you both taking this seriously?"

Before Lilah or Cassidy could reply, Reed cut in smoothly, "I've got a few people I can add to detail. And between Baldwin and Buchanan and the family members Gabriella offered up, we can map out a plan to make sure everything goes off without a hitch."

"I'm not sure—"

Reed patted Violet on the shoulder before pulling her in. The move was part protector, part older brother, and if she weren't already in love with him, Lilah thought that might have been the moment to clinch it. "We'll manage."

"I can't risk all those people on Saturday. They're depending on us."

"And they've put their trust in the right place." Reed guided her to one of the large wingback chairs in the sitting area. "Now I need you to put your trust in us."

They continued to discuss prep, walking through various scenarios as Tucker and Max identified every ingress and egress point in the hotel.

"What is the plan to deal with your stepfather?" Max kept his voice casual as he glanced up from a detailed layout of the hotel, but Lilah sensed the bigger question underneath and knew Max only voiced what they all wondered.

"I have to find him first and I don't know who I can trust in the department not to tip him off. There's no way of knowing how deep his influence goes."

"Is there anyone you trust implicitly?" Tucker asked. "It might be a place to start."

"Jessie, of course. She's my partner, but she's my friend,

too." Lilah watched as Reed processed the question, his subtle frown saying far more than his lack of another name.

"Anyone else?"

"No one I can be absolutely sure of."

Lilah wasn't sure if that was the truth or a by-product of learning of his stepfather's deception, but she couldn't blame Reed for being spooked.

Nor did she want him to accidentally pick someone under Tripp's influence.

Lilah caught Tucker's eye before the man pressed his point. "What about us, then?"

"No way."

"Before you leap to a no, Reed, why don't you hear Tucker out?"

Five pairs of eyes were trained on her, full of varying degrees of curiosity, concern and, in Reed's case, that continued, stubborn *no* in his stormy gaze. Unwilling to wait for him to give that no a voice, Lilah rushed on, "Max and Tucker are military trained. They're as well versed on ops as you are."

"I'm not putting anyone at risk. No way."

"Yo, man. We're not—" Max chimed in immediately and Tucker had already stood, nervous energy driving him from his seat when Reed held up a hand.

"It's not a matter of capabilities. I won't put anyone else at risk. Not over this."

Tucker spoke first, his normal, easygoing demeanor nowhere in evidence. "What part of we're involved and committed hasn't hit you? Your stepfather is a risk to all of us. And he's not stopping until someone stops him. You say he has influence?"

"Yes." Reed nodded. "Even without knowing how deep his unsavory connections go, he's one of the city's most respected businessmen. He's got almost limitless access to cash and he's clearly got some percentage of the police in his pocket."

"Then it's guerilla warfare and you don't have the time to be choosy."

As arguments went, Lilah knew Tucker was absolutely right.

But the look of pain that washed Cassidy's face in sharp lines telegraphed her fear as clearly as if she spoke the words. The man she'd only just found was putting himself in mortal danger.

Lilah knew exactly how she felt.

Cassidy and Tucker called a break in the planning so they could go home and feed Tucker's boxer, Bailey. Reed suspected Tucker was going to get an earful on the car ride over his adamant decision to enlist in this suicide mission, and Reed couldn't say he blamed Cassidy.

If it were up to him, he'd handle this with Tripp all on his own.

Which would be the true definition of a suicide mission, the rational side of his mind leaped out to remind him. He'd been successful on the force by remembering he was part of a team. He used the resources at his disposal and brought in backup, help and others' guidance when he needed it.

And now he was on his own.

The cancer of Tripp's influence couldn't be underestimated. So the people he'd considered friends—those he'd have taken a bullet for—were no longer trusted allies.

"The pizza's almost done. You want to snag a few plates for me?" Lilah pointed in the direction of the fridge. "The second cabinet over there."

"Sure." He moved through the motions, the rich scents

of yeasty dough and sausage registering through the fog in his mind.

"The guys will be good eyes and ears on Saturday."

He trusted Baldwin and Buchanan. Both had more than proven themselves, first to their country and then in their loyalty to Lilah and her friends. They'd already appointed themselves bodyguards to the women of Elegance and Lace and he knew both would follow him through a door, his back covered.

None of it changed his innate distaste in drawing civilians into a police problem. "I don't like the idea of putting them in the line of fire. Of putting any of you in the line of fire."

"Vi, Cassidy and I vowed that we weren't going to let whatever's going on ruin our business. And while the chances are slim anything's going to happen on Saturday, we're taking proper precautions to ensure no one unwelcome gets into the wedding. So Max and Tucker are in this."

"Have you told the bride and groom?"

"Violet let them both know two days ago. We felt it was only right."

"Were they upset?"

"Since the groom is the grandson of a congresswoman, there was already a pretty significant layer of security in place. Our little problem was seen as small potatoes."

Reed wasn't sure he agreed with the assessment, but he couldn't argue with the measures already in place. "So everyone in attendance will expect extra eyes and ears around the ballroom."

"Exactly. A few more won't bother anyone. And your eyes—" she pressed a quick kiss to his chin "—can focus where they need to."

He dragged her close and wrapped his arms tight

around her shoulders. Her response was immediate, her arms banding around his waist with a tight squeeze. "It's going to be okay."

"This time. What about the next time? The next wedding you do where the bride or groom isn't heir to a political dynasty. What then?"

"Then we handle it. I'm not hiding." She shifted from his arms and took a few steps toward the pizza cooling on the stove. "Not anymore."

"This isn't like before. You knew your opponent. You knew how to avoid him."

Lilah stilled before the stove, then turned to face him. Head cocked, he saw the light of awareness finally click to bright. "How close do you think Tripp's going to get?"

"Close." *Deadly close.*

The thought was on the tip of his tongue when Lilah arrived at the answer all on her own. "He wants the rubies he still doesn't have. And now that we know who he is, he wants us, too."

"Yes. Men like my stepfather don't get this far without having an exit strategy."

"Then we need to cut him off. You said it yourself he has eyes and ears in on the force."

"Which means I can't trust a damn person."

"It also means he has help."

"That's the whole point."

"Exactly." The lighthearted pixie with the quick smile was back, an aura of excitement seeming to fill the air around her. "He might have power, but he can't use it by himself. He needs other people. Arms and legs on the ground."

"Which his unlimited reach gives him."

"It's only unlimited if we don't find them first." She transferred the pizza onto a large serving dish, then nodded her head toward the entryway into the front room. "Come on. We need to put our heads together and dig into his background. Let's cut off those extra arms and legs of his."

As ideas went, Lilah knew she had a good one in theory. In practice, however, it was an entirely different matter.

"The Dallas–Fort Worth Metroplex has nearly seven million people in it. How do you propose we find the handful that act as Lange's eyes and ears?" Violet had set up her laptop in the main area and had commandeered Cassidy's as a second workstation.

"Keep searching for any stories on Tripp." Lilah tapped away at Cassidy's computer. "Look for anyone who seems to pop a few times in search results, too."

Reed took the seat next to her, his gaze roaming over the screen. "Wait. Right there. Scroll back."

"What?" Lilah stilled and turned the screen closer to Reed.

"Right there. That photo link." He tapped on the track pad, an image of Tripp and Diana in full formalwear filling the screen.

Reed stiffened next to her and Lilah laid a hand on his knee. "It's okay. You talked to her a little while ago. She's all right."

"I know. Damn it," he muttered under his breath. "She's fine. I know she's fine and I need to keep that in the forefront of my mind every time I start to panic he got to her."

Lilah refocused him on the computer screen. She knew his mother was as safe as she could be under the circumstances and they had the added assurances from Max. He'd been keeping tabs on his grandfather and Mrs. B. and had gotten several updates from the town sheriff he trusted to keep an eye on things. The three of them had stayed at the house as directed and hadn't left since their arrival.

"What stood out about this article?"

"It's the scroll bar of photos. This is a function my mother and Tripp attend every year for one of the mayor's major charities. All the top department brass attend, too."

"Do you attend?"

"I've gone before but found it uncomfortable. It's—"

When he hesitated, Lilah finally pieced together the challenges he must have had in his position. "It's a difficult place to be. You're the stepson of a wealthy man, yet you want to fit with your peers."

"Exactly."

Lilah reached for the computer when another thought bumped up against his comment. "Have you always felt like that?"

"Pretty much. It's a strange thing, you know. I don't come from wealth yet he's my family. It's been important to me to carve my own path."

"Does Tripp know that?"

"I suppose." Reed hesitated and she saw the moment he arrived at the exact same place she had. "He does know, as a matter of fact. We've discussed it. And that would have worked well to his advantage."

"Extremely to his advantage, I'd say. Not having you there while he worked his contacts."

She flipped through the other photos, the captions highlighting the movers and shakers of the city. She flipped through several current and former professional football players, a senator and three congress members before Reed reached out and stilled her hand. "There. That's the captain. Joshua Finney."

"Your captain?"

"Out of my precinct, yes."

Lilah leaned closer, the image pulling her in. Tripp had his arm around Diana's shoulders, a convivial smile playing about his lips. Despite the fact that he was dwarfed by the large bear of a man Reed had pinpointed as his captain, there was no mistaking Tripp was the alpha dog in the photo. She couldn't explain how she knew that, but something in Tripp's eyes—the clear green almost reptilian— had her pulling away from the screen.

As she took in the other participants, she could only assume she was correct. Finney's wife was on his other side and her smile didn't quite reach her eyes. Even Finney himself had small lines of strain hovering around his mouth.

"Would it be strange for a captain to be at a function like this? Such an obvious photograph of the two couples?"

"I wouldn't say it's strange. But it is interesting. Although I've avoided attending functions like this, Tripp and my mother entertain extensively. I've yet to mix and mingle with any department brass at one of those events."

"Yet here's a photo of two couples looking awfully chummy for the press."

She left the observation hang, waiting for his response, when Violet interrupted, "I pulled up Finney's wife's Facebook page."

"How'd you find that?" Lilah held up a hand. "Ignore me. You're Violet Richardson and you have more mad skills than the CIA."

Violet flashed her a quick grin. "And I'm connected to two of her friends. I found a loop and back-doored in through one of their profiles. You'd think she'd be a bit more careful about keeping her page locked down, actually."

Reed got up to peek over Violet's shoulder and Lilah followed, taking the other shoulder. "Anything interesting?"

"When was that photo taken? The one you were both looking at."

"May," Reed answered, his gaze on Violet's screen.

Lilah watched as Vi scrolled through the catalog of a life. Baby showers, grandchildren, a few birthday photos before she'd gotten to the same time period as the event. "There. That's the dress she wore."

Violet clicked into a photo, scrolling through image after image of the Finneys getting ready to depart for the event, followed by a few images from the evening.

"What's that she wrote there?" Reed pointed toward the computer and Violet paged back one photo. "In the comments."

"'Looks like a fun night.'" Violet read off various posts one by one. "'You and Josh are going to have a blast. You look gorgeous.'"

Violet unpinned the comments so all were visible and it was the last few that had them all leaning forward in unison. "Here. It looks like she answered some of the comments the next day. 'It was Josh's big night. A cop's wife's work is never done.'"

"And look at that last one," Reed said. "'Doing my wifely duty.'"

Although it was hardly conclusive evidence, it was odd that Reed's captain would be so well acquainted with one of the city's wealthiest entrepreneurs. It was even stranger his wife had publicly proclaimed she was "doing her duty."

Lilah knew about duty—she'd had her fair share of nights out with Steven during their marriage—and she vividly remembered when they had shifted from being fun evenings out on the town to a requirement. "In spite of the pretty dress and fancy night out with her husband, it sounds like she didn't want to go."

Max reappeared from Violet's office, where he'd taken another call, and joined their huddle. "You find something?"

"It's inconclusive, but it is a possible link." Reed quickly walked Max through their theory.

"It works. Do you think your LT's involved?"

"Tom? I haven't taken him off my list, but it might be worth reconsidering him. The captain would have a considerably better shot at flying under the radar than Tom if he was the one changing paperwork and pushing down orders."

"They could be working together." Although she hated to point it out, Lilah knew it was only fair to consider it.

"Before this I never would have doubted Tom's integrity. Maybe it's time I started trusting my gut." Reed's phone rang and he pulled it from his pocket. "It's Jessie's Dave."

Lilah straightened from leaning over Violet's shoulder. "Does he call you often?"

"No." Reed swiped the phone with a frown. "What's up, man?"

Lilah sensed the panic before Dave's voice registered through the handset.

"Jessie. It's Jessie. Someone's got her."

Chapter 18

Reed had begun to think himself numb to the realities of his stepfather's depravity and was only too shocked to realize just how wrong he had been. A cold, greasy panic filled him as he tried to stay calm for Dave's sake. "What did they tell you?"

"Fair Park. They've got her somewhere over in Fair Park. I was told to call you and confirm you'll be there by midnight. He's going to give further instructions after confirming you're coming or he'll kill her."

A hard sob echoed through the phone and Reed pushed every ounce of training he'd had at the academy into his voice. "Dave. I need you to calm down. We need to work it through and I need you to stay calm, buddy."

"I need to go there. I need to get to her. I'll tear every building apart until I find her."

Reed thought about the sheer area to cover at the city's fairgrounds and knew the vow was heartfelt, if not a fool's errand. "We'll come to you and then we'll figure out how to handle this. Stay there. You hear me?"

"Y-yes."

"Fifteen minutes. I'll be there. I'm calling Gannon in the meantime. I'm sending him over."

"Okay."

"Dave. We're going to get her back."

Even as the promise hovered in the air, Reed prayed he was right. Images of Steven DeWinter lying on the floor of Lilah's kitchen, bleeding out from his injuries, had been proof enough Tripp Lange meant business.

He knew Lilah, Violet and Max waited for answers, but he flipped through his contacts and dialed Gannon, using his side of the conversation to update everyone at once. "I need your help."

Reed caught his friend up on Jessie's disappearance and before he'd even finished, he heard the crank of a car engine rumbling through the phone. "I'm on my way."

Cassidy and Tucker walked back into the shop, their somber gazes no lighter than when they'd left to feed the dog, but Cassidy must have sensed the problem immediately. "What is it?"

"Tripp made his move."

Lilah and Violet filled Cassidy in and Reed took Max and Tucker.

"The mention of Fair Park. That's where Barrington was discovered." Tucker made the connection with his fiancée's ex immediately.

"It doesn't make sense." Reed knew the area was dodgy to the extreme, but there had been concerted development efforts. "There're several bars over there and some renovated lofts. It's too crowded and Tripp's going to want to go for something more private. Even the homeless population is a risk if someone sees him."

"They haven't developed it all." Max snapped his fingers, then sat down at Violet's computer. "What was that development project, Buck? The one we considered then ended up passing on."

"The Exposition Expansion."

"Yep." Max's fingers flew over the keyboard, a triumphant grunt filling the air when he found the property. "There it is. DGL is the title holder on the property."

Awareness tickled the back of his neck with icy fingers. Even with the discomfort, Reed took solace that they finally had a solid lead. "DGL. It's got to be one of Tripp's corporations."

"DGL?" Max glanced up from the computer.

"They're my mother's initials."

Tripp kicked the pile of beer cans that filled the corner of the warehouse, proof that he hadn't fully driven out the riffraff that squatted inside the loft for shelter. What the hell were they doing? The damn building was a million degrees. The homeless would be better off sleeping out under the stars this time of year instead of baking in the oppressive August heat.

"It is you." Jessie stared up from where Alex had bound her on the floor, her arms fastened behind her back with duct tape and a bright, shiny bruise rapidly discoloring her right eye socket.

"Who were you expecting?"

"I couldn't believe it was you. Even with the evidence Reed had, I didn't believe you could do it. Don't you love them?"

He'd always liked Jessie. She was a bright, eager girl and she'd made Reed's transition to his new school easier to bear. He knew Diana had spent years hoping they'd marry, only to be shocked when the depth of their friendship hadn't manifested into something more.

"What makes you think this has anything to do with love?"

"What makes you think you can separate the two? They're your family. Your wife and your son."

"He was never my son."

The lie tripped out and he waited for Jessie to call him on it. Instead, all he got was a sneer, her argumentative attitude at odds with her vulnerable position. "He was in all the ways that counted."

The barb sank deep and his hand was already out, his palm flat against her cheek before he could even think to check the response. "You're awfully vocal for someone in your position."

"And you're nuts if you think Reed's going to make this easy on you."

"You'd do well to remember my family is my business."

Her dark gaze never left his, even as she spat a wad of blood on the floor. "You don't have a family. You never did."

Gannon had already arrived, his soothing voice filling the living room of Jessie and Dave's town house when the rest of them got there. "We're going to get her back, Dave."

The moment Reed walked in, he had known Gannon was the right call. His large, soothing presence and deep baritone went a long way toward keeping everyone calm, even as distress swirled like a tornado in his dark gaze.

Lilah relieved Gannon, taking a seat beside Jessie's distraught husband and drawing his hand into her own. The bright, happy pink streak in her hair was at odds with the horror that had fallen into the center of their lives, but he couldn't argue with her methods. She maintained a short, reassuring monotone every time Dave's voice rose on a sob.

"What are we up against?"

Reed trusted Gannon implicitly, but he was curious to see if their theory about the captain had legs. He'd avoided sharing those details on the phone in favor of watching his friend's face when he told him. "I need you to walk me through the papers again."

When Gannon only stared at him, Reed added, "The paperwork earlier this week on Robert Barrington. I know you dug into it. Do you remember who signed off on it?"

"Yeah, sure. I did end up finding it. The captain had signed off on it. It just ended up being a case of misplaced paperwork, nothing more."

"Captain Finney?" Reed asked.

"Sure, Finney. Who else?"

"We believe he's in this. With Tripp."

"Finney kidnapped Jessie?" Gannon shook his head and Reed felt for the guy. They'd had a few hours to process every twist and turn and he'd been thrown into the deep end. "There's no way."

"No, my stepfather kidnapped Jessie. But we think Finney's been his inside connection at the precinct."

"The captain's straight, Reed. There's no way."

Reed knew Gannon had faced a world of disillusionment during his time in active duty and he hated being the one to add another layer to the man's struggles to overcome the fear of things outside his control.

"I haven't fully proven Finney, but I don't think I'm wrong. And I'm not willing to gamble Jessie's life waiting to find out."

Lilah caught the concern in Violet's and Cassidy's eyes and motioned toward Dave with her gaze. Cassidy caught the signal and came over, relieving her of her seat and quickly adding her reassurances.

"I've got an idea."

Violet followed her into Jessie and Dave's dining room, where the men already stood huddled, deep in conversation.

"We've pinpointed the location. We need to build out the op to get in there," Tucker said.

"We have no eyes on the man, inside or outside the warehouse. No idea who he's got in his pocket or how much firepower he's got." Max shook his head. "It's a risk. And not one that calculates in our favor."

"I know that area." Lilah interjected herself into the conversation. "Down there at the fairgrounds. I know a way in."

"Lilah—" She shut down Reed's protest with a hard wave of her hand.

"You need all the help you can get now. Eyes and ears, right?" When Reed said nothing, Lilah went for the jugular. "For Jessie."

Reed nodded, her hit as direct as she'd intended. "Yes."

"I know that area. I enter the cake show at the state fair every year and I've provided desserts for several events in the various halls. There's a warren of roads and streets that weave in and out of the grounds."

"Wide-open roads and streets. They're going to be watching," Max argued. "It's too dangerous."

"They're watching for you. For something that screams police. But there's no way they're going to care about a run-of-the-mill vendor delivering goods."

"In your pink truck?" Reed's voice nearly exploded on the word *pink*. "Like that's not a flashing neon sign inviting attention."

"I had something a bit more subtle in mind."

"What?"

"Come on. We don't have a lot of time."

Reed had to give Lilah credit. Her idea was brilliant. He'd partnered with good cops through the years—smart, well-trained operatives who knew how to manage and defuse a situation—and he'd be hard-pressed to name one who could have come up with a better plan.

Gabby's brother was one of the city's leading produce suppliers and it took less than twenty minutes for them to mobilize his help and his agreement to loan them one of his trucks. An hour later, they all met in front of Gabby's storefront, plans already under way.

The white refrigerated truck was nondescript beyond the simple paint on the side advertising its wares, and the expansive refrigerated unit gave them plenty of room to hide. More important, it gave them plenty of space to pack an arsenal of weapons for the attack on Tripp and room left over to take prisoners.

Their only possible hiccup was Dave.

The man wouldn't be persuaded to stay behind and if Reed were being fair, he didn't blame Dave in the least. There was nothing on earth that would keep him from Lilah if the situation was reversed, and he had no right to tell the man no.

But his presence was a concern.

Violet had taken over the reassurances, her steady voice and repeated reminders to let Reed, Max and Tucker act on their training had become a litany. Even with her firm hand, Dave's bone-deep upset and lack of police training had Reed worried.

The man was a wild card and they needed nothing but aces right now.

Lilah stepped out of Gabby's building and walked up to

the truck, clad head to toe in black. "Dave needs to make the call and get the meeting point from Tripp. Then we need to get going."

"You're not going."

"We've had this argument before. So let's skip it so we can get out of here and bring Jessie back."

"This isn't a joke."

"And I'm not laughing. You need me on this." Her eyes were dark pools, and even with the reflection of the streetlamps, her sheer, stubborn force of will was more than evident in her gaze. "I can help you navigate through the warren of roads. And I'll be your getaway driver."

He'd ridden the waves of adrenaline since the day before as he walked in on a dying DeWinter, and the excessive spikes of stress finally took their toll.

"There is no freaking way you're going with us on this!"

"You need me. I can help you."

"Aw, Lilah." He ran a hand through his hair, dragging hard on the ends as he stared at her. He'd intended to soften his voice, but the ragged and hoarse sound that came out was a surprise even to him. "Don't do this to me. Please."

"You need me."

"Yes. I need you healthy and well and unharmed."

She moved into his arms and he attempted to reassure himself with the simple act of touching her. Her arms. Her face. Her back.

Nothing worked. All he could imagine was the horror of Dave's situation and the risk that she'd end up the same way. Trapped under his stepfather's control with him unable to get to her.

Helpless to save her.

"I can't let you go. You're a civilian."

"I'm not going in—"

He cut her off with his mouth, a hard kiss against her

lips meant to silence, even as he took the deepest solace in the feel of her. The kiss was hot and hard and spoke of promises and desire.

Of a lifetime of secrets, just waiting to be uncovered.

"I can't risk losing you."

"You have to know I feel the same."

"Then why won't you let me do my job?"

Her brow furrowed, at odds with the light sheen of moisture that painted her lips, bee-stung from passion. "I'm making sure you do the job right. Every one of you admitted you don't know the area as well as I do. Add on the endless construction happening around the city and you won't get in with the same degree of precision and focus that I will."

"And then you're a sitting duck. Stuck in that truck with no help or backup should one of Tripp's men find you. We have no idea how many people he's got working for him."

"You're assuming I'm a bad shot, Detective?"

Fear, raw as vinegar, coated his throat with acid. "I don't want to put you in a position to have to answer that question. And besides, I thought you hated guns."

"I do hate guns. But for the record, I'm a very good shot." She locked her fingers with his. "And I know the area like the back of my hand. I can get you in and out. You need me on this."

"I need you safe."

"No. You need a partner. Someone who has your back and who won't let you down." She kissed him once more, lingering an extra few moments. "I won't let you down."

"Left at the light."

Reed navigated through the most remote entrance onto the fairgrounds, his stoic features in sharp relief under the spotty streetlamps. Voices rumbled from the back of the truck and she knew Max and Tucker were giving Dave a quick overview of the weapons they'd brought along.

"He's calmer." When Reed said nothing, she added, "Dave."

"It's the lull. Calm before the storm. He's going to have to work harder to keep it together when we get there."

She pointed through the windshield. "Make that right down there. The turn that looks like a small road out of the parking lot."

His nod was the only indication he'd heard her, but he made the turn as directed.

Lilah glanced through the small opening into the back of the truck, then shifted her attention firmly back to providing directions. Max and Tucker were well versed in what needed to be done.

They'd handle Dave.

Now it was up to her to handle herself.

Despite her best efforts, the last few minutes before they departed Gabby's still lingered in her mind. Cassidy hadn't even attempted to hide her tears as she helped Tucker into a Kevlar vest. Although Reed had his with him, the others would have gone in vulnerable, and Gannon had made a quick run to the precinct, retrieving vests for everyone.

With Tucker and Max occupying Dave, Lilah addressed Reed. "We've got the advantage of surprise."

"None of it changes the fact I'm dragging four civilians into the middle of a war zone."

Done listening to the mix of frustration and resignation that hadn't left his voice, she laid into him. "Enough. We're here and we're going to get Jessie and bring her home."

"What's possibly left of her. My stepfather has made it abundantly clear he's willing to kill for what he wants. He's equally prepared to kill those who are of no use to him any longer."

Lilah exhaled on a sharp breath, the bleak words at odds with the man she knew.

Throughout this entire ordeal, he'd coaxed her and cajoled her, willing her back to life. Oh, she'd thought she was living before, but Reed had shown her otherwise. She'd lived a half life, going through the motions, avoiding risks and sinking deeper and deeper into a shell that could have swallowed her whole.

Yet she was here. And she *was* whole.

"We're going to get to her in time. And then we're going to make sure Tripp pays for his crimes. All of them."

"I never even saw it." Reed's voice was low and, she suspected, not meant for her to hear.

But she *did* hear.

And in that moment, as one second ticked over to the next, she finally understood the real problem. "The hurt will fade, you know."

"What hurt?"

Lilah's heart broke in half at the bleak question, so at odds with the pain he'd carried like a lead weight since discovering the truth about Tripp. "The pain of betrayal. Of understanding that someone you love is incapable of loving you back."

"What makes you think this is about me?"

"How couldn't it be? Even if you felt nothing at all, you love your mother and you know she's in pain."

"She'll survive."

"It's not about survival, Reed. It's about living. Thriving. Trust me, I know. I've spent a lot of my adult life focused on surviving. It's not a way to live."

"Bastard!" He slammed a hand on the steering wheel, his anguish as tangible as if a rock had hurled through the window. "He's such a miserable bastard."

"He is."

"We trusted him. Believed in him. Blended our world with his. Things weren't so bad before. We got by. But then they got better and she was happy."

Lilah let him get it out, the stream of consciousness going a long way toward filling in whatever gaps she'd had. His mother had struggled, as she surely would have, a single woman raising a child on her own. Tripp's arrival in their life had metaphorically kept the wolf from the door.

Only, neither of them understood Tripp was the wolf in disguise.

"She was happy. And all this time, she's had no idea what he is. What he's capable of."

The line of warehouses came into view and she knew Reed needed to focus on dealing with Tripp. She directed him to a small parking lot, out of view from the warehouse's windows, and prayed that anger would carry him through the matter at hand.

"You okay?"

"I've got this."

"That wasn't my question."

"It's all the answer you're going to get." He unbuckled his seat belt, then leaned into her. "Actually, I've got one other answer for you."

He kissed her, his lips hot and carnal against hers. She knew this wasn't the time or the place, yet as the kiss transported her to a world of pleasure and need and desire, she knew a singular desperation.

She loved this man. She wanted to make a life with him and she wanted a lifetime to do it in.

And if Tripp Lange had his way, there was no way she was getting either.

Reed crouched on the ground, Max, Tucker and Dave at his side. Dave had kept his calm, his hard breathing the only sign he wasn't fully keeping it together. Reed had calculated their physical distance from Lilah and knew they weren't that far, even if the truck was much farther away than he'd have liked. He'd also given her explicit directions to leave and call for backup on the way if she needed to escape the situation.

He might not trust his colleagues to manage this job with him, but he trusted them enough to rescue an op gone bad. And once they got what they'd come for, he was calling in backup to book his stepfather as fast as possible.

Of course, even if the op went textbook perfect, he'd surely be off the force when his little mission was discovered. With a strange sort of clarity, he had to admit that knowledge didn't bother him nearly as much as he expected it would.

Whether Captain Finney was at fault or not, someone high up on the force was involved. Now that he knew his department was tainted, he couldn't see his way to going back and serving in an environment that had placed him in the position of being Tripp's information shill.

"Three o'clock." Tucker's low whisper barely registered, the monotone designed to pass information without alerting others.

Dave's anxiety continued to rise, his gaze never leaving the wall of windows above their heads.

"Dave. You with us, buddy?"

"Yeah."

Reed shot Tucker a quick glance and saw his answer in return. He knew Tucker and his friend had decided on a plan to keep Dave in line until Jessie was rescued if necessary. Reed hoped like hell they didn't need to use it.

Tucker tapped his ear the same moment Reed's own earpiece registered. Max used the same nearly soundless monotone as he relayed the position of the men in the warehouse.

He also confirmed he had eyes on Jessie and she was moving.

"She's okay, buddy." Reed patted his friend's back. "We're close."

A loud burst of fire lit up the night and Max's holler echoed in his ear, in tinny counterpoint to the shout evident on the other side of the building.

"Looks like our discovery's been noted," Tucker muttered through gritted teeth. "Let's move."

Lilah heard the gunfire and it took every ounce of self-control she possessed to sit still. She'd promised Reed she would stay where she was and function as getaway driver only. The gun in her hand and the one strapped to her ankle were meant for protection, not backup and reinforcement.

That promise didn't stop her from craning her neck through the truck's window to see what was going on.

Shadowy figures crouched along the building, Reed, Tucker and Dave all lined up just as they'd planned. She'd watched them since they got out of the truck, their crouched poses hiding them from view of the warehouse. The three of them had remained in position, but the gunfire had them moving in the opposite direction of the conflict. Lilah watched them go, her heart stuck in the middle of her throat.

"They'll be okay." She put more force into the words. "They know what they're doing and they *will* be o—"

Lilah broke off as a shadowy figure rose up next to the truck, the glint of a pistol more than obvious in the light of the moon. A face filled her window, a mix of dark planes and angles, as he waved the gun.

"I wouldn't be so sure about that."

Chapter 19

Reed heard Jessie before he saw her, her sassy bravado filling the air in a reassuring confirmation she was still okay. He kept a firm hand on Dave's arm, subtly giving him the signal he still couldn't move and the man nodded, his face grim even as he accepted the need to wait. Tucker pulled up the rear of their small party and pointed to his eyes, then held up two fingers.

They only had two opponents?

It wasn't possible.

While he knew it was unlikely his stepfather would have his police department flunkies here with him, he had to have some help. Eyes on two people indicated Tripp thought he could handle the situation with the help of only one other person and likely a third outside?

There was no way.

His stepfather's voice overpowered Jessie's, filling the hot warehouse with sharp, menacing teeth. "You may as well come out, Reed. I already know you're here, and hiding is only going to prolong the inevitable."

Reed eyed Tucker and nodded. He patted Dave and pushed them both forward, leaving Buchanan in the shadows as backup. Tripp knew they'd arrived, but he didn't necessarily know numbers. Reed and Tucker gambled on that fact as Reed moved into the light of the warehouse.

"Where's your mother?"

As an opening gambit, Reed was surprised by the approach, but he quickly shifted gears to see how he could use Tripp's comment to his benefit. "She's safe."

"She should be here with me!"

Tripp's shout echoed in the still air of the warehouse, but it was Dave's hard cry before he ran toward Jessie that provided an unexpected distraction.

"How could you?" Dave crouched from his position next to Jessie, his hands on her arms and shoulders as he frantically reached for the restraints at her back. "We trusted you. We know you!"

"Alex." Tripp gestured with a brief nod.

A large man stepped out of the shadows and Reed had his gun up and in hand when the man knocked Dave in the back of the head, his large body falling next to his wife at the impact.

She laid down another rant of pure vitriol and Alex moved to stand above her, the message clear that she stay put.

"Where is your mother?"

Reed saw Jessie's subtle shake of her head and decided to play things out. "Safe."

"She won't take my calls."

"She's devastated to find out her husband is a murderer, a thief and a psychopath."

The gun in Tripp's right hand trembled. "Where is she?"

"Don't play the concerned spouse now. We know what you've done. What you're responsible for. I told her all of it."

"You know nothing. I'm a well-respected businessman. I'm revered in this town."

"Tell me. How long have you been leading this double life? Living a lie?" Reed stepped closer, the anger that had ridden him hard over the past few days winning the battle for his self-control. "How long have you been a murderer?"

"You know nothing." Tripp shook his head, his eyes gleaming with menace. "And you're not going to have a chance to find anything out, either."

Reed stepped closer and he sensed Alex poise for action. "Correction. I haven't known anything. But I will find out everything about you. Every last bit of what you've done for however long you've been doing it."

"That's rather difficult since you won't live to see the morning." Tripp smiled, a cold, oily thing that had Reed retracing his steps. Who was this man?

And then it didn't matter as a loud scream filled the air and a man perp-walked Lilah into the center of the warehouse, a gun to her head.

Lilah fought to remain calm and levelheaded, even as one horrific image after another flowed through her mind. A man—a large man—had a very large gun to her head. And now she was here.

With Reed and Jessie and Dave.

Where were Tucker and Max?

Bile rose in her throat as she imagined the gunshot she'd heard earlier. Was Max hit? Was he lying somewhere dead?

The man who had her had taken her gun and she hadn't even bothered reaching for the one at her ankle. She wouldn't have been quick enough and it was no use tipping him off. There still might be a chance.

She met Reed's gaze, a world of longing and hurt reflecting back at her before he turned to his stepfather.

"Why?"

"Surely you can figure that out. I know you've never been much for money and power, but you like nice things. Good clothes. A nice car. From me, you've come to appreciate the finer things."

"So you're killing people for a few rubies? You're successful. You have a good business. A highly profitable one, too. What you're doing here is wrong. It's greed and avarice and it's evil."

"Possessing things is in my blood."

"You possess plenty."

"It's never enough. But it will be soon." Tripp pulled the stone out of his pocket, the rich red of the ruby refracting the fluorescent lights of the warehouse. "When I have all of these, I'll have everything. These stones have power."

"They're jewels. Nothing more."

"Once I have them they'll be something more."

Lilah watched as understanding filled Reed's gaze. She'd sensed it earlier, but now she knew.

Whatever he believed he knew about Tripp Lange was gone, replaced by a man he'd never really known.

A man he had no desire to ever know.

The goon who had her tightened his grip on her arm, the tip of the gun still pointing into her neck. She knew she couldn't move—and knew the time was fast approaching when Tripp would exhibit the same ruthless finality he'd shown everyone else.

A loud thud reverberated through the room, shaking the floor and tossing her and the man behind her to their knees.

Suddenly free of the gun at her nape, Lilah scrambled as fast as she could, Reed shouting for her to come closer.

The whole moment shattered, the walls shaking even harder as the refrigerated truck they'd driven over slammed a hole in the wall of windows.

Max.

Before she could move, Reed had her down on the ground, his gun extended as he leveled two shots at the man who'd taken her from the truck.

Although he'd aimed at a moving target, Reed managed to slow the man's movements with a shot that grazed the leg. The goon turned his gun, his aim directed at them, but Reed used the man's stilted movements to deliver the kill shot.

As the perpetrator fell to his knees, his gun clattering to the ground, another set of shock waves reverberated through the building, knocking out a wall on the far side of the building.

Another round of screams echoed as Jessie struggled against her bonds, and Lilah raced to her, tugging at the duct tape that bound her wrists. Jessie leaped on her husband, her frantic shouts of his name bringing him around.

"Come on. We have to go."

Lilah took Dave from one side and Jessie had him on the other as they moved to the truck. Max was already out of the cab, clearing a path of debris to get them all into the back of the refrigeration unit.

"Buck! Reed! Come on!"

The man Tucker had wounded bled, his hand crushed against his stomach, while Tripp stood, his face a mask of fury.

"I'm not leaving him."

"I set the charges," Max hollered. "Come on! They've already started."

Lilah raced to Reed, dragging him on. "Leave him. Come on. Please, come on."

Reed gave his stepfather one last glance before he followed her out into the warm Texas night, leaving the men to be buried alive.

Reed pulled Lilah close, unable to believe she was safe. Unable to believe they were *all* safe. They finally called for backup, the explosion the cover for what had gone down.

"Are you sure you're okay?"

"I'm fine."

"When I saw you come in." He clenched the shaking fingers of his free hand, wondering if the tremors would ever stop. "I thought—"

"I know what you thought. It's what I thought, too." She tilted her head toward him, her lips brushing against his. "But it's over. We're safe."

Cops rushed here and there, along with what looked like half the Dallas Fire Department. Reed had already instructed them to look for bodies and knew he needed to help—needed to lead—but he wanted one last minute with her.

Just one damn moment that he'd never take for granted again.

"I love you."

The words—ones he never thought to say—spilled from his lips with a fervent desperation. He'd come so close to losing her. Too close.

Yet they'd been spared. And he was never going to miss the opportunity to tell her how he felt. To share everything that was in his heart. "I love you, Lilah. I want to marry you. Have babies with you. Grow old with you."

"I want that, too. More than you can ever know."

Although he hated the chaos that spilled over into their private moment, he refused to wait.

Refused to delay their future.

"Then let's do it." He shifted their position so they faced each other, his hands taking hers before linking their fingers, pressing his forehead to hers. "Let's make it official. As soon as possible."

"I'm yours, Reed. Always."

As he took her lips once more with his own, Reed couldn't think of a better promise to start the rest of his life.

"Yes. Always, Lilah."

Epilogue

Tripp pushed at the rubble covering his legs, the throbbing pain there only spurring him to work harder and move faster. He'd been bested by his stepson and his friends.

But he still had the stone.

He quickly dropped the ruby still clutched in his fist into the inside pocket of his suit jacket, then used his anger to fling the debris off his body. Sirens filled the night air and Tripp hollered to be heard.

"Alex!"

A stifled moan greeted him before he heard a crisp, professional "Yes, sir."

Before Tripp could respond, Alex towered over him. Cuts painted his face and arms, but he extended a hand to pull him up. Tripp took the offering and struggled to his feet.

They were okay. Trey was buried in the rubble, already dead from Reed's shots, but he and Alex were okay.

And they had a lot of planning to do.

"Far wall, near the windows," Alex shouted over the infernal noise. "It's the shortest way out."

It was how his stepson and his friends had left.

The hot night air was oppressive, especially with the combined debris and dust still lingering from the explosion. But it was the line of cops, all in a row waiting to greet them, with Reed standing point on the far end, that caused his skin to crawl.

So Reed had called for backup.

With a glance down the line, Tripp nodded slightly at the man on the opposite end, receiving the same signal in turn. Clearly his stepson didn't know everyone on his team.

Or where their loyalties lay.

He and Alex would be free in no time. And once they were, they'd press on and find Reed and his friends. Each and every one of them.

* * * * *

If you love Addison Fox, be sure to pick up her other suspenseful, sensual stories:

SILKEN THREATS
SECRET AGENT BOYFRIEND
THE MANHATTAN ENCOUNTER
THE ROME AFFAIR

Available now from Harlequin Romantic Suspense!

REQUEST YOUR FREE BOOKS!
2 FREE NOVELS PLUS 2 FREE GIFTS!

ROMANTIC suspense

Sparked by danger, fueled by passion

YES! Please send me 2 FREE Harlequin® Romantic Suspense novels and my 2 FREE gifts (gifts are worth about $10). After receiving them, if I don't wish to receive any more books, I can return the shipping statement marked "cancel." If I don't cancel, I will receive 4 brand-new novels every month and be billed just $4.74 per book in the U.S. or $5.49 per book in Canada. That's a savings of at least 12% off the cover price! It's quite a bargain! Shipping and handling is just 50¢ per book in the U.S. and 75¢ per book in Canada.* I understand that accepting the 2 free books and gifts places me under no obligation to buy anything. I can always return a shipment and cancel at any time. Even if I never buy another book, the two free books and gifts are mine to keep forever.

240/340 HDN GH3P

Name _____
(PLEASE PRINT)

Address _____ Apt. # _____

City _____ State/Prov. _____ Zip/Postal Code _____

Signature (if under 18, a parent or guardian must sign) _____

Mail to the **Reader Service:**
IN U.S.A.: P.O. Box 1867, Buffalo, NY 14240-1867
IN CANADA: P.O. Box 609, Fort Erie, Ontario L2A 5X3

Want to try two free books from another line?
Call 1-800-873-8635 or visit www.ReaderService.com.

* Terms and prices subject to change without notice. Prices do not include applicable taxes. Sales tax applicable in N.Y. Canadian residents will be charged applicable taxes. Offer not valid in Quebec. This offer is limited to one order per household. Not valid for current subscribers to Harlequin Romantic Suspense books. All orders subject to credit approval. Credit or debit balances in a customer's account(s) may be offset by any other outstanding balance owed by or to the customer. Please allow 4 to 6 weeks for delivery. Offer available while quantities last.

Your Privacy—The Reader Service is committed to protecting your privacy. Our Privacy Policy is available online at www.ReaderService.com or upon request from the Reader Service.

We make a portion of our mailing list available to reputable third parties that offer products we believe may interest you. If you prefer that we not exchange your name with third parties, or if you wish to clarify or modify your communication preferences, please visit us at www.ReaderService.com/consumerschoice or write to us at Reader Service Preference Service, P.O. Box 9062, Buffalo, NY 14240-9062. Include your complete name and address.

HRS15

Flipping through the chart, Eric Colton barely noticed
when the nurse bustled off. Unbelievably, all Jane Doe
appeared to have suffered was a concussion and some
bruised ribs. No broken bones or internal injuries. Wow.
As far as he could tell, she was the luckiest woman in
Tulsa.

He might as well take a look at her while he was here.
Chart in hand, he hurried down the hall toward her room.

After tapping briskly twice, Eric pushed open the door
and called out a quiet "Good morning." Apparently, he'd
woken her. She blinked groggily up at him, her amazing
pale blue eyes slow to focus on him. He couldn't help but
notice her long and thick lashes.

"Doctor?" Pushing herself up on her elbows, she
shoved her light brown curls away from her face. "You
look so familiar."

"That's because I rode with you in the ambulance last
night."

"Ambulance?" She tilted her head, giving him an uncertain smile. "I'm afraid I don't know anything about that."

Amnesia? He frowned. "How much do you remember?" he asked.

"Nothing." Her husky voice broke and her full lips quivered, just the slightest bit. "Not even my name or what happened to me."

He took a seat in the chair next to the bed, suppressing the urge to take her hand. "Give it time. You've suffered a traumatic accident. I'm quite confident you'll start to remember bits and pieces as time goes on."

"I hope so." Her sleepy smile transformed her face, lighting her up, changing from pretty to absolutely gorgeous.

Unbelievably, he felt his body stir in response. Shocked, he nearly pushed to his feet.

This kind of thing had never happened to him.

Ever.

Don't miss THE TEMPTATION OF DR. COLTON
by Karen Whiddon,
Available August 2015,

Part of the **THE COLTONS OF OKLAHOMA** series:

COLTON COWBOY PROTECTOR by Beth Cornelison
COLTON'S COWBOY CODE by Melissa Cutler
PROTECTING THE COLTON BRIDE by Elle James
SECOND CHANCE COLTON by Marie Ferrarella
THE COLTON BODYGUARD by Carla Cassidy

www.Harlequin.com

HRSEXP0715

THE WORLD IS BETTER WITH

Romance

Harlequin has everything from contemporary, passionate and heartwarming to suspenseful and inspirational stories.

Whatever your mood, we have a romance just for you!

Connect with us to find your next great read, special offers and more.

f /HarlequinBooks

🐦 @HarlequinBooks

www.HarlequinBlog.com

www.Harlequin.com/Newsletters

H HARLEQUIN®

A *Romance* FOR EVERY MOOD™

www.Harlequin.com